OUR DARK SECRET

Also by Jenny Quintana

The Missing Girl

JENNY QUINTANA

OUR DARK SECRET

MANTLE

ISBN 978-1-5098-3946-9

Typeset in Sabon by Jouve (UK), Milton Keynes
Printed and bound by CPI Group (UK) Ltd, Croydon, CR0 4YY

For Derick, with love

THE BEGINNING

1978

I met Rachel in the summer of 1978, the year before they found the first body.

I was cycling home from Spar when my front wheel hit a stone. Flying over the handlebars, I landed on my back. Spilled milk and broken eggs. Dazed, I thought I was dead. I closed my eyes and then, when I opened them again, first one and then the other, seriously wondering if the next creature I saw would be an angel or a devil, there was a girl, staring down at me, red hair haloed by August light.

Hallelujah. Praise the Lord. Despite my almost fourteen years of sins and misdemeanours and the fact that most of my teachers thought I was stupid and my own mother said I was obtuse, I'd made it up to heaven.

The girl blinked down at me, chewing gum. 'You all right?'

I grinned and then, I suppose since I was smiling, she shrugged and walked away, leaving me with a daydream.

That summer, *the girl* remained *the girl*. Occasionally I glimpsed her mooching along by the river, chewing her nails, bored and beautiful; walking about town, hands in the pockets of her grass-green dress, staring at shopfronts, or drinking from cans through a straw.

Alone, yet not lonely, she intrigued me. At the same time, I was certain she'd never be interested in someone like me.

I had no idea that one day we'd connect, like planets spinning and colliding in a starry constellation. That one day our fates would entwine.

1

1999

The news comes in the morning.

I'm on the bus, driving through the villages, queuing on the toll bridge, speeding alongside the fields and crawling into Oxford.

It's early, but still . . . that August heat.

A few more minutes; I concentrate on my novel. I'm reading a paperback: a 1950s detective story I picked out from Oxfam. Dog-eared with a lurid cover, it's not the kind of book I used to choose, but it's light and stops me thinking.

I scratch my head, turn a page and then my mobile rings.

People around me narrow their eyes as though I've done something terribly wrong. Usually it's my size that affronts them. Sometimes it's my clothes: mid-calf skirts and buttoned-up blouses. (I've never known how to dress.) Now it's the way my phone cuts through their silence, disturbing their crosswords and their naps.

I flip open the phone.

'Elizabeth,' a voice says.

It's Mrs Joseph, my former next-door neighbour, keeping me posted with local news. Normally she calls at the start of the month, on the first or maybe on the second, and always in the evening. Calling now, mid-month, early morning, knocks me out of kilter.

'They've found a body.'

Pause. Blink. Take a breath.

'Elizabeth,' she repeats in my ear. Her voice is strange, oddly excited, and I know it's because of all the stories she's ever told me, that this, she believes, will shock me the most. 'Did you hear me? A body – a skeleton actually, I think – at the back of the orchard. Imagine that? Do you remember that strip of wasteland?'

Another breath and yes, of course I remember the wasteland. My den was there – a hidden dip surrounded by bushes and trees that blocked out the light. It was like a tomb and even now I can picture Rachel that first time she came, head tilted as she listened, as fragments of light slid through the leaves and brightened her long, red hair. She had an aura, I used to think – a halo of holy light.

It was a tomb and yet, she felt safe, she said, cocooned amongst the leaves and the soft, damp soil. No one would find us unless they were searching. It would be like digging up a grave. And I remember how I'd wanted to protect her from the demons and devils that hid in the trees and beneath the earth and inside the hearts of people. Sometimes you found them in the most unlikely of places. And sometimes they didn't even bother to hide.

'A skeleton,' Mrs Joseph repeats. 'Can you imagine? The builders found it.'

My heart thuds.

'Elizabeth? Are you there?'

I grip the phone, force myself to speak. 'I thought

they'd stopped trying.' My voice sounds far away, like a forgotten echo. Around me, the light has faded, people's faces blanking over. 'The construction company, I mean. I thought they'd decided not to buy the wasteland.'

'No. They never stopped trying. And we never gave up fighting either, but there was only so much we could do.'

Mouth dry, I moisten my lips. At the end of the line, I can imagine Mrs Joseph, gesticulating as she speaks, bangles jangling, bright scarves flying. She's wearing orange or purple, and she's pacing, multi-tasking – dishing out Trill to the birds, or sardines to her brother, or taking a tray of muffins from the oven.

Always doing something for somebody else. That's Mrs Joseph. Volunteering, campaigning, and in those days, back when I was young, it was all about stopping the houses from creeping across the countryside, preventing the construction company from buying more land. So much wrangling about who that stretch of wasteland had belonged to. A sentimental rich woman who had moved to Australia, it turned out, and a son who'd wanted to sell but had been forbidden. Well, I suppose his mother must have died.

'Sold at last,' Mrs Joseph confirms. 'And when they flattened the wasteland, they bulldozed the hollow and hey presto.' She pauses dramatically.

The hollow. The dip, she means. My den.

I open my mouth. I've been expecting this moment for most of my life, but now it's here, the words don't come.

'Elizabeth,' she says. 'Can you imagine? A skeleton.

Hardly covered in leaves and dirt; it's a miracle it wasn't found before. You'd think it would have been, wouldn't you?'

'I don't know,' I manage. 'Wasn't it cordoned off as private property?'

'Yes, it was, but still, children don't take notice of that kind of thing, or dogs for that matter.'

True. It's sheer luck no one has found the body until now, or maybe it's coincidence. People turning away at the very last moment, taking a different path, ignoring their dog rummaging in the bushes – small decisions, huge effects.

'Do they know what happened?' I say at last.

'They're talking about murder.'

'Murder.' I whisper the word and listen to how it sounds.

'Do you think it might be connected, you know, with the other one?' She drops her voice. 'Think about it, Elizabeth, think about it. This skeleton – this body – it might have been there when you children were playing, when us adults were picking apples, when those people were walking their dogs. Do you remember Mr Evans?'

'Yes.' He was my other next-door neighbour, had a dog called Nip.

'Well, you know he died not long ago. Heart attack. I told you, didn't I?'

'Yes. Yes, you did.' I was sorry when I heard that. I really was. I can see him still, hunched, crooked and old, commenting on my weight. In the end, though, he was my champion. My saint. Nip too.

'When did they get the go-ahead?'

'The builders? Last week. That's all. And then this morning when I heard about the skeleton on the local news, I thought I must phone Elizabeth. I must tell you.'

Hot off Mrs Joseph's press. She always was the first to know the news, always keen to share with anyone who would listen. And still she can't resist phoning, keeping me abreast, which of course I've encouraged over all these years because I knew that one day she'd say something like this. Besides, once upon a time, Mrs Joseph was my champion too, and I haven't forgotten that.

Now, though, I need time to think.

I make my excuses, saying I'm sorry, but it's my stop and I must get off. Reluctantly she says goodbye, asks if she can call me later, and when she's gone, I shut my phone and picture her pausing, staring down at her own phone momentarily and then dialling a different number, speaking to another person and starting the spiel again. *They've found a body . . .*

The bus stops near the train station. Crowds emerge, groups of people flustered by the heat; more appear from buses and side roads, on foot or by bike.

I take off my gabardine, fold it neatly over my arm, hitch my bag more firmly onto my shoulder and walk, thighs chafing, along with the commuters, through the dry streets and towards the canal with its motionless water, slick with slime, and wine bottles from some late-night party or other littering its banks.

There's a smell coming from the canal – raw and acrid, made worse by the heat. What is it? It reminds me of something. Metal rusting? I can't recall. Crossing the bridge, I glance down and see a dead gull spread-eagled on the bank, guts spilling. Poor bird, savaged by some creature. What? A cat, an urban fox, one of those devils I used to imagine amongst the trees?

Dizzy, I lean against the rail. People continue, dashing past me, eyes fixed on their goal of being on time. No one speaks to me or asks if I'm all right. I'm invisible. I always have been. Glances slide across me like warm butter, or chocolate melting in the midday sun.

Sugar. I need sugar. It's a habit of mine when I'm not quite right. In my bag, I find a half-melted Twix. I eat fast and root around for the currant bun I know is in there. The bun is stale, but I force it down. The world stops spinning, but the past comes back.

Automatically I think of the beginning, calming myself, ordering my thoughts. Rachel. That day when I fell off my bike and was entranced by her beauty. Or Melissa. I smile vaguely at the memory of her. Melissa always did exaggerate. She was petulant and whining. Nothing like her sister. Nothing like Rachel.

But perhaps it's not with a person at all, where this story begins. Perhaps it's with a place. The dip in the wasteland at the back of the orchard. Yes, perhaps the story starts there: where the trees dance a circle, where brambles and branches block out the sun. It's dusk. We're talking, voices hushed, faces turned up to the glittery light. And she lays her head on my lap and she closes her glorious eyes and her skin is damp and stained with salty tears and her hair is a twine weaving amongst the leaves.

Two friends – or so I liked to think: Rachel and Elizabeth. Elizabeth and Rachel. The crazy girls. The abandoned girls. The lost girls. We had so many connections, although really there was only one that made a difference.

That day when the world changed forever. When I became somebody else. When I metamorphosed from weak Elizabeth, ignored Elizabeth, inconsequential Elizabeth whom nobody wanted; when I became loyal, required, depended on, loved even. That, I suppose, is what I can't let go.

But I cannot predict what will happen now they have a skeleton in the morgue. Now they know where else to search. I have no idea how long they will take to identify the who and the how, to trace it back. But they will. There's no doubt about that, is there?

A war-scarred pigeon with scraggy feathers and missing claws drops in front of me, struts and pecks at the crumbs of my bun. I throw it some more and then suddenly, I remember the stench of the canal. Thick. Acrid. The smell of rusting iron. Or blood.

I look at my watch. It's half past eight.

I need to come up with a plan. I should have thought of one years ago.

How many other people have lived like this? Knowing a terrible truth, waiting for someone to find out. The blue light flashing outside their window. The heavy fist pounding on their door. They wait, ready with their story. Yet no one comes to demand they speak. The hours turn into days and then weeks. Months. Years. No one comes. No one asks. No one knows.

I'll give myself a day to think things through, to get my story straight, to remember the details, write it all down, at least inside my head. A kind of confession. Or a justification. One more day of normality, and then I'll be ready.

2

1969

I was trouble from the start.

According to the story, I made my mother groan and writhe and gasp in agony until they had to split her open to get me out. Even then I lay in the cradle, a limp lump of flesh, while my parents prepared for the worst.

But I survived.

Elizabeth Constance Valentine.

I sometimes think my mother gave me the longest name to prolong my life with letters.

Mum made a living from looking after other people's children, which meant there was a daily horde that invaded our terraced home. She called them her *charges* and complained so often I was mystified as to why she had chosen the job.

In the end, I decided that she liked the idea of losing me in a crowd. A bit like diluting squash.

Every morning, she came down to breakfast clipped and groomed. She wore cigarette trousers – gingham or black – a white shirt and clip-on earrings. Her hair was curly dark brown, secured by an Alice band, or a scarf when she was going out.

The charges burst through the door any time after half past eight. Mum spent most of the day feeding them, cleaning them, scrubbing their sticky fingers. The rest of the time, she spent devising quiet activities and shushing them when they made too much noise. Dad worked as a bouncer in a nightclub so he slept during the day. And me? I was left sitting on the edges watching and waiting, drawing pictures of empty houses.

Lesson one: I didn't belong in a crowd.

The children who came regularly were my age, which in 1969 was four or five. They were a ramshackle lot of boys and one girl nicknamed Lovely Amanda who had shiny blonde hair and big blue eyes and a pointed face like an elf.

I wanted to be friends and so I invented games: tea parties with our dolls, mums and dads, sisters. But every time I settled down to play she would wrinkle her perfect nose and walk off, preferring the boys.

'Here she comes,' people said when Mum was marching us to the park. 'Lovely Amanda!'

I hoped they'd call me lovely as well, but they never did. Instead, Mum would draw herself up, straighten her back and say, 'This is Elizabeth. Isn't she pretty too?' And I was happy with that because Mum was defending me, complimenting me. (The rest of the time I was *foolish* or *nosey*. *Maladroit* when she took evening classes in French.)

I put Mum's loyalty down to the fact that *blood was thicker than water*, which, along with *always be prepared*, was one of Dad's favourite sayings.

Dad had a maxim for every aspect of life and whenever he heard about the people who slighted me, his face darkened and he roamed the house spouting his sayings and berating bloody small towns and bloody small-town attitudes.

Eventually, for the sake of peace, Mum avoided telling him, but I could never keep quiet, and then he would whisk me off to Maggie's Cafe for chocolate eclairs and lemonade, which I drank through a crazy straw. There I would relate the details and by the time Dad had finished raging, gone outside to calm down and *have a smoke*, Maggie would be ready to keep me company.

Maggie was young, early twenties, a newcomer. One day, she had appeared from nowhere with a rucksack on her back and a set of rusty keys and had taken over the cafe which had been boarded up for years. According to my parents, with her honey-coloured hair, long, colourful dresses and feminist views, she had caused quite a stir.

People said she was a mystic, a white witch, an activist who had once been arrested in some London demonstration or other and kept in a cell overnight. So many stories which seemed like a mass of contradictions – I didn't care about any of them. Maggie gave me crazy straws and free cakes and entertained me with folklore and fairy tales, devils and demons. It was Maggie who first told the tale of the Devil hiding in the heart of the orchard – a story which, in a way, turned out to be true.

We lived in a small part of Chelmsford, more like a village in those days than a suburb.

The main street sliced through the middle.

On one side was Maggie's Cafe with the orchard nestling beyond and a couple of fields which sometimes had cows and sometimes had sheep; sometimes sprouted wheat and then sprouted patches of new-build houses. The other side was built-up. There was an estate of identical homes with dormer windows and pocket-sized gardens, a Spar, a newsagent's and a park.

The rest of the houses and shops, The Dog and Duck, the schools, the police station and the church were scattered along the network of roads that radiated out from the main street. Our house stood at the end of a lane amongst a cluster of homes that looked like alms houses and backed onto fields.

Locals prided themselves on the fact that the area was safe.

There was the odd dispute about the size of a neighbour's hedge, of course; the occasional disappearance of tools from a shed or chickens from their coop; the more frequent incidents of a husband slapping his wife (although generally people said that didn't count, so long as it happened behind closed doors) and once the theft of a corset from a washing line.

So, when the body turned up at the back of the barn in the orchard, it was no surprise that the foundations of the neighbourhood shook for quite some time.

When I was five, the orchard was my favourite place. A fairy-tale playground full of sprites and elves with just enough shadows to intrigue me.

In springtime, I walked with Dad along the blossom-covered paths. One day, I glimpsed eggs falling from a tree. Dad said it was a cuckoo, a fledgling, abandoned in an alien nest by its mother. It was throwing out the original eggs. 'A bit like a murderous squatter.'

The eggs were broken save one which I rescued and took home to Mum. She pulled a face. 'It's lovely, dear, but germs?'

I looked at my mother, pretty and petite, so different from me, and I wondered, was I a cuckoo in *her* nest? If not a cuckoo, maybe I was one of those changelings I read about in my fairy-tale books, and maybe one day my real mother would come and fetch me. I didn't think I would go, because I loved Mum and I would never leave Dad.

Later I found a box, wrote *Keep Out* on the lid and put the egg inside. I covered it with cotton wool and waited for the bird to hatch which, of course, it never did.

In late summer, Mum had a second job picking apples in the orchard.

The pickers climbed stepladders in thick green aprons with baskets strapped to their fronts. Their children, including me, ran off to explore. Sometimes the farmer gave us rides on the back of the tractor, but usually the others would split off into pairs and groups that didn't include me. I'd walk alone, breathing the scent of apples and quince, inventing imaginary friends who trailed behind me like ghosts. When I was brave, I would stray to the back of the orchard and slip into the wasteland, a piece of land which carved a space between the orchard and the field beyond.

The field was a building site, transforming as it was into a housing estate. A no-go area. Too dangerous for little girls. I contented myself with watching from a distance: the cranes and cement mixers and shells of half-finished houses; the men in hard hats roaming and hollering. I'd see them lifting steel bars and shouldering bricks, ploughing up shrubs and churning the earth. Then my heart would break for all the creatures – the voles and the field mice and the rabbits – chased away or pierced by the prongs of the diggers.

For me, the wasteland with its tangled weeds and purple shrubs, its patches of blighted trees and tall and wayward grass, became a place of hidden adventures. A place to take my magnifying glass and hunt for bugs beneath the stones and amongst the leaves, which I would catch in a matchbox, examine carefully and then let go. It was a place to find slow worms which I sometimes took home in a jar, along with twigs and leaves and interesting flowers. I'd wander, skin prickling, as my imagination spotted grinning faces in the shapes of the leaves, or weird creatures hanging from branches and hiding in the hollows: the sprites and demons that Maggie had told me about. I left little gifts sometimes, like tiny offerings: biscuits, a pencil, a hair slide. I thought doing that would make the demons think well of me and keep me safe.

I found a hideaway. I was exploring, crawling through a bush. The earth dropped, forming a flat space at the bottom, big enough for a couple of people to lie down. Trees like sentries clasped their branches overhead. Thorny plants surrounded the dip. It was my secret place. My den. I dragged in stones and rocks that worked as seats and dug a hole to store plastic bags filled with chocolate bars and cans of drink, a torch and a penknife which Dad had given me. I hid there, half wishing I were a sprite myself, whittling wood, reading, or communicating with my imaginary friends in our own special telepathic language.

One warm September day, I was in the wasteland crouching in the grass helping an upturned beetle right itself, easing it over with a twig, when I spotted a figure beneath the trees on the fringe of the orchard.

Sunlight in my eyes, I blinked a few times, thinking it would be one of the usual – if malevolent – fairy-tale creatures that littered my imagination, and that in a second it would disappear. But I kept on looking and the figure stayed.

Biting my lip, I considered my options. Wait until my imagination fizzled out; race to the building site where there were men to protect me, but where I was forbidden to go; or else dash straight past and run top speed to Mum.

The beetle flipped and scuttled away. What was I going to do?

Slowly I stood up and now I could see that this was no apparition, but a man in a long coat. I bit my lip harder to give myself courage. I wanted my mum. It wasn't far across the wasteland, but it seemed like a hundred miles. I crept forwards, reciting nursery rhymes to give myself courage: 'Jack and Jill', 'Hey Diddle Diddle'. Soon I had moved so close I could have thrown a stone and hit him.

I looked around, thinking that might be the solution, but there were no stones within reach, so I tried to relax. It was just a man, *having a smoke* like my dad did, maybe, or *taking a bit of air*, and as I got closer and saw his face, I saw that it wasn't malevolent at all, but quite ordinary: a scratch of stubble on his chin, hair a little longer than my dad's. It was his expression that struck me the most, though, because it was blank, like an unfinished drawing.

Nearly at the orchard, I could smell the fresh, sweet scent of apples. The man hadn't spoken, but he hadn't taken his eyes off me either. Not once. Even when I had focused on my feet for a good half minute and recited 'Little Miss Muffet'.

I stepped across the line into what I thought was safety. Quick as a flash, he opened his coat. I stared, transfixed by what I saw, which was so awful I thought there was something wrong with him. A saggy lump of grey flesh was attached to his body, like a rotting mouse. My eyes travelled to his face, but his expression hadn't changed; he still had that same dead look.

I ran fast through the orchard, around the contorted trees, finally reaching Mum who was busy by then stacking apples into crates. Breathless, I threw my arms about her legs.

'Hey!' she said, trying to push me off. 'What's the matter?'

I shook my head, not wanting to speak, blubbering into her skirt.

'Elizabeth, tell me, what's wrong?' Grabbing my arms, she prised them away, knelt down and took me by the shoulders. 'Elizabeth, speak.'

I hung my head.

'What's wrong?'

'It's him.'

'Who?'

'*Him*. There's something wrong with *him*.'

I told her what I'd seen and her face turned a few different shades before settling on red.

'Where is he?' she said, lips thin.

'Will you help him?'

'I'll help him all right.'

She gave me a hug, sat me down on a crate, told me not to move and went off to talk to the group of pickers. A couple of men disappeared and that was the last I heard. Mum never spoke of what happened next, but that evening, when she said goodnight, she stayed with me for a longer time. She stroked my cheek and said that I should stay away from devils like him.

The problem was, how did you know how to spot a devil? The man in the orchard had had no cloven hooves or forked tail or burning eyes. He'd been ordinary. Hardly any different from Dad.

So that was how I learned lesson two: that devils and demons not only hid amongst the trees, they sometimes hid inside the hearts of people.

3

1999

The past steps back and I push on, crossing the bridge, averting my eyes from the ravaged gull.

Along the way, I stop to look at an ancient building. The walls are fading – yellowing limestone. The windows are different shapes: rectangular, arched, semi-circular. A doorway leads to a flash of green and the rest is invisible. I can imagine the alleyways, secret rooms and shaded cloisters. Sometimes, I visualise another me moving through them clutching my books: Hardy, Dickens and Pope.

My life – if only things had turned out differently.

The other buildings on the street are tall, elegant houses. I pass restaurants – Moroccan, Greek, Italian – doors open to let out the heat, wafts of garlic and cinnamon and frying meat. Further along, there's a second-hand bookshop I often browse in, a pub with a literary name I never drink in, the picture house where I sit from time to time, enjoying the peace and the darkness.

A car sounds its horn. A man in a vest appears at a window and yells at someone in the street. A woman pushes a pram while two small children trail behind. People come and go, in and out of shops and houses.

Which of them keep secrets? Which of them are masters at dissembling?

Secrets are parasites that devour the best of you. The only way to survive is to pretend they don't exist. A bit like ghosts and demons.

A queue trails from the cafe on the corner. I spot Tess through the glass, red-faced, wiping the back of her hand across her brow, serving customers. Tess is my boss though she's younger than me; tall and slim, even her brown-checked overall looks good on her, and she has a lovely Thomas Hardy name. Sometimes I think I only took the job because of that.

Tess spots me and beckons me in. *Hurry up*, she mouths as I squeeze past the customers. *You're late.*

I smile apologetically, keeping my head down as I walk through the cafe and out into the back, trying to be normal.

Normal means hanging my gabardine on its usual peg, taking the freshly laundered overall from my bag and putting it on. Five minutes in the toilet. Transition time as I morph from home Elizabeth into work Elizabeth. Past Elizabeth into present Elizabeth. Academic Elizabeth that might have been to ... *Stop. Breathe.* I splash my face with cold water. It cools me down and it's good for my skin, constricting blood vessels, decreasing blood flow. A throwback to those magazines I used to read, sharing beauty tips with Rachel.

There's a pile of dirty crockery on the draining board which means the dishwasher must be broken. I look through to the cafe. The queue's long and Tess moves fast, piling chosen fillings into rolls.

'There in a minute,' I call out, and then duck away before she can beckon me over.

I need time to think.

Turning on the taps, I watch the water splash into the bowl, add washing-up liquid and swirl it around. My fingers look swollen beneath the water, like fat, grey sausages.

I won't miss this job.

It's been a few months and that's not bad. The longest time I've had any job is two years. That was in a library. I was at home there, moving quietly, pushing my trolley along the rows of books. I liked working in the museum too – the hush, the reverence for the past. It made sense being there. It was as if I was making my peace. I might have stayed if my boss hadn't left. As it was, the man who took over was too loose with his hands, too close for comfort. His breath too often on the back of my neck.

I am restless. Changing jobs distracts me. It makes me believe I'm moving forwards, kicking away at the past, moving upwards like a swimmer heading for the surface.

I make a great show of plunging in crockery and banging it down on the draining board. I want Tess to know that I'm busy so she won't call me in. A few more minutes to collect myself.

There's a mug. *I ❤ you*, the writing says. It belongs to Tess, of course. Her boyfriend gave it to her. It's exactly the kind of object that Tess would like. I would have liked it too, back when I was fifteen, back when I was trying to be accepted, trying to be loved. Love hearts and face packs. Those beauty tips in magazines. None of it made a difference. I didn't have that kind of face, or body. I still don't. Even the man in the museum told me I should be grateful.

Piling more mugs into the bowl, I scrub them with the brush. When I take them out, I discover the handle on the heart mug has cracked. My hand trembles as I set it on the side and I'm not sure if that's because I'm afraid of what Tess will say, or because I'm remembering the man in the museum, or because I'm still thinking about people in white coats brushing earth from bones.

Eventually I come out and join Tess at the counter. The queue has shortened, but even so, Tess says, 'About time, I need a break.'

She doesn't mean to be rude. She's young, no more than twenty-five, and she's pretty. I expect she's had a charmed life; nothing bad has happened to her yet; she has no understanding of misfortune, or of people. She certainly doesn't understand me.

Perhaps she thinks because of the way I look I don't have feelings. Perhaps she thinks my heart is so deeply buried beneath the layers of fat that it's been stifled, that it barely beats at all. She doesn't realise that, actually, it's so full of love and loneliness it could burst. That I want to cover my face with my hands and cry.

Tess tells me the area manager is coming in later so the cafe must be *tip-top*. Then she heads for the back room.

I wonder if she'll notice the crack in her cup.

I wonder if the people in white coats will notice any cracks in any bones.

There are two people left to serve. I give the first a pot of tea, the second a black coffee and a croissant. The croissant looks sweet and sticky. I badly want to eat one, but I resist. Tess doesn't like it if I take food without asking, so I don't.

Besides, despite the Twix and the currant bun, I'm supposed to be on a diet. I'm always on a diet. I don't know anyone who's been on a diet who's ever stopped being on a diet.

There's a car outside the shop. A girl jumps out. She's tall and slim and has long, red hair. She swings her shiny shopping bags with their cord handles and gold lettering. She wears a loose dress and flat shoes, and she's walking, moving effortlessly, like water downstream, like Rachel used to do.

A customer comes in. He orders a prawn mayonnaise sandwich which I drop into a paper bag and swing round to twist the edges. As an afterthought, I put it into another bag and twist that too.

Tess returns. I avoid her, staying at one end of the counter, cleaning items that don't need to be cleaned, working up a sweat. When it's my turn, I go to the back room, stare at the wall and, since I'm allowed to eat on my break, wolf down a bacon roll, and then a chocolate eclair, and then a Chelsea bun. I can't stop eating. Fear has wakened my hunger.

Once upon a time, I used to make myself sick. That was *after* what happened, when controlling my food intake was a bit like not stepping on the cracks – but all that retching saps your energy, it undermines your self-belief, and if there were two qualities I needed in the end, they were energy and self-belief.

Finishing the bun, I close my eyes. It's hard to stay normal. To keep my mind from returning to the skeleton in the morgue, to stop imagining the plain walls, the strip lights, those people in white coats searching for clues. I try filling my head with thoughts: my almost empty house with its bare walls and sticks of furniture, its tiny, paved garden. Not much to show after all these years, but then I've never wanted much.

Mid-morning, and there's a lull. We clean the sides and the surfaces and polish the coffee machine until it sparkles. Tess is pleased with my work. She says I'm thorough, she says my experience shows.

She doesn't know I've worked in bookshops and museums and libraries. I never told her I was on my way back from giving in my notice at the museum when I saw the card in the window and enquired.

I said I'd worked in a cafe before, but she didn't ask where or when, only suggested a trial. I was diligent and got the job. No references required. Maybe Tess thought I had an honest face, the kind of person who wouldn't steal from the till or cook the books or take more than her fair share of giveaway cakes.

It's early, but already Tess is sorting through the cakes and sandwiches she predicts will be left over. She likes to do this before lunch as it saves time and means she can leave immediately with her boyfriend who comes to meet her every day.

Now she blushes a bit and says they're going out for dinner. A special date apparently. The way she looks makes me wonder if she anticipates a proposal. She won't tell me because she assumes I know nothing about boyfriends – not that I'm a virgin, if that's what she thinks. I made sure of that when I left school. Who wants a label burdening them for the rest of their life?

I was eighteen. It was my first year in London. I lived in a bedsit in Canning Town which was so dismal I just wanted to get out. I have a vague memory of a pub and a man's face, narrow and unshaven, and his smell – oil (I think he said he worked with cars) mixed with a citrus aftershave. I have a vague memory of what we talked about – his breaking away from his wife, my breaking away from my mother. His ambition to work hard and retire to Spain. My ambition to keep my head low. I was a watcher. He was a seeker. I didn't tell him how I'd given up my ambitions long ago.

Tess puts some of the food into a paper bag for me. The cakes will be from yesterday, the sandwiches will be a little stale, bread curling at the edges. I know she'll take the best for herself but still I accept them gratefully.

Beggars can't be choosers.

And yet . . .

I can't stay here, serving and sweeping and polishing. Smiling at customers as if nothing has changed. Listening to Tess and her good-natured chat.

The feeling grows as time ticks on and when Tess disappears to the loo, I make my decision.

Shedding my overall, grabbing my gabardine, stuffing the cakes into my bag, I step into the street.

Outside, it's still muggy, the air close. People are quieter than usual. The atmosphere is dreary, colours are muted as if the world's gone monochrome. It might be my imagination, of course. It might be that I'm the one whose senses have been deadened.

A car zips past, weaving shamelessly around the rest, music cascading through the window, jarring and insistent. It's Prince. '1999'. Singing about judgement day and running out of time. The turn of the century. How did so much time pass? Who would have thought it possible to build a life on such a precarious past? Like building a house on crumbling foundations. Or is that image too grand? It's more like a rickety old shack and, let's face it, how could that ever last?

I hurry away, throwing a guilty look over my shoulder. Has Tess noticed that I'm gone? Is she wide-eyed and spinning in circles, wondering how she could have misplaced somebody as big as me?

In the street, there are fewer people around – everyone is red-faced and flustered by the heat. I hear them talking. A woman remarks on how suddenly the hot weather has come. A man joins in, pronouncing it will break. They nod sagely, agreeing it won't be long.

And I am lost, standing there.

What should I do?

Write it down.

Think the story through.

Stare backwards and wait for the fog to clear.

I am like the fortune teller I visited once, waving her hands over a crystal ball. Mind you, she was searching the future, I'm still looking at the past.

A woman walks past leading a child in a red and grey school uniform.

My uniform was blue and grey. Mum made the skirt, laying down the tracing paper, kneeling on the floor with pins in her mouth. There she is, cutting the shape from a pattern, measuring and fitting and turning me around, hemming and sewing and saying I look fine. There I am, still a way off meeting Rachel, wearing the skirt on my first day at school.

It was raining. A fine mist had fallen on the playground.

I held Mum's hand, in shoes that were a little too big and a cardigan that was a little too small. As it was, it was two sizes larger than was average for my age.

Mum, in another rare act of loyalty, had seized a pair of scissors and snipped out the label. 'Puppy fat,' she'd said. 'You'll grow out of it. Wait and see.'

I didn't believe that, any more than I believed that my scattering of chicken pox scars would heal, or my hair would thicken like Lovely Amanda's, or I'd become suddenly lovable to people on the street. Or that anyone in this school would like me.

A few of the children were crying; some were alone, digging in the sand or climbing on the frame; others were forming groups or pairs already.

A teacher appeared and clanged a bell.

'Time to go, love,' said Mum.

I bit my lip and swallowed hard.

'Time to go,' she said again, unpeeling my fingers from where they gripped her wrist.

My eyes filled as she bent down to kiss me.

'Be good,' she whispered as the bell clanged again.

She walked away and I watched her go, down the path

and out through the white wicket gates. Her hair blew in her face as she turned to wave and then she was gone.

I dug my hands in the pockets of my skirt and lined up with the rest.

Most of the children were small and wiry. Some wore glasses, a few had grubby coats, one had an eye patch. None of them had thin, pale hair that stuck to their foreheads. None of them filled their uniforms like a bag of stodgy suet. My stomach felt empty as I stood there, turning around, as if in slow motion. Empty and cold as if the life had been sucked out of me, leaving only a shell.

'Doughnut,' said a boy jabbing his elbow into my ribs. 'Jelly belly,' he added when I didn't react.

I closed my eyes. *Sticks and stones.*

What next?

Memories, like those flip books – tiny drawings, each one different, creating a story.

Back to school. A few weeks in, waiting in vain for someone to ask me to make up the numbers in a game. Teachers insisting on pairs: for lining up, for walking to assembly, for reading practice, cartwheel practice, cat's cradle. For taking the register to the office. For fetching the register from the office.

Being alone wasn't possible.

I needed friends.

I looked around again and saw that there were more people like me. A small, quiet boy with dark hair called John Cox and a stick-thin girl called Debra March who wore the same dirty dress every day and tied back her hair with string.

John was brilliant at spelling and adding. He had a scar on his face and no mother, and I didn't know why until a few years later when he told me. Four years old, shopping in town, she had bought him a football, told him not to play with it, only he hadn't listened. He'd chased the ball and she'd chased him, throwing him to safety and herself beneath a bus.

John preferred silence. Debra on the other hand was so relieved to have someone to talk to, she didn't stop. She talked incessantly about her mother and a man called Frank. 'He takes me shopping,' she said, 'and buys me stuff and he's much better than my real dad, 'cos he's a waste of space, that's what Mum says, and he left when I was two, so it must be true.'

School became more bearable. John and Debra and me. We were the misfits and our friendship became cemented by that fact.

Now, of course, I realise those early school years were my easy years, when my biggest problem was avoiding the kids who called me names or jabbed their elbows in my ribs.

They were straightforward playground issues.

It was only later when the darker side of life appeared that it became obvious. The Devil hiding inside that flasher I'd seen had merely been the beginning.

4

1977

It was my thirteenth birthday and one year before I met Rachel.

All was not right in the world.

Two days before, Elvis Presley had died from a heart attack. That very morning, the pet rabbit belonging to Dorothy Metcalf at number nine had escaped its hutch and been ripped to pieces by a bird. I'd stood along with the other kids on our road staring at the messy entrails, knowing it didn't bode well.

I thought it was my fault. (The bunny, not Elvis.)

It might have been Maggie's influence, but I was sure I could predict the future. Sometimes my prediction was based on a strong feeling, like when I went into the bathroom and knew, just knew, there'd be a hairy spider the size of a saucer hunched on the wall. Other times it was due to a sign or a portent. The lone magpie forecasting the injury of a builder on the site. The croaking raven signalling the demise of Mrs Faraday at number five – the woman who'd lost her corset.

In the case of Dorothy Metcalf's pet rabbit I put its death down to three crows which had taken off simultaneously from the ledge outside my bedroom window three days before.

Every year my birthday went the same way. The

tradition was tea for the three of us, except one year when John and Debra had come. On that occasion, Debra had piled up her plate, bolted it down, turned a peculiar shade of green and vomited on the floor. Mum had watched aghast, bottle of Vim in hand, and ever since then I hadn't invited my friends.

Mum and Dad gave me a Polaroid camera and a Starsky-style cardigan. Mid-morning, Mrs Joseph popped round with a plate of biscuits. Dad offered to buy me an LP, so we left Mum baking birthday cake and sausage rolls with the charges lined up on the plastic-covered sofa, each with an etch-a-sketch to minimise the mess.

The record shop was a treat for Dad as much as it was for me. He liked to flip through the albums, pick one out, slip the vinyl lovingly from its sleeve and scrutinise for scratches.

Dave owned the place. He was tall with a big nose and overlong, mousy-coloured hair that he constantly swept from his face. He and Dad were a duo. Not that they had much in common. Dave was into heavy metal – Judas Priest and Alice Cooper. He wore black T-shirts painted with skulls and a metal cross on a chain. Dad loved disco music and Barry White. 'You're the First, the Last, My Everything'. Dave was playing his song.

'One day,' said Dad, tapping his foot, 'I'm gonna quit security and fly to California, get a job as a bodyguard with Barry.'

'That's still security,' Dave pointed out.

'Yeah, but it's high-class security. That place' – he meant the nightclub where he worked – 'is full of low lifes, I couldn't care less what happens to any one of them.'

Dave shrugged. He didn't care about much either so long as Dad came in for a mosey and bought a couple of records while he was there, which he did – Barry White for himself and David Soul for me. Dad said I could get a poster too, so I chose Starsky, mournful in his cardigan.

After that we went off down the street, Dad bouncing along as if Barry was giving a personal performance inside his head, me clutching my LP and my poster to my chest.

Dad announced we were going to The Grand Hotel, which was a way off and overlooking the river. I would have been happy in Maggie's Cafe, but Dad said he thought I should have a proper birthday treat.

The Grand Hotel had an old-fashioned gentility that didn't fit with their menu. The lighting shone darkly on heavy wood tables and chairs and chintzy sofas set around a fire which was blazing even though it was the middle of August. The place smelled of lavender and dust and a hint of pot pourri. Dad said the hotel made you think of old ladies eating Dover sole and consommé, cucumber sandwiches and cream teas, not the fish and chips and chicken in a basket that dominated the menu.

We settled at a table by the bar. The waitress came. Younger than Mum, plump, with brown eyes and glossy lips and dark hair tied back in a ponytail. She wore a short black dress and a frilly white apron and she was chewing gum, quietly, but I could tell. Dad called her Peggy and she called him Ted, so it was obvious to me that Dad had been here before. He introduced me as his daughter and she looked at me and then right through me.

Dad gave our order – chicken and beer for himself, battered fish and lemonade for me. Peggy licked her pencil and scribbled. She brought our drinks and when she put Dad's down, their fingers touched. I liked her jewellery: skeleton earrings, a necklace with a pendant shaped like a bull's skull that hypnotised me as she leaned across the table.

There was something different about Dad. His hair was combed as usual; he wore his tan flares, his good brown jacket and a thin mustard-coloured polo-necked jumper which was also standard, and when he took his jacket off and hung it on the chair, his muscles strained at the cloth. He had a habit of scratching his stubble, but now I noticed he was smoothing his skin which meant of course that he'd shaved.

Dad hated shaving and avoided it, but if I got the chance, I liked to watch – the way he twisted his chin and pulled at his skin, working the razor through the foam and then knocking it into the sink. Sometimes he nicked himself and then he cursed and stuck a scrap of loo roll on the cut which bloomed red as it absorbed the blood. He was proud of his stubble, boasting that he could strike a match and make it burn. I watched him do it one year on my birthday to light the candles on the cake.

Another thing struck me that was different about Dad. There was a scent I didn't recognise, an animal, slightly rotten smell. A new aftershave, I decided.

Peggy came back with the food. I studied her more

closely. Her body was plump but the rest of her was small. Short, with tiny hands and feet, slim legs and arms. Beside her, I was the Incredible Hulk. Dr David Banner, after he'd got angry. Maybe I was a bit green because a flame of jealousy flickered inside me as she commandeered Dad's attention. Quickly I extinguished my feelings with a gulp of lemonade.

Halfway through the meal, Dad pushed away his food and lit a cigarette. He watched Peggy wafting past serving other people before coming back to clear our plates and offer dessert. I asked for a knickerbocker glory.

Dad talked to me about school. 'What's your favourite subject?'

'English.'

He made a face and I knew what was coming next. 'What can you do with that? Maths and science, that's what you need. What does your form teacher think?'

'She's all right.'

He supped his beer and frowned, trying to work out if I'd actually answered his question.

In fact, Mrs Townsend wasn't all right at all.

I *exasperated* her, she said, which seemed to be far worse than any of the emotions the other pupils caused her to experience. Boys made her *furious*. For example, when they flicked balls of paper at people's heads. Girls made her *very annoyed indeed*, when they combed their hair or read *My Guy*, or applied mascara and lip gloss in class. One anonymous person *sickened* her when he or she put a used sanitary towel in the classroom bin. Yet no point was made with the same level of frustrated eye-rolling as when she said to me, 'You're a bright girl, you could go on to great things. I mean *great* things. Oxford. Cambridge. But you need to *listen*. You can't go day-dreaming your way through life.'

Couldn't I?

Zoning out. It worked as well as anything else to mute the advice or criticism I didn't want to hear. Like now, when Dad was going on about school: tests and exams and qualifications and respecting teachers (unless they were wrong). I'd heard it all before. I also knew from experience that working hard in class gave me labels: *swot* and *teacher's pet* to add to *tubs*, *fatso*, *weirdo*. It was only Mrs Townsend I hadn't fooled. All the rest of the teachers thought I was useless.

Dad was still going on and now I imagined a cloud of his inky words gathering over my head – the letters clashing, evaporating, re-forming.

I zoned back in time to hear, 'I could have been a teacher – if I'd gone to a better school. I could have gone to university and studied law. I could have been a doctor if a career's advisor had bloody advised me. Don't make the same mistakes I did. A bouncer working in a night-club. Do you really want to end up like me?'

I had a flash of myself dressed in a black suit, pale hair greasy with Brylcreem, standing at the entrance to the club, flanked by John and Debra with a red cord strung between me and all the people I didn't like. *You can come in. You can't come in. No way, José. Get the hell out of my club.*

'Elizabeth. Are you listening?'

I jumped.

'I said this small town, it's got zero to offer. Not to me and definitely not to you.'

He stubbed out his cigarette and that's when he brought up the subject of Mum.

'It was your mother,' he said, 'that brought us here in the first place, with her silly suburban ways. Nothing's ever good enough for Phyllis.' He finished his beer and lit another cigarette.

I ate a chip, chewing it slowly. Was he being serious? 'Where would you rather be?'

'S'easy. London. One day.' He flicked ash onto his plate.

'When?'

My panic must have shown. 'Don't worry. No time soon.'

'What about me?'

'Hey, I told you, no time soon.' He smoothed his hair.

Peggy appeared, plonked the knickerbocker glory in front of me and hurried away to serve someone else.

Watching Dad watching her, I stirred the ice cream with a long spoon. What if the spoon was a wand? What if I could flick it through the air and cause amazing transformations to happen? The couple by the window would turn into toads. The woman with the perm and the kaftan would turn into a bat. Lights would come on. Music would begin. 'Daddy Cool'. The man at the bar, in the beige suit, would disco dance like Boney M.

And Peggy? What could happen to her? She would melt, like candle wax. I pictured her face collapsing, her body dissolving, thick liquid pooling on the floor.

Dad was still smoking and gazing at a spot over my

shoulder. I was still stirring, harder and harder. The spoon was my wand. The glass was my cauldron. The ice cream sploshed over the sides.

Peggy was on her way back to the kitchen, arms piled with dirty crockery. She passed the man in the suit. He muttered words I couldn't catch.

'In your dreams,' she said, her voice shrill, loud enough for the whole restaurant to hear. She let out a peal of laughter. He said more and she laughed again. I could still hear her giggling as she pushed the swing door into the kitchen.

'There's a lesson for you, Elizabeth,' said Dad. 'If looks could kill.'

I followed his gaze to the bar. The man was scowling, his face dark with anger, as he knocked back his beer.

'Men like that,' said Dad, tapping his ash onto his plate, 'hate to be laughed at.' He gave his own little chuckle. 'Remember that, Elizabeth, when you start to knock 'em dead.'

Peggy came out of the kitchen and over to us. Grimacing, she mopped up the spilled ice cream. Pretending not to notice, I announced I had to call home.

'There's a telephone at the bar,' she said, glancing at Dad.

'No thank you,' I replied in my politest voice. She wasn't going to get rid of me that easily. 'I can use the phone box when we get outside.'

Dad looked at me oddly.

'It's my birthday, you see. And Mum's making a special tea. For the three of us.' I said *three* loudly and very clearly and then repeated it in case she hadn't heard. 'We need to get home quickly.'

She frowned, wondering what I was talking about. Dad paid. I drummed my fingers as he dithered, pulling out notes, counting them into Peggy's hand. At the door, he said he'd forgotten his wallet and hurried back to the table. Peggy was still there, stacking the plates.

A few words, a slow smile, a brush of fingers.

'The wallet?' I said when he came back.

'What?'

'Did you find it?'

His face cleared. 'Oh yeah.' He patted his pocket. 'Here all the time.'

Later, after I'd called Mum from the phone box and she'd asked me what on earth I was doing disturbing her and didn't I know she had enough to do with the charges and the cake and the birthday tea, we walked along the path by the river.

Stopping at the ice cream van, Dad bought us both a 99. Around us, children played games on the grass – catch and badminton, French cricket – while their parents sat in clusters, picnic hampers at the ready. Girls shrieked, all arms and legs and messy hair. Boys barged and yelled, all smelly armpits and untucked shirts. Younger children fed the swans near the boathouse while gulls made daring forays into the melee, and mallards and moorhens darted amongst the lot of them.

Some of the older children stared at me. A couple of them whispered behind their hands. I imagined what they were saying. *She's the weird one. Look at her. Fat. Ugly. Never speaks.*

A hollow feeling grew inside my belly. I tried filling it up, eating my ice cream as fast as I could. I clung to Dad's arm, keeping my face turned away. I was invincible so long as I had him. Yet when we stopped to contemplate the passing boats, his mind seemed locked in a place that didn't include me, and my emptiness remained.

'It would be a good life, wouldn't it?' he said as a white yacht as bright as a beacon passed along the river. 'Imagine lying on the deck in the middle of the ocean stargazing.'

I took a photo of the disappearing yacht and the camera churned out a bleary Polaroid. Dad posed and I took one of him too, but it wasn't any better.

We stayed in silence. It was a lovely day. The sky was cloudless, the trees alongside lush and green; light pooled golden and bright on the water. Yet I couldn't get rid of the emptiness, and my mind drifted back to the hotel, to Peggy with her glossy lips and dark eyes, to the corpse of Dorothy Metcalf's rabbit sprawled on the road. I was nervous and I couldn't pinpoint why. I only knew that a change was going to happen. Maybe not now, maybe not tomorrow or next week, but soon.

Blood is thicker than water.

Did Dad still believe that?

No. I was losing him, I felt it deep inside me. But it was more than just about Peggy and whatever was happening today. This was a blip, drifting away like the boats we were watching. No. When the change came, it would be bigger than anything my imagination could conjure.

5

1978

The day when I met Rachel arrived. August 1978. Saturday, a few days before my fourteenth birthday.

The night before, I had woken to the sound of a thud against my bedroom window. In the morning after breakfast, Mum sent me to buy milk and eggs from Spar. I fetched my bike from the shed and found a bat on the ground. I shivered and looked around me. Since when did bats fly into barricades? Was it a sign or an unlucky accident? Gritting my teeth, I shovelled up the corpse and buried it in the garden. Then, considering the nature of death and the afterlife, balancing notions of paradise, chaos and nothingness, I cycled to Spar. Afterwards, I took a detour, trundling around the park and back through the orchard and the wasteland.

A hundred near-identical houses had sprung up on the field. The builders had ravaged the land. Modern-day warriors in hard hats and donkey jackets.

Not that it was peaceful at home. The house was like an institution for tiny offenders with groups of children standing to attention in varying places: outside the bathroom, in front of the sofa, behind their chairs. There were too many rules; the larder was full, but food was rationed, prioritised for the charges.

Mum bought food that made the least mess: biscuits in

individual wrappers; plain crisps that left no residue. The children ate their meals in regimented sittings at the kitchen table with an easy-wipe-down vinyl tablecloth and tissues at the ready. I ate with them: macaroni cheese and rice pudding; coronation chicken and spotted dick. Thick custard with skin on top, bread pudding, apple pie. Stodgy food that filled me up and weighed me down.

Mrs Joseph was one of the few people who didn't comment on my weight. In her forties, short and round, she wore layers of brightly coloured clothes, beads and bangles that clanged when she walked. She was always busy, darting around, hands fluttering like the canaries she kept in cages, though Mrs Joseph smelled of sweet perfume while the birds had a rancid scent.

She liked to bake and whenever she heard me in the garden, she'd call me over because I was *a tonic who brightened her life*. Mum said it was because she didn't have any children of her own. Her son had died of scarlet fever shortly after her husband had died from a stroke. Now she lived with her brother, Victor, who hadn't been right since an accident he'd had in his twenties. A builder, he'd fallen from a crane.

I didn't understand what not being *right* meant, so when I was in their house, I would study him sitting in his armchair beside the three-bar fire, which was always on whatever the weather. Apart from the fact that he had the longest legs I had ever seen, wore the same burgundy V-necked jumper almost every day, rarely spoke and never smiled, he seemed exactly like anyone else. I liked him because it felt as if we had a special connection: the way he was silent like I was, the way he fixed his eyes on me. Once I swore that he winked.

Mrs Joseph had given me her late husband's bike because she had no more use for it. 'No balance,' she'd said, holding out her arms and giving a kaleidoscopic twirl, releasing a cloud of perfume that smelled like Parma Violets.

The bike was heavy and old-fashioned, and what I really coveted was a chopper – even though Debra had reliably told me that choppers were for boys and roller skates were for girls.

Still, I'd gratefully accepted the gift and was glad that I had because after I left the orchard with my mind still full of death, it was from that old bike that I fell and landed at the feet of *the girl*. If I'd been gliding by on a chopper, the accident might never have happened and the first connection wouldn't have been made.

In September, she turned up at school.

Mrs Townsend marched into our form room, clutching the register and parading the *new girl*.

I gripped the sides of my desk, unable to believe my luck: the angel was back in my life.

'Class,' said Mrs Townsend, 'this is Rachel Wright. I'm sure you'll make her welcome.'

Rachel Wright. I whispered the words and listened to their sound.

There were a few whoops from the boys and much banging of lids on desks. The girls, I noticed, were watching, silently assessing. Did they see what I saw?

A skirt that was a tiny bit too short for school

regulations, a heart-shaped locket on a silver chain, a jaw muscle working where she was secretly chewing gum, hair like a billow of red silk. It must have been brushed a million times to get that shine.

Green eyes. Bright and flecked with black.

She had an aura. A glow. She was plump, but not like me with a body that sprawled out in every direction. Rachel seemed older, more like a sixth-former, and her face was round and pretty. She wore lip gloss, a trace of blue eye shadow. She was flouting the rules with a message of defiance.

I stared while inside my head choirs of angels sang.

Mrs Townsend scanned the room.

'Now,' she said, 'who wants to look after Rachel?'

A raft of hands were raised, including Debra's. Mine failed to make it, rapt as I was, mesmerised by my celestial thoughts.

Mrs Townsend frowned at those, including me, who hadn't volunteered. It was a silent reproach. Had Rachel noticed too? The spell was broken, my hand shot up. *Pick me. Pick me.*

'Amanda, you'd be perfect.'

My shoulders slumped. Naturally Lovely Amanda would get the job. Let's face it. Why would someone like Rachel want to spend time with someone like me?

At home a girl called Melissa joined Mum's horde. Nine years old, Mum would pick her up from school. Skinny, she wore princess dresses and tossed her highly brushed dark-brown hair and stamped her teeny tiny red-patent-leather-clad feet when she didn't get her way.

I'm not sure when I discovered that her sister was Rachel, but since Mum knew pretty much everyone in the neighbourhood, having taken care of so many children, and since these people loved to stand in the doorway and waste Mum's time, as she put it, feeding her the gossip that flew like carrier pigeons around our streets, all the missing details soon fell into place.

The Wright family had moved here for no other reason (apparently) than that they'd wanted a change, an escape from the countryside, which turned out to be a village in Norfolk. They were renting. A twelve-month trial to see how they liked Chelmsford.

Mrs Wright worked for the council. She had a body like Betty Boop and hair like hers too: black and flat on her head with kiss curls on her cheeks and on her fore-head. Secretly I tried teasing my hair to replicate hers, but the curls were more like tentacles and the rest of it just looked greasy. In my mind, her eye colour was a poor imitation of Rachel's: green mixed with brackish brown. She wore thick, dark make-up, which I also tried to copy, but the mascara and eye-liner I found in Mum's room weren't equipped for the job.

They lived on the new estate off the main street, opposite Maggie's Cafe. Mr Wright was a builder with a clapped-out rusty old van.

'An eyesore,' Mum declared.

I wasn't certain if she meant the van or Mr Wright himself because he was huge – tall and solid with hands like spades – but then I heard Mum say that despite his size, he was a handsome fellow on account of his dark eyes and clipped beard. 'He's a bit like one of those Spanish Armada chaps,' she said.

As intrigued as I was by her sister, I didn't like Melissa at all. She whined and complained and bullied the snivelling boys, prodding and poking them and stealing their biscuits.

Mostly, it was her dad who came for her. He squeezed into our narrow hall, and waited there, scratching his beard or flexing his hands as if he didn't know what to do with them; and while Mum was persuading Melissa to put on her coat and to find her shoes, he'd be perusing the hall, his black-eyed gaze slipping from me to Mum to the table to the coat stand with an equal level of interest.

Occasionally, though, Mrs Wright came and when she did, she stood on the doorstep with a smile in the style of a grimace and her arms crossed over her chest.

One day she arrived later than usual, having missed her bus. Dad came home as she and Melissa were leaving, smelling of vinegar. He had a bag of fish and chips and a few bottles of brown ale. It was his night off and he had promised Mum he would spend it with us. 'Not before time,' she'd said, which was fair enough since he usually went to The Dog and Duck.

'Who was that?' Dad asked, raising his eyebrows as Mrs Wright tottered past.

Mum had gone inside, so I explained.

'Wowser,' he said. 'Not the usual type for these parts, is she?'

*

46

A few days later, I was lying on the sofa eating crisps when the telephone rang. It was Mrs Wright. Her husband was working and she'd missed her bus. Could Melissa stay later?

Mum suggested I entertained Melissa by playing KerPlunk.

KerPlunk. How old did she think I was?

Cramming the last of the crisps into my mouth, I dragged myself off the sofa and went to my room in search of the game.

Melissa was her usual fussy self. She complained each time the marbles dropped into her section. Eventually, I pulled out a stick, balanced it behind my ear and escaped to the bathroom. When I came back, Melissa said she was bored and didn't want to play.

Fine. It was more trouble to argue. I packed away, muttering to myself. I didn't see her crossing the room, or climbing up and kneeling on the bed, or examining my shelves, or taking down the box I'd filled with stuff I'd collected with Dad: the egg we'd found abandoned; stones and shells from a day trip to Bournemouth; a postcard from the London Planetarium.

I didn't notice what she was doing until she said, 'Eww. What's this?'

She was holding the egg, collapsed now and rotten.

'It's a bird's egg.'

'Where did you get it?'

'Nowhere.'

'Did you steal it from a nest? My dad says it's cruel to steal from nests.'

'No,' I said, making a grab for the box. 'Of course I didn't.'

'Don't snatch. My mum says it's rude to snatch.'

I hesitated, reminding myself that Melissa was only nine. 'Maybe you shouldn't touch other people's—'

'I'm a guest,' she interrupted. 'That means I can do what I want.'

I bit my lip.

'And . . . my mum *pays* your mum which means she's more important.'

I glared at her.

'She says you should lose weight. She says you're weird and that if me or Rachel ever got fat like you, she'd lock us in our rooms so we couldn't eat.'

I turned away, humiliation making me hot. Was Melissa making it up? Or were she and her mum and, worst of all, Rachel, laughing at me behind my back?

'Mum says I'm just right but that Rachel's on the plump side.'

She put her hands on her waist and swivelled as if she was swinging a hula hoop.

What was she talking about? Rachel was perfect.

'Mum says she wears too much nail varnish. She says she won't get herself a boyfriend unless she smartens up her act. Boys don't like tarts.'

'Rachel's not a tart,' I retorted finally. 'You don't even know what that means.'

She tipped her chin. 'Yes I do. Mum says she'll end up being a little tart and that you're a disgrace and that your mum's prissy.'

A gust of anger swept through me. 'Prissy?'

'Yep. And a prude. She says your dad should get rid of her.'

I had a sudden flashback of Dad staring at Mrs Wright flouncing along in her tight dress and my temper broke. Swift as an arrow, I whipped the KerPlunk stick from behind my ear and launched it in Melissa's direction. Missing by a mile, it clattered on the fireplace.

For one second Melissa stared at me and in her eyes, I saw what I needed to know. She had the power and I was in trouble.

I was right.

Later, when her mother arrived, she took one look at Melissa's miserable face and said, 'What the hell has happened here?'

I looked at Mum. She pursed her lips.

Melissa was crying, but it wasn't *proper* crying. It was dry, like a dog with a cough.

'A misunderstanding,' said Mum. 'The girls had an argument.'

'She stabbed me,' said Melissa.

'What?' I said. 'That's not true.'

'Look!' She pointed at her neck.

Mrs Wright leaned forward and squinted at her daughter. 'Elizabeth did this?'

I protested. 'There's nothing there!'

She ignored me and glared at Mum, towering over her, lipstick mouth open like the gates of hell.

'Well, I'm not surprised. Melissa has mentioned behaviour like this before.'

Mum's face was getting redder. There was an atmosphere that reminded me of the moment before the first thunderclap of a storm.

'I think you'll find Elizabeth was provoked,' she said finally. 'Melissa has a foul mouth. And I'm sure I don't know who she could have got that from.'

I sucked in my breath. It was one of those rare and special moments when Mum was defending me.

Mrs Wright scowled. 'What do you mean? What did she say?'

'You'll have to ask her,' said Mum dramatically, 'and now, if you don't mind, I'm rather busy.'

Their eyes locked until suddenly, Mrs Wright grabbed Melissa's arm and pulled her out of the house. 'We're going,' she threw over her shoulder as she tottered down the path, 'and we *won't* be coming back.'

Later, Mum told me not to tell Dad. She was making tea, wearing her red and yellow striped apron. 'I don't know exactly what happened, and I probably don't want to hear, but there's no point bringing it up.'

I sat down at the table, my stomach growling. 'Why?'

She sighed. 'Don't be obtuse, Elizabeth. You know very well how he'll react.' She fixed me with her gaze before producing a plate of sausage rolls. 'Promise me you won't. We don't need any excuses for more . . .' – she hesitated – 'absences.'

There was a note to her voice that made me uneasy. I reached for a sausage roll and grasped nothing as she moved the plate away. 'Promise me,' she insisted.

I nodded and she put down the plate. Choosing the

biggest, I bit into the pastry. As quick as a flash, Mum leaned across and wiped away the crumbs.

I filled the hour before Dad came home brooding about what had happened.

I was still angry with Melissa – the way she'd insulted me. She was only nine. Who did she think she was? It was bad enough at school when people my own age called me names, and then there was the stuff about Mum. Dad would be furious if he knew Mrs Wright had called her prissy. I was beginning to think the woman was a siren trying to steal Dad away, just like Peggy had before.

I waited until Dad had had his tea and was sitting in his armchair, having one last smoke before he left for work.

'She said what?' His face had slowly been turning red while I'd talked.

'She said I was fat and weird.'

He blinked, took a drag, blew the smoke high into the air. 'Well, that's not on. Phyllis, did you hear?'

Mum was dusting the bookshelves. She turned. 'What's that?'

'The Wright girl called Elizabeth fat.'

'And weird,' I added helpfully.

Mum frowned across at me and shook her head, and then replaced the book she was holding. 'It's nothing, Ted. Kids being silly.'

'It's not silly if they're not coming back. That's money lost and we can't have it.'

Ignoring Mum's warning stare, I carried on. 'She said

I was the ugliest girl she'd ever seen and I should stay in my room and never come out.'

'Ridiculous,' said Dad, his eyes blazing. He shifted in his seat, rubbed the back of his neck.

'And she said Mrs Wright thinks that you're too good for Mum and should leave her.'

'What?'

'Mrs Wright thinks Mum's prissy. And . . .' – I paused and sifted through the insults that were regularly levelled at me – 'frigid.'

Silence. Dad was staring. Mum had stopped dusting and turned to look, face filled with colour.

Had I gone too far?

Almost immediately, Mum started dusting again. Dad folded his paper and searched for his cigarettes.

'I'll have a word,' he said eventually, 'before work.'

Mum spoke to the bookshelves. 'Don't. It won't bring Melissa back and, quite frankly, I don't want her here.'

'No,' said Dad slowly, 'but it might give the signal to these people that they shouldn't call Elizabeth names. Blood's thicker than water. That man needs to sort his daughter out. What did he say?'

'It wasn't him that collected her,' I said.

The atmosphere thickened. Dad scratched his stubble. 'Well then, what did she say?'

'It doesn't matter, Ted. I've dealt with it.'

'Even so. I'll have a word.'

Mum's lips were so tight they were almost white.

Frozen out, I went to my room and threw myself onto the bed. Chin in my hands, I gazed at my posters, trying to find solace. I'd wanted to unite Mum and Dad by telling Dad about Melissa, not make them argue. I'd expected him to be angry, but I hadn't imagined he'd go to their house. He'd never actually confronted anyone like that before.

I heard him come up the stairs and visit the bathroom. Twenty minutes later he knocked on my door.

'Gotta go,' he said, leaning to give me a kiss.

I noticed that his stubble was gone and he was wearing his new aftershave: Musk. There was a bottle of it in the bathroom cabinet next to the Brut I'd bought him last Christmas.

'Don't go,' I said suddenly, grabbing his neck.

'I have to. It's work.'

'I don't mean to work.'

'Hey, don't worry. I'll sort it out.' He loosened my grip.

'But I shouldn't have—'

'Stop. Don't worry. You did the right thing telling me.'

He sat down properly and gave me a hug. I rested my head on his chest. I had a terrible sense of foreboding. If only I could undo what I'd said.

'See you tomorrow.' He kissed me once again, and then he was gone.

The door slammed. I dashed to the front of the house to look out the window. He was swaggering along the street, hands in his pockets, Barry White singing inside his head. A Siamese cat darted across the road. A car swerved, narrowly missing it. Was it a sign? What did it mean? A lucky escape or an accident that would have brought Dad back home?

Later, when I'd got into bed, I heard Mum's footsteps

on the stairs. 'I told you not to tell him,' she said from the doorway. Her voice was ice cold as she closed the door quietly behind her.

Switching off the light, I tried to sleep, but the scent of musk hung heavy in the air, making me queasy.

Mum was right, I shouldn't have told. I'd exaggerated what Melissa had said. Would Dad repeat my lies? Worse. What would Rachel think?

6

1999

A horn blasts and there's a shout: 'Get out the way!'

I've stopped in the middle of the road. Stuck in a reverie.

Zoned out.

Cheeks burning, I lift my hand as an apology and hurry across to the other side. My legs ache. I've been walking for too long. Going in circles, screwing my courage to the sticking post, as they say.

I breathe, get my bearings. It's so hot, I'd like a drink – a cold glass of white wine, perhaps two – just to dull the sharpness of my thoughts. Maybe I should find a cafe or a pub where I can sit outside and watch people passing by, or go for a walk in the gardens, or along the canal.

On Broad Street, a mass of tourists is grouped around a thin, bespectacled guide who's pontificating about history and ghosts. The tourists are dressed for the heat: summer dresses, T-shirts and shorts with light jumpers tied at their waists or draped across their shoulders. They move on, going to the Bridge of Sighs, perhaps, or to one of the colleges, or the Bodleian Library. All those ancient places, what hopes and dreams and secrets they must hide. What unwritten stories.

I am outside them looking on and my heart aches at

the untouchable and the unreachable. The what-might-have-beens woven in-between my acceptance of how life is. I'd miss Oxford if I had to leave it. Even being on the outside is better than having nothing at all.

A man bumps into me and tips his fedora as an apology. I smile back and watch him saunter confidently along the cobbled street, swinging his gold-tipped cane like a character in a storybook. Out of his time yet with a sense of belonging that I envy.

Sweat trickles down my skin. I regret wearing my gabardine. I don't know why I brought it this morning, grabbing it from its peg in my tiny stone cottage, putting it on out of habit. As soon as I got to the bus stop and saw everyone else in their dresses and shirts, I knew I'd made an error. They did too, judging by the smirks from the younger ones, the quick glances of sympathy from the others.

My cottage in the village is the fifth house I've rented around Oxford. I've lived in several places – spiralling around the nucleus of the city. Before that, I lived in London. I got on well enough and it served its purpose, but the frantic pace made me nervous. I like being close to Oxford better and I like the village where I live now the best. It's quiet enough to feel safe, but large enough to maintain my privacy. I can shop, sit in the square, walk along the river and no one bothers me. They don't know me, or if they do, they pretend that they don't.

Thinking about home makes me think of Jude. These days I avoid relationships. When I get close, I move on, before the urge to confide becomes too strong. But Jude – well, she can't repeat the words I whisper in her ear and besides, she found me. Turned up one morning mewling at my door, so thin you could see the ridges of her bones. Who could turn her away? I fed her titbits – chicken liver and tinned salmon. She's grown plump and sleek and fast on her feet, bringing in offerings – broken fledglings and ravaged mice. It revolts and pleases me at the same time.

It's funny that I call her Jude.

Inspired by Mrs Townsend, naturally, who ramped up the pressure as I grew older, making lists of books and films and programmes I should watch. 'Your future starts here, Elizabeth Valentine,' she'd said, handing me a copy of *Jude the Obscure*.

Passing the church feels like serendipity. A refuge from the chaos of thoughts raging through my mind.

Pushing the heavy door, I step inside.

The church is small, set back from the busier streets, harder for tourists to find. I discovered it by chance not so long ago: a pale building with spires and pinnacles and gargoyles and intricate stonework.

The temperature drop is welcome. I take a moment to get used to the darkness and then, sliding into my usual pew, an organ starts. The music rises. I imagine the organist – I've seen him before. Small, with Friar Tuck hair, insignificant until he plays.

The notes are birds fluttering beneath the vaulted ceiling. I try sending my thoughts there too, a form of release, but they are heavy and they sink – down to the stone floor where I imagine them dissolving and seeping into the tombs below. I've never been down there, but I can picture the scene. Statues prostrate above crumbling skeletons, stone hands clasped in eternal prayer.

Sometimes when I'm here I try to pray too; other times I light a candle. But my prayers never seem to go anywhere and my candles flicker emptily. I'm not religious. I don't seek out churches for that. It's the silence I enjoy and the richness of the stained-glass windows that cast a mosaic on the floor, and the way the light holds the dust. I love the painting and the art and the feeling that if I'm wrong and there is a God after all, he'll look lightly on my well-intentioned past, while if there's a Devil, he'll punish where punishment is due.

My mind steals back again.

I'm alone in my room. Mum's eyes are piercing, making it clear I've done something wrong.

Me knowing and yet not knowing. That precarious sensation children have when they're not quite sure what they've done, what they've unleashed.

The organ music soars, crashes, climbs again. Its pattern holds a mirror to my life: the dips of loneliness, the elevations of love, the rise of fear and the levelling out.

I sigh and cast a last look about the church. The old stone font, the stained-glass window, so textured it's like a tapestry – a depiction of *The Last Supper*. What meal would I choose if I were condemned to die?

The door creaks and a woman appears. She bows her head, makes the sign of the cross, walks steadily to the dark-wood tiered table set with candles lit for the dead. She lights her own. Should I follow her lead? Light a candle for the soul that's been uncovered. Only you do that for people you love, don't you? Not for those you hate or can't forgive.

I make my exit from the church.

I wish I could say I've had an epiphany, but as I walk and the ghosts from the past slide back into my mind, as the emotions rise and the old voices clamour, I know that I haven't.

7

1978

The morning after I told Dad about Melissa, Mum's voice blasted up the stairs.

'Slashed,' she shouted. 'Four tyres slashed. Do you hear me? Four tyres slashed. But I don't need to tell you this, do I? Because you already know.'

Dad responded, voice too low to catch.

'Well, who was it then?' Mum boomed.

Dad again.

'No, you're right. I don't believe you.'

Holding my breath, I crept onto the landing. What was going on?

Tiptoeing down the stairs, I listened.

They were talking about Mr Wright's van, which had been vandalised overnight. Mum was accusing Dad of doing the deed, but that was impossible. He'd never do that. It was ridiculous to even imagine.

I was worried that Rachel would hold the trouble against me, but she gave me neither more nor less attention than she ever did.

Even so, I kept my head down and focused on Debra and John.

The problem was, I'd begun to notice habits I didn't

like about them and that made me feel uneasy and guilty and irritated all at the same time.

There was the way Debra wrote so slowly, showing the tip of her tongue, and her chatter about Frank, and the fact that occasionally she sucked her thumb. John was too serious. He never watched TV. Looked blank when I mentioned the charts. Neither of them were interested in fashion. Debra never wore make-up and although I knew I would never be a model in *Vogue*, I wanted to put on mascara and lip gloss with the practised ease that other girls did.

I longed for someone to confide in. How I envied those whispered conversations: the discussions about boys and sex and who had started their periods. Debra blushed if I mentioned my period. Mum gave me packets of sanitary towels in plain paper bags and talked about my *unwelcome visitor*.

It was hard to navigate life alone. Labels were important and confusing. Girls were slags and sluts, especially if they put on weight and dropped out of school. You had to be sexually willing, yet not easy; hard to get, but not frigid; and at the same time, not careless enough to get pregnant. They called me a lesbian at best, sexless at worst. A life-long virgin. No one in their right mind, male or female, would touch my body with a bargepole.

Life was complicated, and yet what I wanted most was simple. I yearned to be noticed for a positive attribute other than my brain. Surely everyone had something attractive about them? I only had to identify what that was and then accentuate it.

I spent hours staring in the bathroom mirror itemising

the parts of my body: eyes brown, too light to be mysterious; hair flat, an insipid kind of blonde; body, big and bloated in all the wrong places.

My hands were good, I decided, stretching out long, slim fingers. Maybe they would be my saving grace. I wore cheap rings I bought on the market and painted my nails pink and went around making excessive hand gestures, drumming on the desk, scratching my face for longer than was necessary, until Mrs Townsend asked me if I had a rash.

I needed to observe more, look for clues amongst my classmates, work out how to make the most of who I was. Rachel drifted from the periphery of my vision into the direct line. Who better to learn from than her? She gathered friends as easily as I repelled them. She sparkled like a jewel in a rusty crown and seemed oblivious to the discord, the dark jagged edges of life at school. Not for her the sharp elbow in the ribs, the muttered comments: *Bulging Elizabeth*; *Trashy Debra*; *Scar-faced John*.

In my head, Rachel was charmed – the type of person who never had bad luck or came across prejudice. I put her on a pedestal. She was otherworldly, an ethereal being, the angel I'd first thought – although somehow, instinctively, I knew she needed her own angel, a guardian angel, and who better to take on that role than me?

The idea buoyed me when I was waiting for Dad to get up for work, or come home from work. He was a bouncer protecting the vulnerable, throwing out drug addicts, thieves and fighters. Wasn't he a kind of guardian angel too?

*

One cold November evening, Dad had a night off. After fish and chips for tea, we sat around the kitchen table. I got out my homework – an essay on Keats.

'Waste of time,' said Dad. 'How does poetry get you through life?'

'Empathy,' said Mum, looking up from the art book she was browsing.

'What?'

'Understanding people's thoughts and feelings.'

'I know what it means. I'm asking what's the point of poetry when science is the thing. Science makes the world work.'

'There's more to life than making the world work,' she said. 'There's refinement, and beauty and . . .' She faltered, thinking of more to add. 'Poetry.'

'Are you planning on doing another evening class?' said Dad suspiciously.

Mum didn't answer. I happened to know that she was. She had a leaflet about the Romantic poets stashed in the drawer and another about amateur dramatics.

Dad grunted and reached for the paper. His view on Mum's classes was proof she was sinking further into the suburban life he despised.

I changed the subject, asked Dad if we could do some stargazing.

'Sorry, Lizzie,' he replied, 'I'm meeting Dave in The Dog and Duck.'

Mum threw him a look. 'It's your night off.'

'It's just a few drinks.' He reached for his cigarettes. 'I won't be late.'

There was silence, solid and impenetrable.

Dad went back to his paper. I returned to my essay and then Mum spoke. 'Why do you take me for a fool?'

'What?'

'I said, why do you take me for a fool? Why don't you tell me what you're really planning?' There was a pause. 'Come on. What's going on?'

I held my breath, scribbled some words of my essay.

'Nothing's going on,' said Dad.

'You're a liar.'

'What the hell do you mean by that?'

She gave an empty laugh, slammed her book shut and pushed back her chair. Then she leaned forward, snatched Dad's newspaper, ripped it down the middle and threw the pieces in his face. Leaving the room, she slammed the door behind her.

The next morning when I went downstairs, Mum was in the kitchen, ready for the charges as usual. Neither of us mentioned the fact that Dad was asleep on the settee.

I dragged myself to school. The sky was dirty white and the wind pinched sharp and cold. At break time, I wandered about with Debra and John. Debra was chattering, describing the gorgeous new dress Frank had bought for her mum: multi-coloured, multi-patterned, ribbons and bows, collar and cuffs, buttons and zips – it sounded like a whole wardrobe in one.

Debra wore the same clothes every day, even though the skirt was too short and the blouse was greying when it should have been white. Her coat was thin too and she shivered as she talked. To me, it didn't seem fair. Why should her mum get new clothes while Debra had hardly any?

I asked her how Frank – who last I heard cleaned toilets in a department store – could afford it.

'He's got a new job – in the chicken factory. He has to leave very early in the morning and sometimes works all night.'

My dad worked most of the night too, so I could sympathise with that.

Rachel caught my eye. She stood on the edge of the field with a scrawny boy with short-cropped hair. Karl, another new pupil in our form. He kept touching her shoulder, giving her a nudge each time he spoke. I was sure she didn't like it – the way she turned away and blushed.

Her usual friends were huddled nearby, whispering and pushing like fidgety deer. It was as if they had given her up like a sacrificial virgin. I imagined her in a white robe with a golden cord and me as high priestess, bringing down my sword, surprising everyone, slaying Karl instead of her.

After break, we had RS, taught by Mr Hinton, the most sarcastic teacher in the school.

He droned on about the value of trust and faith and belief and wrote the words on the blackboard in capital letters while a flurry of paper aeroplanes flew across the room.

'Do you know what a parable is?' he said, whipping round and pointing straight at me. Heads swivelled.

I sat up straight. 'No, sir.'

It wasn't true, I knew exactly what a parable was,

thanks to Mum having forced me to go to Sunday school when I was small.

'No, Elizabeth. I didn't think you would.'

Mr Hinton was holding the board rubber, weighing it in his palm like a weapon. He thought I was the most useless person he had ever had the misfortune to teach and not only was he the most sarcastic teacher in the school, he was also the teacher with the least discipline and the one most likely to launch a board rubber at a pupil. Not that he had ever done that to a girl. Yet.

'Do you even know how to spell it?'

His voice was tired, eyes weary, complexion patchy and red. He was plotting revenge on his rowdy class and he had decided to pick on me.

'Perhaps you'd like to come to the board and try.'

More swivelling. Everyone glad it was me, not them.

'I'm not sure.' I kept my voice low. My expression neutral. It was like being with a wild animal. One wrong move and it would pounce.

'Not sure,' he said. 'Not sure you can spell it or not sure you can make it to the board?'

From out of the corner of my eye I could see Rachel a few rows in front of me, head turned like the others. Was that a hint of sympathy in her dark green eyes?

Karl was sitting beside her. Was that a smirk?

I licked my dry lips.

Mr Hinton held out a piece of chalk and waited.

John's hand shot up. 'I can spell it, sir.'

I looked at him gratefully.

'I'm sure you can,' said Mr Hinton. 'But I'd like to see what Elizabeth can do.'

All eyes on me.

My chair scraped the floor as I dragged myself up and trudged down the centre of the classroom. It was tense. I pictured myself in a dust bowl in the Wild West with a hot wind blowing in my face and tumbleweed bowling along and the theme tune to *The Good, The Bad and The Ugly* drowning out the sound of my heart.

Perspiration pooled on my skin. Someone sniggered. Sweat patches. That was all I needed. My world was doomed.

But hallelujah. Praise the Lord. Rachel was looking straight at me. She smiled and the dust bowl disappeared and it was as if the classroom was illuminated. I reached the blackboard and made my decision, writing the word *parable* in the biggest letters I could fit on the board, spelling it exactly right. The class laughed. Mr Hinton spluttered and, before he could speak, the lunchtime bell rang. Without waiting for permission, we shut our books and disappeared.

Lucky for me. Incident forgotten.

In the dinner hall, I said thank you to John for offering to step in.

He grinned. 'Any time.' Then blushed scarlet.

I ate all of my shepherd's pie and tapioca pudding and most of Debra's too. She was off her food even though she seemed half-starved, sitting in her place, rubbing her legs.

'What's the matter?' I asked.

She shrugged. 'My legs hurt.'

'Why?'

'Dunno.' She stretched them out and I saw that her shins were bruised above her grubby socks.

'What happened?'

'Dunno,' she said again.

'You must do.'

She shrugged. 'Might have banged them on the side of the bed.' She yawned, showing yellow teeth. Her lips were cracked too.

'Why don't you go to the office? They might let you go home.'

'Frank's asleep.'

'So?'

'Mum's out cleaning. I'd rather be here.'

I shrugged and glanced at John, but he was flicking through his maths book and hadn't heard.

Rachel and Karl were in the corridor when we came out of the hall. I narrowed my eyes, seeing his arm resting on her shoulder. Who did he think he was?

'What you looking at?' he said, catching my eye.

'Nothing,' I replied, flushing.

Karl turned to Rachel and spoke in her ear. I caught the words *stupid* and *bitch* and moved on quickly.

I was used to name calling, but it felt worse when Rachel was listening. Tears stung my eyes and I didn't dare to turn back and check her reaction.

I carried on walking. Why did Rachel's opinion matter to me so much? She was just another girl. He was just another boy. Maybe that was the problem. People were all the same and I was different.

*

At home, the house smelled of detergent.

I poked my head round the front room door. The charges were seated in a row on the settee, watching *Woody Woodpecker*. One boy sat in his pants with a towel wrapped around his shoulders.

Mum was in the kitchen pulling out washing from the machine and dumping it into a basket. The boy had been sick, she said, on his clothes and all over the floor, as if she didn't have enough to do.

I asked her where Dad was.

'Gone into town before work.' She took the basket to the Sheila Maid.

'Is he coming back?'

'Your guess is as good as mine.'

She hung up the clothes and then hoisted the dryer to the ceiling. I grabbed a few biscuits and disappeared.

In my bedroom, I ate standing at the window. The fields beyond were stark and dead, the sky dark and ominous, storm clouds gathering.

Next door, our neighbour was sweeping his path. Mr Evans wore a long coat whatever the weather, carried a stick and walked practically bent right over. He'd been around forever, always on the edge of my existence, seeming ancient, but I suppose he couldn't have been more than sixty. His terrier, Nip, yapped a lot and drove Mum crazy. She didn't like dogs. Especially in the house. All that dirt and dust and fleas and traces of who knew what on its paws and fur. But she liked Mr Evans.

Now Nip was yapping at his feet, trying to attack the broom head.

I left the window and lay on my bed, flicked through a

magazine checking the beauty tips and the problem pages. I read about a girl whose boyfriend was pressuring her into having sex and another whose parents wouldn't let her wear make-up. I threw the magazine down. What was the point? Beauty wasn't for me. Boys weren't for me. Sex wasn't for me. I was ugly and fat. Everyone said so.

Turning on my side, I stared at my posters. Starsky and Hutch. David Essex. David Cassidy. Blondie. If only I looked like Debbie Harry. People would notice me properly then. Life would be so much easier.

Karl's face came back, his mean eyes and his lips shaping the word *bitch*. What right did he have to call me that? I jerked upright. Why should he get away with it? The more I thought about it, the angrier I became. I should have confronted him, told him, in front of Rachel, that he should have more respect. He deserved some comeuppance.

The doorbell rang and the first of the charges left. Fifteen minutes later they'd all gone home.

Downstairs, Mum was chasing around the house, tidying.

'Where's Dad?' I asked for a second time.

'Do I look like your father's keeper?' she replied.

I waited in the front room until I heard the gate click and then his familiar whistle.

'How's Lizzie?' He kissed the top of my head.

I grinned. Dad called me Lizzie when he was in the best of moods. I leaned against him and breathed in his scent. Musk mixed with a sweeter smell, like mushy fruit or flowers. My mind was full of Karl. Should I tell Dad?

I wanted to, more than anything. Dad was Dad. He sorted problems out and Karl needed sorting out, and even though I'd been down this path before and even though the path had ended badly, I couldn't resist following it again.

At teatime, Dad launched into a story about Dave's shop. It had been vandalised: windows smashed, records snapped in half.

'What did they take?' asked Mum, dishing up. 'Lay the table, will you, Elizabeth?'

I pulled out the knives and forks.

'Nothing,' Dad replied. He was sitting at the table, leaning back in his chair, wearing his work uniform: a black suit and narrow tie. His hair was slicked back. He looked handsome and apart from the concern he was showing about Dave, he was still in a good mood.

'But that's senseless,' said Mum, putting down our plates – sausage, peas and mash. 'Who would do that? What are the police doing?'

'Not a lot. They don't think they'll find anyone. They're saying it's kids.'

'Kids? It sounds a bit much for kids.' She sat down and attacked her food. Mum had a habit of eating fast so she could be on to the next job as soon as possible.

'Depends,' said Dad, leaning forward and reaching for the gravy boat. 'You should see 'em at the club – what they grow into. Last week, in the toilet, vomit all over the floor and on the walls, drugs, needles, the lot. One woman, skirt so short I swear she was a—'

'Ted,' said Mum, interrupting. 'Do we really need to

71

hear this?' She gave him a stare and then looked across at me meaningfully. I pretended to be fascinated by how many peas I could load onto my fork.

'Ah, Phyllis,' he said, shaking his head and addressing his food. 'It's the way the world's going. We gotta face it. There's no point being prim.'

'Prim? Why are you calling me that?'

'I'm not calling you that.'

Another couple of exchanges and they were off again. I zoned out. Let their argument wash over me.

I thought about Dave and his shop. Vandalism wasn't new. Last week the off-licence had been targeted. Mind you, they'd taken stuff – cigarettes, mainly – and they'd been caught. Turned out they were kids I knew. Boys in the fifth form. Too bad it hadn't been Karl. It would have been good to see him in borstal.

A flash of his scrawny figure dressed in a suit of arrows popped into my head. His hair was short enough to fit the picture. I'd heard his dad was in the National Front. Went around in big boots and braces handing out leaflets. Dad would say he was a lowlife. Mum would say it wasn't what good men and women had died for in the war, including her older brother, my uncle Albert, who of course I'd never met.

The argument was petering out.

I zoned back in.

'Please yourself,' said Mum.

I wondered what Dad was supposed to please himself about since neither of them looked very happy.

Mum left the table, taking her plate. 'By the way,' she

said, scraping her unfinished food into the bin, 'talking of vandalism, they found Mr Wright's van.'

Dad raised his eyebrows. 'I didn't know it was missing.'

'Didn't you?'

He sighed and dropped his knife and fork onto his plate. 'What are you talking about now, Phyllis?'

'It was stolen. From outside his house. And now it's been found, abandoned in Pump Lane, burned out.'

'Burned out?'

'Exactly.' She turned from where she was standing at the sink and looked at him coldly.

'For God's sake, Phyllis. Please don't tell me you think I had something to do with it.'

'It wouldn't be the first time.'

'What?'

'You stole a car.'

I stared at Dad. Was this true?

Dad glanced at me. 'It's not what it sounds like, Elizabeth. I was fifteen, Phyllis – you know that. And anyway, that was Jack and Eddie. I only went along for the ride.'

Jack and Eddie were two of Dad's brothers. Eddie had *done a stretch* for burglary and coshing an old man on the head. Jack apparently had *slipped the noose*. He was a *lucky bugger*, Dad said.

Now he got up, brushed down his trousers and went to watch the news. I helped Mum clear away and then we followed him. He was in the armchair, feet on the pouffe, reading the *Evening Post*. Mum fiddled around, dusting the shelves, rearranging ornaments. Dad moved his feet, patted the pouffe and I sat down, heart hammering inside my chest. It should have been a warning, but I was so intent on disgracing Karl, my mouth was open and the words were out before I could change my mind. I told the story while Mum's eyes drilled into me. I could read her mind exactly. *Here we go again.*

As soon as I'd said the words *stupid bitch* Dad's face darkened. I ended my tale and there was a silence broken only by the ticking of the clock and Dad's angry breathing.

'You say it was unprovoked?'

I nodded.

'And this girl . . .'

'Rachel.'

'She heard and . . . how did she react?'

I gnawed my lip. I didn't want Dad to think badly of Rachel, so I said, 'She told him to stop and then afterwards she was nice to me, said he was nasty to her too.'

Fact and fiction. I was muddling them up.

'And this girl,' said Mum slowly, 'is Melissa Wright's sister?'

'Yeah.'

'It doesn't matter who she is,' said Dad, interrupting. 'I'll have a word with the boy's father.'

'For God's sake, Ted. How many times? It'll blow over, if you leave it.'

'I don't care if it blows over,' said Dad. 'He shouldn't get away with it. What's his name?'

Mum glared at me. I grimaced and looked away, taking the hint. 'I'm not sure.'

'You don't know?'

'Not exactly . . . he's new.'

'What does he look like?'

'Short hair.' I tried to keep my voice normal.

'What else?'

'Don't know.'

'Fine, I'll find out. I'll ask at The Dog and Duck.'

'Oh, for goodness' sake,' said Mum. 'When?'

'I'll take the night off. Call in sick.'

'What? So that you can sort out this elusive family?'

'You're not saying Elizabeth's lying?'

'No,' said Mum. 'But she does have a habit of embellishing.' She fixed me with her gaze. 'Don't you, Elizabeth?'

When Dad said goodnight, he stood at the window, chatting about the stars and the possibility of snow, but he seemed distant, as if he was going through the motions.

He sat on the bed and for a long while we didn't speak, and then he said, 'You know you'll always be my favourite girl, don't you?'

I nodded and said that of course I did, but inside me something deep and sad and terrible was burrowing. I was afraid that what I'd said about Karl had been a mistake. Mum was angry. Dad was upset. No good was going to come of it.

8

1978

The next morning, Mum's anger filled the house.

I heard it in the rattle of the cutlery, the twang of the Sheila Maid as she hauled it through the air. I saw it, too, in the way she held herself. Lips pressed, small frame upright and taut.

I edged around the kitchen sorting out my cereal.

'Where's Dad?' I asked sheepishly.

'Out,' she said, eyes down as she wiped up an invisible pool of milk.

At least it was Friday. If I could get through today, I'd have the weekend to hide away. Maybe Karl would forget.

He didn't come to registration or assembly and then it was double English. I was in the top set and he was in the bottom, so there was no chance of him arriving late and finding me.

When the bell rang for break, I made an excuse to Debra and John and wandered alone across the field. I sat on the grass beneath the oak tree trying to guess what had happened and why Dad wasn't home.

Then I spotted Karl, lolloping across the field. By the time I'd struggled to my feet, Karl was in front of me, one eye puffy and yellow.

'Look!' he said, jabbing his finger at his face. 'Your dad's responsible for this.'

I was trembling with anger. Steadying myself, I shot back, 'My dad wouldn't do that.'

'No, *my* dad did it after *your* dad told him a load of fucking lies.'

'Where?'

'In the pub – obviously.'

He dabbed at his eye, almost crying with pain or fury or whatever else he was experiencing. Guilt flooded through me, but I was relieved too. Mum was wrong. Dad hadn't lied about what he was doing. He *had* gone to The Dog and Duck. Exactly as he'd said.

Karl took a step towards me, his eyes small and mean. 'You,' he said, pointing his finger, 'keep away from me. You're crazy. You and Rachel.'

'Rachel?'

'Yeah. What did she say about me?'

I opened my mouth and then closed it again. Dad must have relayed the lies I'd told.

'Fucking crazy girls. Making things up.'

Guilty as charged.

'Crazy,' he said again, tapping his temple with his fingers.

He stalked off. I watched him go, my heart beating hard and fast. But it wasn't only fear that made my heart so wild, it was the thrill that had run through me when he'd said *You and Rachel*. Rachel and me. *Crazy girls*.

After school, I delayed going home and turned into the orchard. The ground felt frozen through the thin soles of

my shoes, birds huddled on branches, and I walked fast
to keep warm. The grey clouds were low. Maybe Dad
was right about snow.

It was quiet beneath the trees. The only sound as I got
closer to the wasteland was the clank and hum from the
building site.

I'd heard that the contractors wanted both the wasteland and the orchard. Mrs Joseph had formed a com-
mittee: Residents Against Estates. They wrote letters and
put forward petitions, complaining about the mess, the
loss of public spaces, the men who came and went,
casual labourers. Who were these people wandering
about the community? Had they been properly checked?
Mum talked about losing the beauty of the trees. Dad
said it was progress and what was wrong with that?

With the trees stripped of their fruit, the orchard
felt abandoned: stark branches and stacked-up broken
crates. I wandered for a bit, going over what had
happened with Karl. John and Debra popped into
my head. I should be content with them, I decided,
and stop messing about trying to be a type of person I
wasn't.

I reached the edge of the orchard and stepped into the
wasteland, thinking for the first time in a long while
about my den.

The undergrowth around the opening had sprawled
wildly. The branches of the trees either side had thickened. I pushed my way through the ring of bushes and
brambles, and slid down to the dip. Here, too, it was
overgrown. I stamped my feet to level the space, dragged
weeds away from the rocks that were my seats. Digging

around, I found the hole where I'd hidden my supplies and pulled out a can of drink. I should take all this stuff away. If the contractors bought the wasteland, they'd demolish my den. I was sorry about that. Right now, it felt safe and warm and hidden.

I sat on a rock, drank deeply and thought about Karl and then Rachel.

'Crazy girls.'

I said the words out loud and imagined them etched on a love heart. I liked the idea of being crazy with Rachel. Though I couldn't think of anything crazy that I wanted to do. Not then.

By the time I left the dip, it was getting dark.

I moved quickly through the trees, anxious to leave.

Close to the barn, I heard sounds: whistling, tuneless and low, and the tread of footsteps. Maybe it was a builder making his way home.

I hesitated, not wanting to meet anyone. There were more sounds. From a different direction. Laughter. A low rumble growing louder and then voices. Stepping from the path, I hid behind a bush, waiting for the people to pass. I saw their shapes: a man and a woman, walking slowly, bodies striped by bars of fading light, faces obscured in the gloom.

I had come across couples in the orchard before and as soon as I saw them, I would melt away like mist. I knew the place so well. Often, they turned out to be people I knew: groping teenagers, occasionally a neighbour with a husband or wife that didn't belong to them.

Now, they passed so close to where I was hiding that I could have reached out my hand and touched them. I held my breath and they moved on, the man leaving behind that same low laughter. Peering into the gloom, I tried to make out what they looked like. From behind I could see that the man was tall. He wore a woollen hat pulled over his ears and a dark jacket. The girl had loose, long hair and was much shorter than him, her body bulky in a fur coat. They stopped not much further on and my stomach dropped. I wanted to leave, but I was too afraid they'd hear me.

She turned then, features still blurred in the half-light. I blinked as I watched the man leaning to kiss her. A few more murmurs. No more laughter. I bit my lip hard. I badly wanted to run, but I was frozen there, my feet rooted to the cold ground. Afraid and yet mesmerised as their kissing became urgent, as the man pushed the girl against the flat of a tree. I watched, heart thumping, heat rising, as he grabbed her hair – her long, red hair – and he twisted it around his hand, pulling her head back, kissing her throat. Rachel? I held my breath and closed my eyes. Suddenly it was as if the orchard had come alive. Birds flew from the bushes in a whirring of wings. The wind lifted, shivering the branches. Tiny creatures leapt amongst the roots.

Abruptly, the kissing stopped. The noises in the orchard stilled and as she stepped back, I saw that it wasn't Rachel at all; it was a woman and her hair was brown, not red.

Backing away, I tripped.

'Who's there?' said the woman.

80

Behind me I heard a crack of wood. Movement. There was someone else. I was sure of it. Watching me watching them. Someone or something.

The hairs on my arms and on the back of my neck rose. Screwing my hands into fists, I willed myself to stay silent. But I could hardly breathe and there was a pain in my chest from the effort of keeping so still.

More sounds. The snap of dry twigs.

A bush swayed. A rat darted from behind a tree.

I had to go, but panic forced me to stay. What if the couple saw me? What if the hidden person grabbed me as I fled? Worse: what if it wasn't a person at all, but a demon, a ghost?

Suddenly, my strength came back. I gasped, flooding my lungs with air. Turning, I took off, pounding through the trees, tripping and righting myself, not stopping until I reached the edge of the orchard.

Mr Evans was coming in, back bent, stick tapping on the ground. He didn't look up as I passed. Even Nip took no notice, more interested in his walk.

There were two plates on the table when I got home: cold fish and chips.

Mum barely noticed as I sloped through the door, my hair tangled from my flight, my legs cut and bruised.

'Where's Dad?'

'Gone.' She turned and fiddled at the sink.

'When will he be back?'

'I don't know. Sit down and eat.'

I did what I was told, taking my place, but instead of

sitting down too, Mum went to the cupboard, took out a bottle of gin and splashed it into a glass. I gaped as she drank it down and poured herself another.

The weekend passed. No sign of Dad. No explanation from Mum. I asked her where he was and she repeated that he'd gone. Each time she looked as if she might explain, her eyes filled with tears. She put her hand to her mouth, shook her head and ran upstairs, saying she was sorry.

In the end, I told myself they had had another row and that he had gone to London to stay with one of his brothers. He would be back soon.

The weather was getting colder. Sunday night, I woke at midnight, struggling out of a dream. Throwing off my blankets, I staggered to the window, cupped my hands to the freezing glass.

The sky was grey and eerie. The moon blurred by a halo of light. The garden was still. Trees and bushes milky in the darkness.

Downstairs, somebody was moving. Dad come home at last? I was hopeful, but there were only light, female footsteps on the stairs. I went back to bed.

On Monday, I woke to the strangest silence and the sense that there was something different going on with the world. I lay, blinking at the ceiling, counting the cracks.

Sitting up, I stared out the window. A patch of white slid down the glass. I swung my legs out of bed. A pile of snow had formed around the sill. Outside, great white mounds covered familiar shapes in the garden. I gazed, open-mouthed, then ran to tell Mum. She was lying in bed alone, on her side, facing the door, her eyes wide and tired.

Creeping away, I went back to my room and stood at the window with my legs pushed against the radiator. Across the fields, a deer stood motionless with its head poised. It leapt, suddenly, front legs bounding in exaggerated steps across the snow.

A loud knocking blasted the silence. A long pause and then the sound of Mum's footsteps and the shot of the bolt as she opened the door.

Tiptoeing halfway down the stairs, I hunkered on the step. Fragments of conversation drifted.

Mrs Wright ... gone ... poor Melissa ... poor Rachel ... Can you imagine?

It was Mrs Joseph, back from church, handing Mum a leaflet about the Christmas bazaar along with the latest gossip.

... run off ... with a married man ... I wouldn't be surprised ...

An icy chill swept through me.

A few minutes later, Mrs Joseph left. Mum, turning, spotted me. Her lips moved as though she was about to speak, but then she walked straight past me, back up the stairs and into her bedroom.

She closed the door.

I went back to my room, back to the window. Breathing on the glass, I made a sad face in the mist.

9

1978

It would soon be public knowledge.

Dad and Mrs Wright had run away together.

If Mum thought I was better off at home until the news settled, she didn't suggest it.

That first Monday morning she cancelled her charges and stayed in bed. I was left to get ready for school. I crept about the house, pulling on my clothes. In the empty kitchen, I found bread, buttered a slice and ate it standing.

It couldn't be true that Dad had gone. Mrs Joseph must be wrong. Mum too. Any moment he'd come home, whistling Barry White, tired and hungry, back from a long night's work.

The front door stayed closed.

I chewed my breakfast, sensing something else was wrong. It took a moment to realise what it was. The smell of dirty crockery and unwashed pots left in the sink overnight. There was a pool of chip fat spilled on the side and the bin was overflowing.

Finishing my bread, I ran hot water into the bowl, squirted in Fairy Liquid and did the washing-up. I wiped away the chip fat and put the pots to soak; took out the rubbish and sprayed air freshener.

*

Outside, I trod carefully on patches of ice. As I passed the cafe, Maggie waved. I smiled back sadly, wondering if she'd heard the news.

I considered bunking off, but in this weather, where would I go? Anyway, Dad said you had to face your fears. Halfway to school I felt a thud on my back and then straightaway a sting on my cheek. A boy had thrown snowballs. I took no notice, plodded on. He couldn't chase me, it was too slippery, and besides, I didn't care if he did.

Already the mechanics of the gossip machine had clicked into action. People watched me as I came through the school gates, some through lowered lids, others more blatantly.

John and Debra were loyal. Both from incomplete homes themselves, they treated me no differently. Debra beside me, John the vanguard, they were my human shield and I was grateful.

In lessons, I kept my eyes down. In the corridor, I negotiated my way staring at the dusty floor. Once I sensed a flash of red. By the time I'd registered it was Rachel, she was way in the distance, walking alone.

I was used to my own company, Rachel was not. How must it be for her? How must she feel about the loss of her mother? People said women who abandoned their children were more wicked than men who did the same. Absent mothers were abnormal creatures working against the natural order. It wasn't like that for me. Dad's absence was the most tragic event in the world.

At lunchtime, I listened to the buzz of gossip and

learned a new fact. Mrs Wright might have abandoned her husband and Rachel, but she'd taken Melissa with her, which meant my dad had taken Melissa too. What did that mean for me and why had Rachel stayed?

Instinctively, I searched for Rachel, enticed by the connection we had. I found her at last, sitting on the field. A few of her friends hovered nearby, but no one approached her.

I took my chance, moved closer and waited, but she carried on doing what she was doing, staring at the grass, pulling out a blade and tearing it to pieces.

Taking a few steps forwards, I cleared my throat. No response. I coughed. Once, twice, and then again until finally, she looked at me with red eyes, frowning as if she didn't know who I was.

'You all right?' I said.

No reply. I grew hot. I'd echoed her words. How stupid was that?

She opened her mouth and I waited for her to tell me to leave, but then she laughed and even though I was miserable, I smiled, pulled the handkerchief from my waistband and held it out.

'Thanks,' she said, taking the handkerchief and dabbing at her nose.

She laughed again and I joined in, although now I wasn't sure if I was happy or sad or a combination of both.

Mum stayed in bed. She was there when I went to school and there when I arrived home. I was pretty sure she moved around the house in the intervening hours because

I found clues: a broken cup in the sink, a smashed plate beside the bin, a ripped shirt on the landing.

On each of those days when I got home, I heated a can of soup and took it to her, but when I went back to collect the tray, her bowl was still full. I tempted her with biscuits, chocolate, bread and butter, but she hardly touched them. At night, she took sleeping pills, crushing them and dissolving them in warm milk.

Free to eat and do whatever I wanted, I tried to enjoy my freedom. I ate standing up with the fridge door open. The shelves were stacked with food prepared for the week. I took forkfuls of beef stew, broke the pastry crust from a pie, nibbled pickles and cheese, dug a spoon into a trifle. I left something of everything, reminding myself that these were Dad's favourites and he'd be back to finish them off.

But no amount of food could untangle the anxious knot in my belly, and nothing felt right with Mum in bed and Dad absent.

I tried to be useful, cleaning the kitchen carefully, making sure it was exactly how Mum would want it. I tried to be considerate, playing records quietly. I tried not to be a nuisance, occupying myself, watching detective shows, staying up late until the test card. I got stuck on *Colombo* – the way he pretended to be stupid to confuse the villain. It reminded me of the way I was at school and it struck me that the best way to get on in life was to pretend to be someone that you weren't. Dad had done that. He must have done. His affair with Mrs Wright hadn't happened in a day. It was as if he'd been pretending to love me, pretending to look after

me, while all along he'd been hiding the deepest secret –
from me and from Mum. He'd been plotting to leave
us behind.

It wasn't the first time. The memory of Peggy still
stung. If before I had pretended to believe his innocence,
now I no longer bothered to hide from the truth. He had
had an affair.

I hated myself. It was my fault he'd gone. I was
trouble from the start. Now I had to change.

Physically, I couldn't do much about my face, but I
could lose weight – with a bit of effort – and I could alter
my clothes and my hair. Maybe Dad would come back
if I looked different. It couldn't have been easy, going
around with a daughter like me, always having to get
angry with the people who insulted me. How much
better must it be for Mr Wright with Rachel?

There was another advantage to changing. If I was
livelier, cleverer and funnier, Rachel might like me. I
could be the class wit. I imagined making everyone laugh,
getting us out of homework because the teachers found
me so amusing. I pictured myself fooling around, the
whole class surrounding me in the playground, not to
taunt me, but to pat me on the back, or to hoist me onto
their shoulders like a footballer. It would all be because
Dad had left. He had forced me to examine myself and
change and when he saw how popular and entertaining
I was, he would come back. Mum would smile again,
and we'd return to the way we'd been. Only this time
I'd appreciate it more and I'd do anything that Mum
and Dad asked me.

*

Eventually, Mum recovered enough to have a proper conversation. She called me in and I sat on the side of the bed. There was a box of tissues on the mattress beside her and a load more tissues all over the floor. Should I clear them away? I grew agitated thinking about it and had to sit on my hands. If Mum wasn't bothered, I shouldn't care either.

She leaned against the headboard, tiny in her long-sleeved nightdress. It was red flannel with a high collar, only she'd forgotten to do up the buttons and I kept catching sight of her narrow chest. I fixed my eyes on different parts of the room. The problem was everything reminded me of Dad. The plumped pillow beside Mum's, the clothes brush on the dressing table, the platform shoes beneath the chair, the photo of Barry White slotted into the mirror. I had an urge to open the wardrobe door and see what was missing. Maybe if it was only a shirt or two, a pair of trousers, one of his polo-necked jumpers, it would mean he was coming home. He'd gone on a jaunt with Mrs Wright, a break, a mini-holiday, but he'd be back for the long haul with us.

'He's gone, Elizabeth,' said Mum, sniffing and dabbing her eyes. 'He's gone.'

I stared at this new version of my mother that didn't match who I thought she was. Mum was smart and fair and efficient. She dressed with precision, her hair pinned in place. This woman was somebody else. Her hair was wild and loose. Her eyes were red from crying. Thin white lines of dried, salty tears smeared her face. She smelled, too, unwashed, and she expressed emotions I'd never seen in her before – misery and anger.

'I knew that woman was trouble, spending time with other people's husbands, stealing them away, destroying families. I knew she was a trollop.'

She said the word *trollop* so fiercely that bits of spittle hit me in the face. Hearing herself, she clamped her hand to her mouth, but still the words, and then her shame, escaped.

'Oh, Elizabeth, look what I've become. Look what he's made me say. I'm so sorry. None of this is your fault. You couldn't have known. That day. That wicked woman. He had no chance against her. She wove a spider's web around him as soon as he stepped through her door.'

I blinked and zoned out, imagining Dad caught on a giant web, wrapped in a sticky cocoon with only his head and his platform shoes visible, while a black widow with the face of Mrs Wright perched beside him, calmly smoking, cigarette attached to each leg.

Mum wept, telling me again that it wasn't my fault, but I was sure that she thought it was – at least partly, since it was me who had sent Dad to the Wright house in the first place. I realised, too, that Mum thought Dad bore zero responsibility for his actions. It was *that woman*, *that jezebel*, *that harlot*.

I pulled out a tissue from the box and handed it to her. She wiped her eyes and carried on crying.

'Do you know,' she said, 'a day ago, I would have welcomed him back. Even yesterday. Even last night. But now, I really don't think I could. No. I won't have him in the house again.'

As I listened something changed inside me, in the way, I know now, that it does for all children, the moment when the scales drop and they see the truth about their parents.

Then, it became obvious to me that Mum had no control over whether Dad came back or not. I was wrong about the mini-holiday. Dad had made and executed an escape plan – exiting the building, abseiling down the walls, landing straight into Mrs Wright's arms.

Mum with her yearning for a better life, her criticism of Dad's friends and petty-criminal brothers, her desire for poetry, art and books – her view of the world just didn't chime with Dad's and so he'd left, preferring the simple pleasure of the kiss-curled, smoky-eyed Mrs Wright.

It was all about timing and for Dad, the time had come. As for Mum, it seemed her time, at least with him, was over.

It was only me left floundering, still searching for a way to bring him home.

10

1978

Dad rang on Saturday.

Mum passed me the receiver.

'Elizabeth,' he said in a subdued voice. 'How are you doing?'

I was silent, chewing my lip, conscious that behind me, Mum was listening, silent and small, a shadow at the door. I could hear him breathing down the line and then he cleared his throat.

'Elizabeth,' he said. 'You know I'm sorry, don't you?'

I heard the uncertainty in his voice and imagined him scratching his stubble, trying to work out what to say.

'Yes.'

'You know that none of this is your fault?'

I pressed the receiver closer to my ear, plucked at the wire with my other hand. There was so much to say, so many questions to ask, but I didn't know where to start.

He carried on. 'You know that a lot has been happening, that things haven't been . . . you know . . . quite right.' Pause. 'Do you understand?'

There was a noise behind me, like a whimper. Mum was crying, one hand pressed to her mouth.

I took a breath. 'When are you coming home?'

He didn't answer straightaway and a sigh came down

the line. 'Soon.' He talked about Christmas, which was only a few weeks away, and I nodded uselessly because I still couldn't think of what to say. Eventually, he said he'd ring again and that we'd sort out a visit. I nodded and managed to say *bye*, but when I turned to tell Mum the news, she'd gone. A moment later, I heard the click of her bedroom door.

It would be another dreary day alone. I trudged about the house, in and out of rooms, feeling as if an iceberg had formed in the middle of my belly. The drinks cabinet caught my eye. I opened it, each dusty bottle reminding me of a moment: sherry for the Christmas trifle; brandy for the cake; a bottle of gin which Mum called mother's ruin; a half-empty bottle of Bell's – Dad's choice when he'd run out of beer.

The last time I'd seen him drinking it, Mum had been out and the two of us had played records, top volume like naughty kids. I remembered Dad standing in the middle of the room yelling out the words to Barry White. He'd given me a thimbleful of the whisky and told me not to tell Mum, it was our secret. But after a few glasses, he'd gone quiet, slumped in his armchair, brooding. Had he been thinking about leaving then?

Taking the bottle, I made myself a drink, pouring in a measure, spurting soda from the syphon. I was clumsy and it spilled. I wiped away the mess with my sleeve and then forced myself to take a sip. It didn't taste so bad with the soda. I downed it and poured myself another.

Drinking made me brave. I was confident that Mum wouldn't appear. I could do what I wanted, make as much mess as I liked.

In the bathroom, I riffled through Mum's make-up. If I was going to change my appearance, I might as well start now. I picked out a mascara, but Mum wore it so rarely, it was blobby and old and left marks on my skin. I washed it off and tried her face powder instead. I looked like a ghost.

I went through the bookshelves. Mum's books were pristine, unread products of some evening class or other: Austen, Richardson, Trollope. That made me giggle. Was there a Harlot too and a Jezebel? I flicked through her art books, picked out a study of Classical Greek. I examined the friezes, the pottery, the statues of Zeus and Aphrodite.

Dad's paperbacks were tatty detective novels with pictures of terrified women on the covers. One of the women resembled Mrs Wright: dark-haired and red-mouthed. I took down a book with the title *True Crimes* and flicked through, lingering on the pages about Ruth Ellis. That blonde curled hair. Those thin painted eyebrows and glossy lips. I scanned the story: guilt and innocence. How blurred was it? Who else had been to blame?

Moving away, trying to get rid of the images, I rummaged through the bureau for something to do. Rooting around, I found envelopes, pens, a paper knife. A few stray photographs. Mum. Young and serious. Dad grinning, arm slung around her neck. There was a photo of the three of us, me as a toddler stretching out my arms to Dad, only he didn't notice. He was looking the other way.

Tears pricked my eyes, blurring my vision to match

my thoughts. I finished the whisky, picked up the paper knife and weighed it in my hand. Knives were useful. *Always be prepared.* That's what Dad had said. *Know your enemy.* Anticipate, plan, be two steps ahead. But Dad had gone and left me no clues. How could I have prepared for that?

Dad would come back, wouldn't he?

Any day, any moment, he'd appear as if nothing had happened.

I let the fantasy linger, my thoughts overlapping as I tried to make sense of it all. Then, driven by hunger, I searched the fridge. The pies and the puddings had long gone and Mum hadn't replaced them. I had a drink of water, then took some money from the housekeeping tin and went to Spar.

Rachel was ahead of me in the aisle.

I hesitated. I'd only spoken to her once since that moment on the field. I'd been waiting to collect my dinner tickets from the school office, and she'd called out *Elizabeth*, making me jump. I hadn't realised she'd known my name, although of course she must have done, since we were in the same class, and her mum had run off with my dad, and somewhere along the line someone must have mentioned me.

She'd pressed a square of material into my hand and for a moment I'd been too busy absorbing the spark of electricity to care what it was. 'It's washed,' she'd said. Then she'd swung around, leaving me grasping the hand-kerchief I'd lent her, all freshly washed and ironed and smelling of spring. I'd tucked it away in my drawer, found another to use.

Now I watched, awkwardness giving way to excitement. Her hair was one long, red plait, reminding me of Rapunzel. She wore a grass-green dress beneath her coat and boots. On me the dress would have been a sack, but on her the material flowed about her body as she drifted down the aisle.

She paused to select a packet of Uncle Ben's, a Fray Bentos pie, an apple. It seemed like a good enough meal to me, so I did the same, added a packet of fig rolls, and hurried to get ahead of her in the queue. Sneaking a backwards glance, I saw her browsing the magazines, not the *Oh Boy* and *My Guy* that I favoured, with their photo stories and advice on going steady; Rachel had picked out a glossy women's magazine.

Outside, I lingered on the pavement, pretending to search my bag for something I'd lost. Rachel took ages and when I peeped through the window, I saw that the woman on the till was talking to her in that way adults do when they think they're making a child feel better. Rachel just looked embarrassed.

When she came out, I hoped she'd smile, but I didn't expect her to stop, let alone speak, so when she did all three, I panicked.

'Hi, Elizabeth.'

She *still* remembered my name. I smiled inanely.

'You all right?' she added.

I cleared my throat. How should I answer? I could say that I was fine, but that wasn't true. I was miserable and lonely and I missed my dad.

Tongue-tied, I stared back at her and thought how the colour of the dress brought out the green of her eyes.

Beside her, I was stupid and clumsy. I had on a pair of old jeans, a scruffy jacket and a Motörhead T-shirt Dave had given Dad which he'd passed swiftly on to me. I took the moment to smooth my hair, and check my fingernails for dirt. So far, I hadn't done a lot about changing my appearance. Not that Rachel had focused on me properly. She was still gazing down the street. Some older boys leaned against the window of the off-licence, smoking. They were short-haired and scruffy – a bit like Karl. Nowhere near good enough for her.

She filled the silence. 'You going to London?'

'What for?'

She looked along the street and then back at me. 'To visit them.'

'Who?'

'Your dad and . . .' She stopped speaking and shrugged.

'London? Why are they in London?'

'Don't you know?'

'Know what?'

She sighed a little. I was irritating her, not understanding, but I couldn't grasp what she'd said.

'They're living there,' she explained patiently.

Heat flooded my face. How could I not know? In my head, Dad was in a hotel somewhere close, on that short break I'd constructed for him, yet this made sense because London was exactly where Dad wanted to be.

Rachel sighed again. 'Granddad's dead.'

I couldn't see the connection.

'She's gone to live in his flat . . . with Melissa.'

And my dad.

Tears pricked my eyes. Automatically, I reached for my handkerchief, but today it wasn't in my waistband. Not surprising since Mum had done no washing since Dad had left. This morning, I'd fished my T-shirt from the laundry basket, sniffed the armpits, sprayed on Charlie to disguise the smell. Rachel on the other hand smelled like apples and her dress was clean and fresh and nicely pressed. Had she done that or had it been her dad?

Funny, I hadn't thought about how life was for him. Was he behaving like Mum? I imagined him cooking and cleaning: giant hands grasping the iron; body hunched over the board. His beard would be long like a wise old man's and scruffy because he was too sad to clip it. I had a vision of him crying as he worked, huge tears splashing down on Rachel's dress, a river of sadness that flooded the house.

Rachel produced a packet of tissues and offered me one because now it was me that was crying.

'Thanks.' I dabbed at my eyes.

'I thought you knew,' she said, looking at me curiously.

I shook my head and blew my nose.

'Well, that makes your family as shit as mine then.'

I wanted to say that my dad wasn't shit, that he'd been led astray, but again it didn't seem right to mention that when Rachel was being so nice.

In the end, she pulled out a packet of Juicy Fruit and offered me a strip. Gratefully, I took it, peeling off the paper, unwrapping the foil and folding the gum into my mouth. Rachel nibbled hers delicately, as if checking its flavour. I caught a glimpse of her small white teeth. Smoothing out the foil, I slipped it into my pocket. A sliver of a silver lining.

Mum couldn't stay in bed forever, but she could stay in her dressing gown. She walked about the house, opening cupboards and doors and drawers as if she was searching for something – Dad perhaps, hiding amongst the clothes or the cutlery.

She must have cancelled her charges permanently because from the day Dad left, none of them appeared again. I was glad at least about that. Now I had Mum to myself even if I didn't have Dad.

Finally she admitted what I already knew. Dad was in London. Seeking his fortune like Dick Whittington.

'You see now what he's like?' she said sadly, shaking her head, speaking as though she'd been feeding me the knowledge for years. 'He's run away, done what he always wanted, put his dreams ahead of us.'

The next day, he rang. Mum answered and it was as if overnight one of the Furies had possessed her – a mythological creature seeking justice.

She began the conversation by denying him access to the house. 'Over my dead body,' I heard her say. 'You forfeited your rights when you vacated this house.' She took a breath and began again, threatening to throw all his stuff onto the street if he didn't collect it, at the same time reiterating that he would never darken our door again.

Her words were like flames, her eyes sparked anger.

I listened, hating to hear Mum berate him but also aware of the break in her voice, the sadness in her face, and the stoop of her body when she put the receiver back in its cradle, when she leaned heavily, hands gripping the table with her back to me, when I saw her shoulders slump and her rage ease.

Quietly I left her and went to my room.

The thought struck me: if Dad wasn't allowed in the house, he wouldn't be home at Christmas, which meant an end to our traditions. There'd be no fetching of the tree from the *dodgy geezer* down the street, no decorating the house with scrappy tinsel, the same old angel and all the silly decorations I'd ever made at school – snowflakes and stained-glass windows, paper chains to stretch across the room.

You're fourteen, I told myself. *You're too old to care about Christmas*. But I knew that wasn't the point. I cared about Dad and he wasn't going to be here.

That night, I lay on my bed going through my photo album, lingering over the milky Polaroids I'd taken.

Dad was gone and I had no one to blame but myself. I'd brought him and Mrs Wright together. Why hadn't I listened to Mum and kept my mouth shut about Melissa? I'd ruined Mum's life as well as mine, not to mention Rachel's and her dad's.

Rachel. My cheeks burned as I thought about meeting her outside Spar. What must she have thought? I'd been crying like a baby. Tears and snot running down my face.

I turned on my side, more tears of self-pity rising. I

was ugly. Inside and out. I deserved nothing. No Dad. No friends. No Rachel.

There was a sound. A pitying whimper like an animal caught in a trap. It grew louder, whispering and rising. Mum's crying winding up the stairs and along the landing, seeping through the cracks of my door.

I burrowed beneath my blankets, but the guilt wouldn't go away. It festered inside me as I fell into sleep and crept into my dreams.

11

1978

An envelope dropped on the mat. It was a train ticket to London.

My mood rocketed as I circled the date on the calendar with a thick, red pen and crossed off the days. I would put misery on hold, show Dad that I was a new and confident me. He'd never have to fight my battles again.

On the day, I woke early and packed my rucksack: *Jude the Obscure*, which I was reading for the second time, along with my Polaroid camera and three apples for the journey.

Rachel had an apple every lunchtime. Her skin was like porcelain and I was on a mission to transform mine. I'd read that certain types of oil softened imperfections. The best I found was reused vegetable oil. I rubbed it diligently into my chicken pox scars. The smell of chips hung about for days.

I had a present for Dad: 'You're the First, the Last, My Everything' on 45. I'd bought it with money taken from the housekeeping tin. I told myself it wasn't stealing since Mum had barely gone shopping since Dad had left; occasionally, food would appear in the cupboards, but not shampoo or sanitary towels or Clearasil. And my pocket money had stopped too, so I considered the cash

I'd helped myself to as a kind of advance on what she owed me.

That day, when I had walked into the record shop, Dave had looked at me sadly. He'd had his hair cut – not short, but enough to stop him needing to brush it away from his face. My heart had sunk when I'd noticed because everything was changing, even Dave.

Still, I'd stayed for a long time with Barry White, standing on Dad's spot. I was sure there were two hollows in the carpet, one deeper than the other where his foot had tapped. Eventually, I'd pulled the record from its sleeve and examined it like Dad would have done; and I'd paid Dave who'd slipped it into two paper bags instead of one. He was generous like that – with bags, although not with words. He'd only ever had a few for Dad and hardly any for me.

For London, I wore my new jeans and the Motörhead T-shirt because I thought it might remind Dad of the past. Then I'd wrapped myself up in my Starsky cardigan because dressing like Starsky made me feel safe. In the bathroom, I sneaked on Mum's cloggy mascara and a slick of blue eye shadow. Trying to make the best of myself.

Mum waved me off. Pale and unkempt, eyes red-rimmed, she stood in the doorway in her dressing gown and hugged me.

'I won't go if you don't want me to,' I mumbled into her chest.

She held me at arm's length and examined my face and for one sad moment I thought she'd ask me to stay.

Then she gave me a push. 'You go, Elizabeth. None of this is your fault. You go and . . .'

She didn't finish her sentence.

I finished it for her: *persuade him to come home.*

Gusts of wind cut through the platform, grabbing bits of rubbish and hurling them onto the tracks.

The last time I'd stood here, I'd been with Dad. Off to the Planetarium. I remembered the dome and the lights going down and the brilliant stars and a deep voice telling us all about the universe.

Later we'd sat in a Berni Inn eating steak and chips and Dad had said, 'Now do you see how big the universe is? Now do you understand its possibilities? Don't make the same mistake I made. Don't stand still.'

I climbed into a half-empty carriage wondering if that was why Dad was so restless. Then I thought: had he moved far enough? From Chelmsford to London. Not much of a leap. There was a lot further he could go.

A Milky Bar Kid doppelgänger hung over the back of the seat in front of mine. He waved his gun at my head and I turned away. A couple on the opposite side were kissing. They made a slurping sound and the man kept saying *oh yeah* and *baby*. I felt weirdly sick and as if I was one of those vultures I'd heard Maggie complain about, slowing down at accidents, reading the details of a murder story. Fascinated by horrible events.

The woman caught me watching and scowled. She had small eyes and thin lips. Her hair was greasy and twisted into a ponytail. The man had hair cropped short and bristling. They both wore great big DM boots.

Quick as a switch I whipped my head away and looked out the window. But now I was thinking about the other couple in the orchard and remembering them gave me a shivery feeling which then turned sad because that was the same night Dad had left.

I read for a bit and then passed the time counting rows of haphazard houses; lonely skeletal trees; a line of crows perched like tiny devils on a pylon, ever alert as they searched for creatures to kill.

Dark thoughts followed me, and the weather didn't help. The wind had turned wild, buffeting and bullying the trees, racing through the fields. Weird weather was a bad omen. So was seeing a magpie and there was one right now flying outside the window. I lifted my hand in salute and spat.

I fantasised about the crows swooping ahead of the train, on their way to capture Mrs Wright, grabbing her by their talons and dropping her into the middle of the sea or, better still, deep inside a volcano. By the time I'd finished imagining her hair sizzling in the fire, followed by a phoenix rising and fetching Dad home, the train had started to slow.

At Liverpool Street, I trundled through the ticket barriers and waited on the concourse. No sign of Dad. The couple from the train came barrelling along. The woman caught my elbow with her handbag. 'Ow,' I said. She gave me a nasty little smile as she passed.

Tears stung as I rubbed the sore patch. I tried conjuring a plan for revenge, but I was too focused on waiting for Dad. At last, he appeared in the crowd. As he approached, I thought there was something different about him. He seemed taller. Was it his shoes? The platforms were higher and he was definitely slimmer and more handsome. He'd shaved too and his hair was longer, which suited him. I forgot the woman and waved.

Spotting me, he yelled, 'Lizzie!'

I fell into his open arms and he staggered, but he didn't mention it. Dad never commented on my weight.

We caught the underground to a place called Plaistow which Dad said was in East London. The train smelled of sweat and someone had written the word *sexist* all over an advert for a holiday that showed a woman in a bikini. Dad was looking at it and I wasn't sure if he agreed that the advert was sexist or whether he was admiring the bikini. I didn't like to think about it too much so I turned away and examined the other people in the carriage, but they were all staring at their feet.

At Plaistow, we set off on a path that ran alongside the train track. At the end, we crossed and went down a street of terraced houses and on to another. The roads seemed to weave in and out of each other forever, and there were hardly any glimpses of green. Just rows of houses and shops with rubbish piled outside. It wasn't windy like it had been on the way, but it was cold and the sky was iron-grey.

I jammed my fists into my cardigan pockets and stole a glance at Dad. He was stony-faced but I detected his sadness floating like an aura.

'How's school?' he asked.

I thought about telling him how I'd made friends with Rachel, but that wasn't strictly true since we'd hardly spoken. Besides, he might think it weird under the circumstances. I thought about telling him how my English teacher said I was getting *brilliant* at English and that I'd started to believe her, borrowing more books from the library, picking out Brontë and Austen and Poe. But then I thought he'd give me one of his lectures, so I told him I was enjoying physics.

He clapped me on the back. 'My daughter, the scientist,' he said.

Dad's place was in a large house in the middle of a miserable terrace. I noted a creaky old gate, chipped paint and broken steps. Why was living here better than living with us?

Before he opened the door, he said, 'You know I've missed you, don't you, Lizzie?'

I wanted to reply, *Well, why don't you come home then?* But I thought it might be a bit early for that. I'd save it for the end of the visit, make sure we had such a good time he'd be unable to resist coming back with me. I pictured Mum's face as we walked through the door, her confusion turning to joy.

The dusty entrance hall smelled of Windolene and bacon. A heavy old bike leaned against the wall beneath a row of rusting post boxes. A load of leaflets had been dumped on the floor. Adverts for double glazing. A few for the National Front showing the angry face of a tattooed skinhead. Dad saw me looking, bent to pick up the leaflets and threw them in the corner. 'Good riddance,' he said, nodding across to a door that said Flat 1. I imagined the same skinhead on the front of the leaflet crouching there, waiting to burst out. Then I thought of Karl's dad and shivered.

'Second floor,' said Dad, leading the way up a flight of stairs. His new shoes clumped on the threadbare carpet. His trousers, I noticed, were tighter than usual, the flares wider.

Stupidly, I hadn't imagined I'd see Mrs Wright, but when we reached the landing I realised that of course I would; Melissa too. I could hear her whinging already, through the closed door. My heart sank. I couldn't believe it hadn't occurred to me they'd be here. I was an idiot not telling Dad I only wanted to see him. I bit my lip and tried to blink away the tears pooling in my eyes.

Inside the flat, I followed Dad along a short corridor leading to a musty room with peeling wallpaper and thick, dusty curtains. It was full of furniture. A dresser, crammed with crockery, took up most of one wall, and there was a whole shelf devoted to plates and cups commemorating the Queen's Silver Jubilee, which made me feel sad straightaway because last year we'd had a street party and Dad had made the bunting outside our house.

Apart from the dresser there was a brown settee, a matching armchair, a nest of tables and a couple of hardback chairs. There was a wheelchair folded in the corner, a TV set that belonged to the 1950s, and a hideous painting of flowers in a vase.

Melissa was on the floor playing with a doll's house. When she saw me, she clamped her hand on her neck – in memory, I supposed, of her imaginary wound. I ignored her and perched on the settee. Dad sat down next to me, hands flat on his knees, smiling stupidly.

Mrs Wright appeared and stood in the doorway, arms folded. She wore a tight pink dress which made me think of a sausage skin. No shoes. Stockinged feet. Her hair was lacquered, each kiss curl in its place, and her face was rouged, lips reddened, lashes blackened. Her smile was tight, her tongue silent as she surveyed me. I looked at her curiously, trying out my new-found talent at aura spotting, but the air about her appeared lifeless. I guessed she hadn't forgotten about the incident with Melissa either.

I was contemplating my fastest escape route from the flat when Rachel came in. I was so surprised, I forgot to say hello. She gave a half-smile and sat on the armchair, tucking her legs beneath her. I tried not to stare, but found myself grinning like an idiot. Everything was different now that she was here. She brightened up the room.

In contrast, it was darker outside. The sky had turned from iron-grey to almost black. The wind had found us and was thrashing the branches of the tree outside the window. Soon the rain began thrumming on the glass, which at least broke the silence, though it did nothing for the awkwardness. No one bothered to turn on the light.

'We could go for a curry,' said Dad, nudging my leg and speaking softly.

What? I'd never heard him mention curry before, let alone seen him eat it.

'But I've made lunch,' said Mrs Wright, still glued to her place at the door.

I stole a glance at Rachel, but she was studying her fingernails, her head bent. In the darkened room, I could hardly make out her expression, but I could see her hands. She'd painted her nails green (I made a mental note to find the exact same colour in Boots) and her hair hung loosely over one shoulder.

Dad was protesting, saying he'd like to take me out, but he had a strangled expression as if he didn't mean it. 'It's all right,' I said quickly. 'I don't mind eating here.'

It was worth it then to see Dad relax and Melissa scowl and to think about all the time I'd be spending with Rachel.

We sat around the table waiting for the food to come. Mrs Wright crashed about in the kitchen, banging pots and pans, slamming cupboard doors.

Dad turned on the light finally, and the tasselled shade cast shadows, like dull, metal bars. He sat back down and jiggled his leg. Melissa dug her knife into the table. If that had been me, Dad would have told me not to vandalise the furniture. Or if Mum had been here, she would have slapped my hand and sent me to bed.

'Maybe you should stop that,' said Dad at last.

Melissa gave him a disdainful look and carried on gouging the wood. Beaten, Dad stilled his moving leg with the spread of his heavy palm and we stayed in silence. Rachel was fiddling with her silver locket, moving it along the chain. In the end, I started imagining the sound, amplifying the squeak of a distant rusty swing; the sound of a saw on metal; the screech of a runaway train skidding on its tracks.

Mrs Wright took so long I thought she must be making a three-course meal from a Cordon Bleu recipe book, but when the food arrived, it was a shop-bought quiche and a salad.

Each of us gazed at our plates. Had I refused the curry for this?

Dad recovered first. 'Thank you,' he said.

He nudged me. 'Thank you,' I said.

The girls said nothing.

The quiche was soggy and eggy. The pale bits of bacon got stuck in my teeth. The lettuce leaves were brown at the edges, the radishes soft, the cucumber slushy.

Mrs Wright didn't eat. She sat at the head of the table, arms crossed, smoking cigarette after cigarette, flicking the ash onto her plate.

'I thought we were having chops,' said Dad timidly.

'We are,' said Mrs Wright, 'for tea.'

So then I knew that the chops were being saved for when I wasn't there, and I knew that the same thought had occurred to Dad. Worse, I knew that he knew that I knew and that everybody else at the table knew too.

Heat crawled across my face. Dark thoughts tumbled through my mind. Mrs Wright was dead. Mum was standing over her with the paper knife. The crows from the fields were scrabbling at the window, banging against the glass, smashing it, swooping down to pluck out her mascara'd eyes, to rip and claw at her fleshy skin.

'Cake,' said Melissa.

I jumped.

'I want cake,' she demanded.

My imaginings disappeared and my jaw dropped at her rudeness. From the corner of my eye I noticed Rachel's lip curl. We exchanged a look and I felt the thrill of connection.

'Go and get it then,' said Mrs Wright, lazily stubbing out her cigarette. 'You know where it is.'

Melissa flounced away and returned with a slab of Victoria sponge which she ate greedily, licking the jam from her lips and the cream from her fingers.

Rachel's face was tight, but her eyes gave her away. I could almost see the spark of her emotions, fizzing and ready to explode. I wanted so badly to know what she was thinking, to delve inside her mind.

No one else had noticed. They were acting normally: Dad eating, Mrs Wright smoking, Melissa licking her fingers, one by one. A sensation rose inside me. It was my old certainty that I could predict the future. Any moment, something bad would happen.

Rachel put down her cutlery.

Mrs Wright frowned and turned to me. 'More quiche?'

I had plenty left. Rachel answered for me. 'She doesn't like it.'

'Elizabeth can decide for herself.'

'I don't like it either. Neither does Melissa.'

Dad gallantly ate another mouthful.

'Elizabeth?' said Mrs Wright, tilting her head.

I glanced at Rachel. Whatever I said would upset someone. I nibbled at a piece of quiche, but my throat had closed and I could hardly swallow.

'I'm quite full,' I managed at last.

Beside me, Dad shifted in his seat.

'You're rude,' Melissa piped up.

'You can talk,' said Rachel. 'Why didn't you offer Elizabeth cake?'

My discomfort gave way to another pulse of pleasure.

Who cared about lamb chops when Rachel had de-
fended me?

'That's enough,' said Mrs Wright. 'It's not your place
to speak like that.'

A moment's silence, and then: 'What *is* my place? It's
not here, obviously.' She pushed away her plate, fingers
finding her locket again.

Mrs Wright narrowed her eyes and put her head on
one side as if deciding whether to speak. 'You had a
choice,' she said finally.

'Not much of one.'

'I offered you the chance to come – several chances,
in fact – and you chose to stay.'

'You chose to leave,' Rachel retorted. 'You're the one
that ruined things.'

Mrs Wright lifted her chin. 'I'm afraid, Rachel, you
don't know what you're talking about.'

'Charlotte,' said Dad. For a second I didn't realise
who he was talking to. I hadn't heard him use her name
before.

'What?' she said, giving him an angry look.

'Now's not the time.'

My dad the peacemaker. It was a side of him I hadn't
seen before. Mum would have argued, but oddly Mrs
Wright nodded. She cleared away the plates and took
them to the kitchen.

No longer the centre of attention, Melissa was quiet.
After a bit, she returned to her doll's house. Dad drummed
his fingers. I practised my telepathy, focusing on Rachel,
trying to get her to respond. The conversation had
intrigued me. Mrs Wright hadn't abandoned Rachel as

I'd thought; Rachel had refused to go. I wondered which of my parents I would have stayed with if I'd been given the choice.

The silence stretched. I produced Dad's present and told him how I'd bought it from Dave. 'He gave me two bags,' I said.

'Course he did.' Dad smiled.

Melissa peered across jealously. 'You can't play it,' she said.

'Can't you, Dad?' I looked around for a stereo. How would he survive without his music?

'No, but I'll get a record player as soon as I've got the cash. For now, it can go in pride of place.' He put it on the mantelpiece. 'In the meantime, we can sing.'

We only got as far as the first *da da da*'s before Mrs Wright needed his assistance in the kitchen.

Soon I heard raised voices. I pretended not to notice, keeping my head bowed and my hands clasped in my lap. Beneath my lids, I examined Rachel. She was listening too. I could tell from the way her eyes flicked to the door. Once again I wished I knew what she was thinking.

After a few minutes, the arguing softened. Mrs Wright laughed. Dad did too. Then there was silence and I thought they must be making up.

Melissa got bored of her doll's house. Spotting the camera in my bag, she asked me to take her picture.

Reluctantly, I pointed the camera across the table and clicked. The camera whirred and the photo appeared, juddering from its slot. I gave her the blurred image and then took another for me, moving the camera at the last moment, so that it captured Rachel as well.

While the photo was developing, Dad reappeared and told Rachel she was wanted in the kitchen. I heard the door close behind her. There was no yelling or bad humour and when the two of them came back, Rachel was more relaxed and Mrs Wright had a choc ice for everyone and a plate of pink wafers. Rachel took a wafer and nibbled it, as she had done with her gum, testing it before she took a bite.

That evening, when I got home, there was a load of boxes in the hall, sealed with tape.

Mum had packed away every single item that belonged to or reminded her of Dad. The boxes would be dispatched tomorrow, she told me, to the church, the Salvation Army or the rubbish heap.

'Things will be better now,' she said, sipping her gin after serving me spicy pancakes and chips.

Maybe she was right. It was the first proper meal she'd cooked since Dad had gone.

Later, I sat on my bed and examined the second blurry photo I'd taken in the flat. I fetched my magnifying glass and took a good long look. Half of Melissa was there, posing on her chair, and then there was Rachel, who sat with her arms folded, silent and bored, just as she had been for most of the day – but even in that flawed image, I could see the secrets flickering in her eyes.

12

1978

Voices hopscotched up the stairs – one of them loud and cheerful, the other soft and small.

Dad? Had he made it home for Christmas?

Bleary-eyed, I groped for my cardigan and ran downstairs.

Halfway and I realised: not Dad; the louder voice belonged to Mrs Joseph. Too late to disappear, though: she stood in the doorway, Mum beside her, clutching a gift and a tin of Quality Street.

'Come on over,' Mrs Joseph was saying, offering mince pies and Christmas cake, perhaps a glass of sherry.

'I'd love to,' said Mum politely, 'but we've company.'

We didn't. She was making it up.

Besides, who would come?

Mum was an only child and both sets of my grandparents had died. I had a single memory of a vegetable patch and a kind woman teaching me how to plant beans.

It was Dad who'd had the family – one of six boys. A succession of men of varying sizes, chucking my cheeks and handing me sweets. Dad was lost in the middle of the age order and wasn't close to any of them – even Jack and Eddie who, according to Mum, were the ones he'd followed into crime. They lived in London. Family gatherings: small houses, noisy discussions, rooms so full of smoke, I lay on the floor to breathe.

Usually, by now, I'd be dressed and on my way to church with Mum. Afterwards, we'd prepare dinner while Dad was having a *swift half* in The Dog and Duck. It was my favourite time, Mum and me chatting and listening to carols. When Dad came home staggering, Mum laughed instead of minding since she'd been at the sherry herself.

Now Mum had no intention of going to church while Mrs Joseph was clearly on her way, wearing a smart red coat and scarf.

I put her gift under the tree and felt the other packages, squeezing them gently and checking the labels. I tried to be excited but the feeling wouldn't come.

There was a parcel from London. I pulled the string and unstuck the thick brown tape. Inside was a book of astronomy and a signed photo of Barry. It was typical of Dad to give me a gift he'd like for himself – although tucked inside the book was a pound note and a message instructing me to spend it at Dave's.

I found Mum in the kitchen. She sat at the table, head in her hands, a pile of parsnips left untouched. Fingers grasping the roots of her hair, as if tearing the sadness away.

Instinctively, I left her alone, backing out of the room. Upstairs, I threw myself down on the bed. What was the point of Christmas without Dad? I lay brooding and then got dressed and crept out into the empty streets.

A mist had fallen, blurring the edges of the houses and the trees. My breath swirled dirty white in the freezing air as I headed for the orchard. Here, the ground was slippery with dark mud. A wintry light struggled through the branches of the old apple trees while the mist curled eerily around the trunks. A crow called out. I walked, feeling separate from the rest of the world. I *was* separate. Always different. I stamped my feet trying to keep warm. Every step reminding me of being here with Dad.

A crackle of twigs underfoot and I turned. It was Mr Evans with Nip. Seeing me, Nip strained at the lead, yapping, and I bent to scratch his head, sank my hand into his warm fur. Mr Evans said, 'Merry Christmas,' but Nip, distracted by a movement, pulled him onwards and they disappeared into the mist.

He was always in the orchard, creeping around in his long coat. Maybe he was a pervert like that flasher I'd seen years ago. Or a peeping Tom. There'd been one of those on the new estate. A woman had reported him to the police and it had been on the local news.

Thinking about the estate made me think of Rachel. We hadn't spoken since the trip to London. At school the distance between us had widened rather than closed. She remained fast with her friends, aloof and untouchable. I wondered how she was spending Christmas. Had she gone to London or stayed at home with her dad? I had a sudden crazy idea of going to her house and inviting myself in.

I let the fantasy play out for a while longer before I gave up on it. Even so, there'd be no harm in going there, just to see.

*

The house was identical to the rest: chalet windows, a paved path and a white, wooden porch. On the front lawn were piles of slates and breezeblocks and bags of cement. No van since Mr Wright had never replaced it.

The place was quiet, curtains closed.

I dared myself to knock, but what excuse would I give? I could say I was passing and had felt ill and then I could collapse, really collapse. Mr Wright would catch me in his great big arms. Rachel would appear and say, *You all right?*

I stamped my feet and blew on my hands. A few more minutes passed and then it happened. Rachel opened the door. My stomach dropped and I stepped backwards, stumbling from the kerb. She must have seen me from the window, watching the house. What must she think?

'Hi,' she said.

'Hi,' I replied, righting myself and then taking a few steps forwards, trying to look normal.

She wore an old-fashioned pink embroidered dressing gown and she was holding a present, gold paper tied with a red bow. For one second I thought it might be for me. I was considering whether it would be possible to dash straight home and find something suitable in return when she said, 'I got this for Melissa.'

Right. Of course she hadn't bought me a present. What was I thinking?

'I wondered if you were going to London soon,' she added.

I recovered my calm and stepped onto the path. Dad had hinted I could visit after Christmas, but he hadn't said for certain when. I told her I didn't know.

'Oh.' Her face fell.

'But I don't mind taking it when I do,' I said quickly.

She smiled. 'Would you?'

'But aren't you going yourself?' I hoped so. Being at the flat would be better if she were there.

She shrugged. 'Don't think so. Not for a bit.'

I was curious. 'Why?'

She shrugged again and tightened the cord on her dressing gown. Maybe it was because she wanted to be loyal to her dad. I thought of Mum earlier, sitting sadly in the kitchen, and felt my own twinge of guilt.

Holding out the package, she gave me another smile before producing a card from her pocket addressed to 'Charlotte'. I looked at it, blinking. Did she call her mother by her first name? I couldn't imagine Mum allowing me to do that. I shifted on the spot, took the package and the card. The warmth of the house and the smell of Christmas dinner seeped seductively through the door. The hall was darkly lit and I glimpsed a thick carpet and pink pinstripe wallpaper. If only she'd invite me inside.

There was no chance of that.

'Thanks,' she said.

I grinned back stupidly, tongue-tied.

'See you around then.' She hesitated and then pushed the door and was gone.

Dad rang in the afternoon.

'Merry Christmas,' he said so quietly I had to ask him to repeat it. 'Thanks for my present,' he added.

I'd sent him a cushion I'd made in needlework, embroidered with music notes and the word *Dad* written in cross stitch.

'Thanks for mine.'

In the background, I could hear Melissa laughing and Mrs Wright's voice and then the sound of music. He must have bought a record player. It didn't sound like disco. Country and Western. 'Stand By Your Man'.

The conversation didn't last long. Dad asked about my other presents and whether I'd watched any good programmes on TV. Then someone called his name and he said he had to go.

'When can I come to London?' I said quickly.

He hesitated. 'I'll get back to you, Lizzie. We're going to Norfolk for a few days.'

'Why?'

'Um ... you know ... Charlotte's parents.'

'Oh.'

'Don't worry, it won't be for long, and then you can come. How about at the beginning of January? We could go somewhere. Madame Tussauds. Fancy that?'

'All right,' I said. But my eyes brimmed with tears when we said goodbye.

I found Mum on the settee in front of *The Generation Game*.

She didn't ask what Dad had said. I sat next to her and we stayed there, hardly speaking, right through *The Sound of Music* and *Mike Yarwood*.

When *True Grit* came on, I wished I was the heroine riding out to avenge her father. I'd gallop to London, picking up Dave as my own John Wayne. I'd clatter up the stairs of that big old house in Plaistow and snatch my dad away.

Later, I stood at my window. Through the gloom, I could make out shapes: the bushes and the cherry tree, its spiky branches pointing, accusing me. Of what? Driving Dad away?

Clouds sped across the moon and the garden dropped into darkness. Laughter drifted from a garden further along the line. Next door, on Mr Evans' side, I heard a sound. A door opening. Squinting, I could see him on the path. Motionless, absorbing the moonlight, waiting for Nip to finish his business, before turning around and going back into the house.

Earlier, Rachel had been watching me from *her* window. My cheeks burned at the thought. Pleasure and embarrassment combined. She hadn't asked why I was there and I hadn't said.

I fetched the present and the card she'd given me. I was sad that I wouldn't see her again in London but pleased she'd trusted me with this task. For now, I slipped them both into a drawer in my room. However glad I was about being the messenger, I didn't think Mum would feel the same.

13

1999

The past closes its curtains and I spot them.

Two police officers: a man and a woman in sturdy blue uniforms. They're walking slowly, hands behind their backs, stepping in unison like clockwork toys.

My first thought naturally is that they've come for me. After all these years, they're going to make me tell them what I know. You can't leave a body unattended. Questions must be answered.

I think about this and my brain fast-forwards to the weight of a hand on my shoulder, the clank of cuffs on my wrists, the push on my back as they manhandle me into a cell. *Tell us what you know.*

I take a breath. They can't possibly have discovered anything. Not yet.

Still. I take a step sideways and try to blend in with a group of tourists walking by. I'm swept with them into Cornmarket Street where they stop outside the church. I give myself the luxury of staring with them at the Saxon Tower. A flock of pigeons swoop and circle, so much more elegant in flight. I imagine myself climbing the spiralling staircase, touching the stones that a thousand people have touched before me, and there I am, a pinpoint at the top, the wind lifting my hair as I gaze at the spires. The untouchable world.

The police officers reappear.

I peel away from the tourists, and duck into a shop to hide. It's a boutique called Second Chance and the irony isn't lost on me.

The rails are crammed with retro clothes: crushed velvet, silk and fake fur. Darkly lit, the shop is low-ceilinged, with mirrors and fans set in strategic places. I allow myself to breathe.

A woman brushes past in a blazing orange dress. Others wear coral or cobalt blue. They're like tropical fish swimming around me in a cool glass bowl.

A teenage girl pays for her clothes at the counter. She has red hair. What are the chances? Oxford today is teeming with Rachel lookalikes, but then I have spent the past several hours fixated on my memories. When you think about a subject for long enough, you see it wherever you are.

She leaves and I move to the window and watch her. To be honest, there's little resemblance beyond colouring. Rachel was plump. This girl is thin. Painfully so. Her legs and arms are like sticks. Her back is narrow. She reminds me of the girls at school who pretended they hated their lunch every day, who were starving themselves, desperate to become the new Twiggy, as vulnerable in their way as I was in mine.

The officers stop outside the shop. A group of tourists surround them asking questions. Turning back to the rails, I choose a few random items then hurry to the fitting room. It hides behind a blood-red curtain and, to my horror, is both communal and crowded and hot. A woman in her bra and knickers smiles as I go in. I avoid her and dodge another woman who's dragging off a dress. Shuffling to a corner, I hang up my chosen clothes: a velvet jacket the colour of the curtain; a canary-yellow cotton affair; a dark-pink summer dress.

I should leave, but the woman in her underwear is looking at me. I imagine that I'm invisible. There's a bubble around me. Slowly, I remove my skirt, my blouse, my sensible shoes. I haven't seen myself in a full-length mirror for a long time. Quickly I pull the canary-yellow thing – I think it's a dress – over my head. The material flutters around my sweaty body. I twist and turn trying to see the back of me, whip it off and pull on the pink. I catch the eye of the woman, still standing in her bra and knickers.

'It suits you,' she says, 'it really does.'

I nod vaguely, try the jacket, but it's far too hot. Abandoning the clothes, I dress quickly, trickles of sweat running down my sides.

'Make sure you buy that,' says the woman as I'm on the way out.

She smiles again and I smile back.

It's a link between us and I think how my life is made up of connections – people and places I'll never see again.

I put the yellow dress and the jacket back on the rail and keep the pink. On the way to the cash desk, I'm distracted by a grass-green scarf and a pair of silver flip-flops with fake emeralds embedded in the straps. They'd look good on a faraway beach in a faraway place beside a turquoise sea where the brilliance of so much colour can eclipse the grey of the past.

I stand stock still, the image running through my mind like a film.

Would it be possible? Flight not fight?

Maybe it's the answer.

Slowly, I put the pink dress back on the rail and take the scarf and the flip-flops to the desk.

14

1979

At the end of January, several weeks after Dad had promised I could visit, I went to Plaistow. Charlotte and Melissa were absent, shopping. I half hoped Rachel might be there but of course she wasn't.

The two of us sat in the musty front room, talking awkwardly for an hour or so, before going out for the curry he'd suggested that first time. Neither of us were hungry. Dad had the look of a guilty man and it made him silent and miserable.

We went back to the flat for the last hour and listened to records on Dad's new stereo. Charlotte had bought it for him for Christmas, apparently.

When I left, I put Melissa's present from Rachel on the dining table, only realising on the train on the way back that I'd forgotten to leave the card. Too busy feeling sorry for myself to care that much, when I got home, I buried it again at the bottom of my drawer.

All the way through January and February and onwards to spring, I kept Dad in my mind. I went to the record shop and looked at the stars. I wandered in the orchard, picking sprigs of blossom. I asked Mum for pork chops and mashed potatoes, steak and kidney pudding, spotted dick – Dad's favourite dishes.

I visited him several times again after that. Not at the flat; we met at Liverpool Street, had lunch in a Berni Inn, walked across Westminster Bridge or London Bridge or Tower Bridge, and we watched the boats and I wondered whether Dad still dreamed of sailing across the ocean or if living in Plaistow was enough.

Mum was changing again, planning a new evening class, trying to find a job. She was dispensing with the past, she told me, as she carried on throwing out objects that reminded her of Dad.

Sometimes I came across something she'd missed: a shoe cloth; a cufflink down the side of the sofa; a ratty shaving brush at the back of the bathroom cabinet. I made it my business to search in out-of-the-way places, to find – and keep – these little remembrances before Mum got rid of them.

Then there were the presents he'd given me: the book of astronomy, the ship in a bottle, the magnifying glass, the camera. I didn't think Mum could justifiably confiscate these, but even so, I kept them hidden and it occurred to me again that each of Dad's presents represented something he was interested in himself. The thought felt like a major revelation. Yet in the end I concluded it only meant he'd lacked the imagination to consider what it was like to be me.

I found his old bike in the shed, a place Mum hadn't ventured yet, along with a donkey jacket, an old cap, gloves, a pair of wellingtons. The smaller items I secreted away. The bike I seized, pulling it out and examining the heavy frame. It was rusting and old, not a prize-bike, not better even than my own, but it was Dad's and, heaving myself onto the saddle, it was as if I was inhabiting his space.

I went back to Maggie's Cafe because that was where I'd always gone with Dad. Maggie spun about the place as usual, her hippy dresses whirling, giving off the scent of herbs and spice. She had a new talisman: a ceramic eye, which she'd attached to a bracelet.

I looked at it curiously. 'What does it mean?'

'It staves off the evil eye,' she said mysteriously.

'What's that?'

'It's a curse cast by a malevolent glare.'

'Who from?'

'It could be anyone,' she said, 'anyone who wants to cause you harm.'

I frowned, thinking that in my case that might be quite a few people. Mr Hinton, for example, who still hadn't forgiven me for the day I'd written *parable* correctly. Or Mrs Wright because I took too much attention from Dad. I considered getting hold of a talisman myself just in case.

One day, Rachel came in. I was reading *A Tale of Two Cities* – another book from Mrs Townsend's list. Lost in the story, I didn't notice Rachel until she was on her way out, clutching a can of Coke.

The second and third time she stayed and did her homework. Sensing me watching, she gave me a brief smile before turning back to her work, reading and underlining and taking notes.

At school, she remained remote, but I noticed how she

behaved in a group, whirling from one person to the next, the centre of attention. I also saw how her expression changed when she thought no one was looking; how her smile dropped and the light in her eyes faded. She had an emptiness about her, a loneliness that I recognised because I felt the same.

So now there were two points that connected us. Our parents' betrayal and our sadness, and with that, I decided I should try harder to be, if not her friend, then someone she might speak to.

I needed an excuse to attract her attention, but I had no courage and although I persisted in going to the cafe, I stayed in my place, heart thumping, too afraid to make the first move, patiently waiting for her to take the lead.

Finally, she did. Familiarity made her friendly. Her nod became a smile. Once she said *Hi* and another time *OK?* Then she asked me to help her with her homework. She didn't understand a passage from *Hamlet*, the one with the slings and arrows.

We went over it line by line, sitting so close our shoulders touched, and I smelled her apple scent. I noticed while she studied the book and listened to my explanations that she fiddled constantly, with her locket, her hair, a pencil. Or she bit her nails right down to the quick.

'So,' she said, 'it's about indecision and revenge?'

I nodded, pleased.

'Great.'

She put her books away and pulled out a magazine. Seeing my interest, she asked me if I wanted to borrow it.

I stared at her. 'Can I?'

'Sure. It's got great beauty tips. Did you know if you

wash your hair in lemon juice and then sit in the sun it makes your hair go blonder?'

I touched my hair. 'Does it?'

'Yep. You should try it.'

I grinned. Rachel had red hair and yet she'd taken the time to absorb a tip about fair hair. *My* colour hair.

'Whereas,' she said, 'if you have red hair, you should keep out of the sun because it makes the colour fade.' She took a strand and pulled it away from the rest. 'Do you think I should keep it red?'

My mind went blank. Rachel wanted my advice?

In the end, I said she should be pleased with what God had given her because he didn't always get things right, for example poor old Debra whose hair was like string and John who had a nasty scar – and me, of course, but let's not talk about that. Then there were the teachers who'd been blessed with unfortunate noses, or sarcastic voices.

'But in your case,' I told her, 'God got everything A-OK.' I made a circle with my thumb and first finger to emphasise the point.

She smiled at me as if I was completely mad and then she laughed and said, 'You're hilarious.'

I beamed. Hilarious was good if Rachel said so.

That evening, I read the magazine from cover to cover. It was so much more sophisticated than the teenage magazines I was used to. Carefully turning the pages so as not to crease them, I absorbed all the information. Then I went over our conversation, picking apart everything we'd said. Happiness surged. Rachel was noticing me: offering tips, asking for help, lending magazines. Our relationship had changed.

Yet I kept on going to the cafe hoping for more. I gave her back her magazine; she lent me another. I began to help her regularly with her English homework.

'You're a genius,' she told me as I explained iambic pentameter and assonance. 'A bloody marvel.'

I blushed at each compliment and told her modestly how one day I hoped to study English at university. Oxford, if Mrs Townsend was right about my ability, and had she read *Jude the Obscure*?

She laughed. 'You're a sensation. A prodigy. Of course I haven't read *Jude the bloody Obscure*. Mills and Boon, that's me. I'll be lucky to get a single CSE.'

'I'll help you if you like.'

She frowned. 'Would you?'

I nodded. 'Yes.'

'With other subjects?' She spoke slowly as if making sure that was what I meant.

I looked at her. 'Yes.'

'You'll explain things?'

'Sure.'

'Lend me your notes?'

'Yes.'

'Write an essay?'

Was she testing me? 'Yes, anything.'

After that, I made sure I was in the cafe and available whenever she needed me and when we'd finished working, we'd chat. She still only talked about superficial topics – beauty and make-up and school – whereas I wanted to know all her thoughts and feelings, to be her confidante, to learn her secrets, so that then I could tell her mine.

Was it an obsession? No. It was a crush. A schoolgirl crush that I was desperate to believe was a friendship. I didn't stop to consider that the reason Rachel stuck to ordinary conversations was because we had no great friendship. I didn't stop to consider that Rachel was a girl who under normal circumstances wouldn't have taken the time to say hello; that we were acquaintances flung together through the misbehaviour of our parents.

I was creating a fairy-tale friendship and the problem with fairy tales is that they're packed with bad characters as well as good.

In fairy tales, it's obvious who those bad characters are; in real life, it's more difficult to tell.

15

1979

It was open day. I was standing in the hall with Mum. Miss Kilpatrick, my art teacher, was droning on, saying I was the most unartistic pupil she'd ever met. I knew Mum was waiting for a break in the speech and then she'd point out how much I was going through at home. She would demand I have extra tuition and mention her own lessons, classical Greek, and suggest Miss Kilpatrick might benefit from taking classes herself.

It was hot. People were sagging, thin shirts and dresses sticking to their backs. On the other side of the hall, Debra was standing between her mum and a sandy-haired man who must be Frank. John was silent beside his equally silent dad.

Mr Wright and Rachel came in. He wore blue jeans and a checked shirt with his sleeves rolled up showing muscly arms. Skin tanned from his outside life. Beard clipped. Hair shining black and brushed. I'd pictured him an unhappy hermit, scruffy, neglected, crying rivers of tears. Not so. His clothes were freshly laundered with sharp creases. He walked with an easy tread.

Mum, about to launch into her tirade, lost her thread. She turned to stare with the rest of the women. Even Miss Kilpatrick faltered and the discussion came to a full stop, which meant a moment later, we were walking across the room in time to meet Mr Wright and Rachel in the middle.

Mum stepped into her role, greeting him politely and asking him how he was getting on.

Towering above her, he had every opportunity not to look at her and he took each one. His gaze slid from the gym ropes to the ladders folded against one wall, from the high windows to the art displays pinned on the boards. Someone had done a fine representation of Salvador Dalí. All those melting clocks. I was sure Mum would also like to dissolve and escape this conversation.

Mr Wright swallowed and I watched his Adam's apple bobbing. 'Ahem,' he managed eventually. It was more of a cough than a response. He smelled of spice – aftershave. I leaned into it, remembering the man-scent I missed now that Dad had gone. I glanced at Mum. Did she smell it too?

'Good,' she said as if he'd answered her question, which he hadn't. 'Life isn't easy, is it?'

He moved his head in a cross between nodding and shaking.

I knew without turning that every pair of eyes would be fixed squarely on the four of us. There were few people who didn't know our situation.

Mum stood ramrod straight and kept up the performance.

'There's tea available,' she said in a bright voice and pointed to the refreshments table in the annexe: a shining urn, a few sad-looking cakes.

He cleared his throat.

'Well then, we'd better get on,' said Mum.

Beside me, Rachel was chewing her fingernail. I thought she'd done a good job of zoning out.

We'd moved on to Mr Hinton when my attention was taken by a raised voice. Karl's dad was talking to Mrs Townsend. He had a skinhead haircut and a couple of tattoos, but he was as thin as a bean and not the burly thug I'd been expecting.

His voice on the other hand was vicious.

'I don't think so,' he kept saying to Mrs Townsend. 'I don't think so.'

What he didn't think wasn't clear, but all of a sudden, he raised himself up on his toes, leaned forward and yelled again right in Mrs Townsend's face.

The room hushed.

Mr Wright stepped in. 'Hey,' he said, poking him on his shoulder. 'I don't think this lady wants to speak to you.'

He spoke quietly, calmly, and it worked. Karl's dad took one look at the size of the man confronting him, scowled and walked away.

There was a collective gasp. Karl, humiliated, had already retreated to the other side of the room.

Mrs Townsend, face flushing, smiled gratefully at her saviour. I almost expected a round of applause.

'Well, I must say,' said Mum, 'Mr Wright is certainly the gentleman.'

I agreed. We turned back to Mr Hinton, but Mum was so enthralled by events that she forgot to challenge him even when he said I had no grasp whatsoever of any religious concepts (not true), my spelling was atrocious (not true either) and my attitude was lackadaisical at best (quite likely).

A few weeks later school broke up for the summer.

July and August stretched ahead – an endless rolling carpet of empty days. I entertained myself with a trip to London. I wandered the orchard alone. I hung about with Debra and John, lounged in the park and by the river, but nothing happened and we hardly spoke. The three of us were separate entities stuck in our own little worlds, our thoughts and interests barely colliding. We were connected by lack of choice.

Rachel stopped coming to the cafe. I cycled past her house a few times, but gave that up when the woman next door – thin-faced with long, blonde, feathery hair like Farrah Fawcett's – noticed me. The last thing I wanted was for her to mention me to Rachel and for Rachel to think I was following her.

Summer crept along: slack days and long nights. Mornings spent reading the same magazines over and over, trying out beauty treatments when Mum wasn't there to ask what I was doing.

I developed an obsession with natural products. Banana hair treatments, strawberry face masks, cucumber eye patches. I followed recipes from the beauty sections and concocted my own, hoping to happen on a new and miraculous way to get rid of my chicken pox scars or to breathe new life and colour into my hair.

I devoured Mrs Townsend's book list; reread *Jude the Obscure* and dreamed of those gleaming spires. At the same time, I added to my collection of posters, and gazed adoringly at each new face, checked out the photo stories in *My Guy* and *Oh Boy*. I had the constant internal battles of teenagers everywhere: the self-doubt that warred with ambition; the belief that I could do anything coupled with the suspicion that I had no power at all.

Late at night, I allowed myself to think about Rachel, to wonder where she was and what she was doing and whether she ever thought about me.

On my birthday, I met John and Debra and we mooched about in the park. Debra had made a card and John gave me a bracelet with my name engraved on it. He blushed when he handed it over and was even quieter than usual. To spare his embarrassment, I went to the ice cream van and bought us all a 99.

Kids from school were standing around, smoking and listening to a ghetto blaster. 'Sex & Drugs & Rock & Roll' was causing a stir and earning a few hard looks from the parents in the queue. A boy and a girl peeled off and disappeared behind the bushes. The rest smirked at them and then at me and I realised how childish I was, buying ice creams. Across the grass, John and Debra were making daisy chains. No smoking or drinking for us. Never mind sex and drugs and rock and roll.

Debra devoured her ice cream, so I bought her another and she ate it just as quickly and then went home because Frank was making tea.

John was still acting weirdly, looking as if he wanted to speak and then changing his mind. Finally, he asked me if I wanted to go to the Little Chef.

He said it so miserably, I hardly thought he meant it.
'When?'
'Tomorrow?'
'What about Debra?'
He shrugged. I wasn't stupid. I knew he wanted the two of us to go alone, but however much I was interested in trying out sex and drugs and rock and roll, I wasn't interested in John.

On the way home, I stopped at the cafe.

Maggie strode about, clearing up crockery, wiping down tabletops. She looked amazing, in a long dark-red dress and a wide leather belt. She'd crimped her honey-coloured hair and it flowed around her shoulders. She was like a druid, I decided, or the white witch that she'd always claimed she was.

'Happy birthday,' she said, plonking a cream slice down in front of me and then retreating to the counter where she'd left her newspaper.

I grinned at her happily and then listened to her grumbling in the background. She was reading an article about how women in Leeds had been advised to stay home at night to avoid getting murdered.

'Shouldn't it be the other way around?' she said. 'Shouldn't men be the ones with the curfew?'

The door banged open and Rachel, a blast of cold air and Karl stepped in. This was all I needed. Quickly I assessed my situation. Could I make a run for it? Since the incident with Dad, I'd kept away from Karl. This summer, I hadn't seen him at all. Now I noticed how he'd changed. His tufty hair had grown longer, his skinny arms had filled out and he was tall. I thought of his scrawny dad. I didn't think he'd get away with punching Karl now.

Rachel asked for a Coke.

'Same,' said Karl.

His voice had deepened. Cheeks flaming, I pretended to find something of great interest in my glass. *Stupid bitch*, he'd called me. I'd not forget that.

Turning my attention to the cake, I took it apart, eating it layer by layer. I glanced up once to see Karl looking back at me, watching me with his mean eyes, which actually didn't seem so mean anymore. Like the rest of him, they'd changed.

Cream, he mouthed, wiping long thin fingers across his lips.

I flushed and scrubbed my lips. I was confused. Was he trying to embarrass me or just being kind?

At home, Mum cooked my requested birthday meal – chicken pie, another of Dad's favourites – but, as usual, she watched me eat over the rim of her glass.

When I'd finished she gave me her news. She'd found a job.

I knew she wanted one and I'd seen her circling ads in the local paper, so I wasn't particularly surprised. 'Where?'

'In the library.'

I frowned. The library was my domain.

'It's part-time,' she went on. 'Mornings only.'

Not so bad.

She fetched another drink and now I saw that she'd

had her hair done – a subtle neatening of her usual style, a delicate covering of the grey, and underneath her housecoat, she wore a dress – pale blue with a white collar. Fitted and flared.

'Are you going out?' I asked suspiciously.

She grimaced and then twisted her glass. She'd painted her nails – pink; and was that a new pink lipstick?

'No,' she said. 'We have a visitor.' I waited for more information. 'Bob,' she said obligingly. 'He's coming over later. He's going to be my new boss.' A blush bloomed on her cheeks.

Bob. She must mean Mr Murray. The man who checked my books in and out. The man who watched me too closely when I was choosing from the shelves, who had bad breath, a comb-over and a paunch. This effort then – the dress, the hair, the nails – was for him?

I put down my fork. 'But it's my birthday.'

'I know, but . . .' – she blushed harder – 'he suggested meeting and I need to get this job.'

'Why?'

'You know why, Elizabeth. There isn't enough money and now that your father has . . .' She stopped.

My skin prickled. 'What?'

She studied her glass as if seeking inspiration. 'Now that he's made other plans.'

'What plans?' No answer. 'Mum?'

She coughed and refilled her glass. I waited for her to explain, but now she was back on the subject of money, talking rapidly about the cost of living. 'His payments barely cover the bills,' she said. 'I need a job.'

What was going on? She refused to meet my eye. I

tried taming my thoughts, seeing things from her point of view, trying to work out what she'd meant by Dad having plans and, worse, what her intentions were with Mr Murray. Was it normal to invite your new boss to your house? She was lonely, I reasoned, just like Mr Wright must be. She should have a life and I should support her even if it meant Mr Murray coming here on my birthday. It wouldn't be so bad.

I finished my food and sat waiting for Mum to whip out my birthday cake. Instead, she grabbed her purse, handed me a few coins and asked me to fetch a cake from Spar. She hadn't had time, she said, to make one. She was sorry, but there'd been so much going on.

I took Dad's bike, my positive thoughts and resolutions already dissipating in the evening air. I had no intention of buying a cake. Why? So I could take it home for Bob to eat? I imagined his yellow teeth clamping down on the delicate icing, his tongue licking at the crumbs on his fleshy lips.

I cycled hard, along the main street and into the park. Mr Evans was there as usual with Nip. I continued past him, with my legs aching and head bowed. It was my birthday and yet there was nothing to celebrate. Dad was in London and Mum had invited a stranger to our house. I was another year older, fifteen, and still wearing my Starsky cardigan and blobby mascara. I was still overweight. Still lonely and despised by my classmates. I hadn't moved on at all.

At the end of the park, I turned around and laboured back the way I'd come. A haze of misery had descended over me. If only I could keep on cycling. Maybe if I kept going, I'd find a way of travelling in time. Any minute a portal would open – a gateway to a different world, a different century. The past or the future. How about that: I'd keep on pedalling, keep on finding some place new where I could be somebody different every time.

There was a sudden noise and the bike jerked to a stop. I had a puncture. Groaning, I threw myself onto the ground and examined the tyre. Now even my means of escape had failed.

A shadow fell across the bike. It was Mr Evans. 'What's this?' He pointed a knobbly finger at the wheel.

What does it look like? I wanted to say, but stopped myself in time.

He peered at the tyre, Nip sniffing at my heels. 'A puncture,' he said.

'Yes.'

'Have you got a kit?'

'No.'

'You should always have a kit. When I was a lad I always had a kit.'

Had kits even been invented then? Had bikes?

'Tape, then, and a pump of course. Which you've got. I can see that.'

The pump was tied to the frame.

'I haven't got any tape,' I said, feeling stupid.

'What about at home?'

'I'm not going home.'

He nodded as if that was perfectly normal. 'In that case, Paracord.'

'What?'

'Paracord. Had it in the war. Cut it off my parachute. Very useful for tourniquets, for example.'

He opened his coat like a salesman with a batch of stolen watches. For one awful moment, I remembered the flasher in the orchard – but Mr Evans simply searched his pockets, producing string, plasters, a penknife and a length of stretchy cord which he promptly cut in half. Deftly he peeled off the tyre, inflated the inner tube, identified the damage and tied the cord in two places, isolating the puncture.

'See,' he said. 'Paracord. Works a treat.'

I was interested. 'What did you do in the war?'

'Medical corps. Nurse.'

'Where?'

'Africa. Egypt, mainly.'

'What about when you came home?'

'Same thing. NHS.'

Mr Evans had been a nurse. I considered him with a new respect. Had he been married? I'd never thought about his life before. I'd never even considered him as a person.

But now it was as if he could read my mind. 'That's how we met. Gladys and me.'

'Gladys. I don't remember . . .'

'No, you wouldn't. She passed away before you were born.'

I was silent.

He handed me the rest of the cord. 'For next time.'

'Thanks,' I said, pocketing it.

'Patching things up can work. Remember that.'

I nodded and watched him go, limping across the

park with Nip. No longer an irritating old man in a raincoat, he'd transformed into my saviour. A saint. I imagined him dressed in robes like a biblical shepherd with a staff.

Creaking onwards with the bike, I left the park.

At the end of the street, I spotted Rachel, walking towards me, heading for home. She saw me and gave a half-hearted wave.

If only I had an excuse to talk to her. If only I was a *normal* person, small talk and gossip at the ready.

Then it came to me. Quickly, I rode home, tiptoed to my room and retrieved the latest magazine she'd lent me. Downstairs, I could hear Mum in the kitchen, humming, waiting for Bob. I went out the door as quietly as I'd come in, left the bike and scurried back towards the estate.

It was now or never. I was going to knock on her door. My heart beat hard with anticipation while above me, the bruised sky turned a few shades darker. A crow flew directly across my path. A sign of imminent doom, but for once I took no notice.

16

1979

Mr Wright opened the door in a red checked shirt and jeans.

'Yes?' he said.

I froze. I'd assumed it would be Rachel at the door, letting me in. No questions asked.

I opened my mouth and forced out the words. 'Could I speak to Rachel?'

'Rachel?'

I gulped. 'Yes.'

He frowned and I pictured the cogs in his brain whirring. When his face cleared, I knew he'd twigged who I was. The girl in the school hall whose father had run off with his wife.

Feeling hot, and then cold, I panicked, sure that at best he'd shut the door in my face. At worst, he'd berate me for the sins of my father.

He was a big man. I quaked and then took the only way out I could think of. I started to cry.

'What the . . . ?'

Next door, the woman with Farrah Fawcett hair appeared, dressed for going out, child hitched on her hip, key clutched in her hand. She looked at the two of us curiously.

Grimacing, Mr Wright stepped backwards. 'Rachel,' he yelled.

Turning sideways, he gestured for me to come in.

I smiled meekly at the woman and stepped into the thickly carpeted hall. Rachel came down the stairs in a mud-brown dress, sleeves hanging over her wrists, hair brushed out around her shoulders. My heart missed a beat.

'Elizabeth,' she said, glancing at her dad as if asking for permission, knowing as well as I did that I was crossing enemy lines.

Mr Wright nodded and then disappeared into a room at the back of the house. A man of few words. He reminded me of Dave.

A moment passed. We stared at one another, Rachel and me. I cringed with embarrassment, scrubbed at the tears on my face. I'd made a mistake. She didn't want me here any more than her dad did. A few kind words, a bit of homework help – it didn't mean much. Why would someone like her want someone like me?

Rummaging in my bag, I produced my reason for being there.

'It's your magazine,' I said as if it wasn't obvious, and then blushed, knowing I sounded pathetic and needy and very young.

'Thanks,' she said, taking it, 'but you didn't have to.'

I looked at my feet, willing the heat in my cheeks to cool.

'Have you finished it?' Her voice was polite, non-committal.

I nodded. I didn't tell her that I'd read the magazine

from cover to cover, poring over each beauty tip, obsessively making notes about diet and treatment and exercise.

'You'd better come in,' she said.

'Really?' I gawped, hardly believing what I was hearing. I'd been about to sidle away and forget I'd ever come here in the first place. Instead, here I was grinning stupidly and following Rachel into the front room.

The dominant colour was a deep pink: the corduroy settee and matching armchairs, the shagpile carpet and paisley wallpaper. It was as different from the plastic covers and dull decor that characterised our house as it could be. There was a shelf packed with china – figurines in ballgowns, chocolate-box cottages; a few books – Jilly Cooper, Jackie Collins, Barbara Cartland, Mills and Boon. I sank awkwardly into the settee. It was so soft it was as if I'd been swallowed up.

Rachel handed me a box of Kleenex then disappeared. I pulled out a tissue and dabbed at my eyes. Sitting back, I let my gaze settle on the photos on the mantelpiece. One of the frames had been turned around and I was dying to see what was hidden. Maybe it was a picture of Mrs Wright, banished by her angry husband, but there were others of her still in pride of place, so that theory made no sense.

In one photo, she was in a park, her Betty Boop curls messed up by the wind, and in another she stood behind Melissa, hands resting on her shoulders. There was a school photo of Rachel looking gawky, with a crooked smile, at about eleven or twelve and another of Melissa in a pink dress.

Rachel came back with a Fanta for me and a plate of digestives. She dropped into an armchair, curling her legs beneath her like a cat. She didn't have a drink or a biscuit. I took mine awkwardly. I was like a child, given a treat. I set the can on my lap, and babbled, telling Rachel all about the puncture and how Mr Evans had rescued me.

She hardly listened. Instead she kept glancing at the door. It was understandable. If Rachel had come to my house, I reckoned Mum would have sent her away.

'Sorry for being upset,' I said when I'd finished my story.

She looked back at me steadily. 'Is it because of the bike?'

I stared at her. Did she genuinely think I'd been crying because of that? I shook my head.

'Why then?'

'Mum's got . . .' I hesitated. I was going to say a new boyfriend, but that would be an exaggeration. 'A new job.'

She was interested. 'Where?'

'In the library.'

'Sounds OK.'

'Yeah.'

Silence. I tried again. 'Are you going to London soon?'

She wrinkled her nose. 'Doubt it.'

I considered suggesting we go there together. Then I realised she'd probably say no. Being with me was an acquired taste, like learning to appreciate Motörhead, as Dave would say.

Thinking about that brought another lump to my

throat. I imagined Dad in London in another record shop with another Dave, and with Melissa instead of me.

Rachel shifted in her seat and glanced at her watch. How could I keep her interested?

I said the first thing that came into my head. 'I saw you with Karl.'

It was her turn to blush. 'Yeah.'

A mistake. I hadn't wanted to embarrass her. Inwardly, I cringed. Why did I say that? Now she would hate me.

'He's different now,' she said. 'He's changed.'

I was silent, uncertain. *Stupid bitch*, he'd called me. He'd have to change a lot for me to forgive that.

'We were kids,' she added, 'then.'

The way she said kids was weird, as if we were adults now. She was older than me, it was true – sixteen in September. But still, it wasn't that long ago that Karl had shown what he was like.

Whatever the truth, I sensed a new awkwardness between us. Feeling unwelcome, I got up to go. Only as soon as we were in the hall, Rachel asked me to wait. She went through to the back room and I caught a glimpse of Mr Wright hunched over the table tinkering with the tangled chain of a necklace. His big hands were loosening the links. He must be doing it for Rachel. My dad would never have had the patience.

They were talking, their voices quietly overlapping, and then she came back with a shopping bag.

'Mind if I come with you?'

I blinked as if a light had gone on. This was more than

a miracle, if that was even possible: not only did Rachel want to be with me, she was asking my permission.

'Yes,' I said, trying not to sound eager, but my face flushed scarlet anyway. 'I mean, no. I don't mind at all.'

Outside, the sky had turned a nasty shade of grey.

It was hot and humid, but Rachel walked so quickly I had to break into a trot. All I could think about was sweat patches, the humiliation of dark stains spreading across my T-shirt. Why had I worn jeans? Better to be free like Rachel in her loose dress, gliding rapidly like water downstream.

But the further we got through the estate, the more Rachel relaxed. By the time we'd made it to the main road, my breath had returned to normal.

'Where shall we go?' she said.

We. Where shall *we* go?

'Spar?' I said, indicating her shopping bag.

She made a face. 'Nah. Boring. I'll go there later – maybe.'

'Won't your dad be waiting?'

She shrugged. 'He'll be at work in a bit.'

'It's Sunday.'

'Overtime.'

I suggested the cafe.

Rachel made a face. 'I don't feel like seeing anyone else. Do you ever get like that?'

All the time.

She looked at me and I nodded inanely. I was still reeling from the fact that she didn't want to see *anyone else*. She only wanted me.

I bit my lip, trying to think of a way to entertain her. A single swallow flew like an arrow in the direction of the orchard.

It was a sign.

'We could go for a walk,' I suggested.

I hardly expected her to say yes, but she agreed.

My body cooled beneath the rows of trees, branches bending low with fruit; the air fresh with the scent of apples. Rachel reached up to pluck one and she ate, grimacing at the taste as her small teeth pierced the flesh.

Leaving the grass, we took the rougher, furrowed path that ringed the trees and led to the barn. Through the broken slats, I glimpsed the old tractor. On the ground beside the doors was a dead owl. Both of us stared at the beautiful creature, its tawny feathers, jewelled eyes still intact. It can't have been dead for long.

'What does it mean?' I breathed.

'The owl is dead,' said Rachel in a matter-of-fact voice. 'Everything dies.'

I nodded slowly, but to me it meant more than that. It was a sign, a portent of death or disease. Bad luck would come.

We ended up at the edge of the trees and stepped into the wasteland. The march of the houses had come closer, but had mainly spread sideways, which meant the building site was still far enough away for the hum of machinery to remain distant, leaving the wasteland in its own world, as it always had been to me, a fairy-tale place, teeming with secrets and possibilities, good and bad.

Together, we watched the men in the distance working on the site, each of us lost in our own thoughts.

A few more minutes passed and then Rachel spoke. 'How long do you think the building will take?'

I shrugged. 'Forever.'

'It's shit.'

I glanced at her. She was still staring across at the site, her face impassive. I wondered why she cared so much. 'A lot of people don't want to lose the fields,' I said, thinking maybe that was her reason.

She nodded, but I wasn't convinced.

'Did your family come here for the work?' I asked.

'Yeah.' She was quiet before she added, 'I wish we hadn't.'

I nodded glumly. It must be as obvious to her as it was to me that if they'd stayed in Norfolk, my dad and her mum would still be at home.

I tried to break the mood, talking about how I used to explore the wasteland. I told her about the insects I collected and the slow worms and even the flasher.

'I didn't understand what was happening at the time,' I said. 'It was only when I got older that I realised.' I was trying to sound worldly and wise.

She gave me an odd look, which made me think she didn't believe me, so I distracted her, describing the den I'd found so many years before.

It worked; she asked me where it was.

I led her over to the spot and crouched down to crawl through the bushes. She did the same and we slid into the dip.

'What is this?' she said, eyes wide.

'My den.' I tried to sound nonchalant, but failed. My voice was high and stupid because now I was convinced she'd think it was childish. Who had a den when they were fifteen years old? 'I haven't been here for ages,' I added.

But she wasn't listening. 'It's great.'

'Really?'

'Yeah. It's the perfect place to hide. And hey, there's seats.'

She sat down on a rock and grabbed at her hair, plaiting quickly, fastening the end with a band she produced from her pocket. I followed her gaze, seeing what she saw. The foliage had grown. It was heavy and lush with dark green leaves clinging to the branches above.

'It's like a bird cage,' said Rachel.

Now sunlight sprinkled through the gaps like magic dust. Delighted, Rachel lay back: eyes closed, arms flung above her head, legs pulled up and twisted to one side. She was beautiful lying there. Like the statue of Aphrodite I'd seen in Mum's art books, the goddess of love, fertility and desire. I blushed all over again.

This was it. This was the moment I'd wanted since we'd first met. I wished I could hold it tight in the palm of my hand and never let go and in the space of a minute, I imagined a whole lifetime of more moments like this weaving and binding us tight.

Anxious to please, I went to the place where I kept my supplies, cleared away the branches and unearthed a can of Coke.

'Oh my God,' said Rachel, sitting up, 'you've got refreshments. It's like the bloody pictures.'

Grinning, I produced a plastic bag full of chocolate. Laughing, she scrambled across and searched for herself, finding the cans, the magazines and then the penknife. Taking it, she pulled out the blade. 'What's this for? Wild animals?'

I laughed too and she snapped the knife shut.

'No one would find us here, would they?' she said, suddenly serious.

In the distance, voices drifted, a few shouts and then the sound of the diggers started. Mr Wright would be there by now. I thought of him, huge and heroic, as he had been at school, dealing with Karl's dad. A big old friendly giant, trying his best, raising Rachel alone. Was my dad a hero too? I used to think so, but now I wasn't so sure.

'Do you miss her?' I said impulsively.

'Who?'

'Your mum.'

A shadow fell across her face. She took hold of her hair again and slipped off the band, slowly unplaiting the strands. 'Do you miss your dad?' she said.

She'd turned things around. Soon I'd discover she was clever at that. Keeping her secrets close. Prising out mine. Answering questions with questions. Giving half-truths, never lies.

Soon it would be a skill I'd learn too, but then I only sighed.

'Do you wish you'd gone with him?' she added.

'I didn't have a choice.' I looked at my lap.

'That's adults for you.' She gave a short, bitter laugh.

But Rachel had had a choice, hadn't she?

'What about you?' I said carefully. 'Your mum wanted you to go with her, didn't she?'

She gave me another strange look. 'Yeah, Charlotte asked me.'

Charlotte. I knew Rachel must call her that because I'd seen it on the card, but hearing her say it was different. It felt so modern. Like in a film. Then I remembered I hadn't actually given Mrs Wright the card and the guilt came back.

'But you didn't want to go?' I asked, sticking to the conversation and trying not to think about my misdemeanour.

'Not then.'

'Did you change your mind?'

She rubbed her arm through her sleeve. 'Yeah. Maybe.'

'Why didn't you tell her?'

'I did.'

'So . . . what happened?'

She shrugged. 'You know what they're like.'

I was unsure what she was talking about.

'Adults. They say they care, but they don't, all they think about is themselves.'

She crossed her arms as if signalling the end to our conversation.

I spoke quickly, trying to prolong it. 'But surely . . . if she knew you were unhappy, she'd let you live with her?'

'Well, I did tell her. I wrote it in a card and she didn't bother to reply, so there . . . that's what she's like.' She lay back down and covered her eyes with her arm.

A sickness rose in my stomach. The card. It was worse than I'd thought. 'When?' I asked, my voice sounding strangled, hoping that maybe she was talking about a different one.

'Last Christmas. Don't you remember? You gave it to her.'

Should I tell her what had happened? If I did, she might hate me. Besides, I said to myself, if she missed her mum so much, she'd ask again. She could go to Plaistow any time. Maybe she'd got used to being here and was happy with what she had.

'At least you've got your dad,' I said eventually.

She didn't reply.

I carried on. 'Do you think he'd have her back? My mum says she wouldn't touch my dad with a bargepole.'

Rachel lifted her arm away. Her eyes were shining, but she wasn't crying. 'They all say that, don't they?'

There it was again: that other side of Rachel. The worldly Rachel. The I-know-everything-about-adults Rachel. It occurred to me that actually she had more than two sides. She was like a whole lot of people wrapped up in one. I couldn't work her out.

We stayed until dusk and then, when it was too cold to stay any longer, we headed back across the wasteland. Around us, the night animals were waking. Field mice and hedgehogs. Yellow-eyed foxes glaring as we passed. A badger lumbering with its steel-trap jaw.

It was late. Mr Murray would be there by now, but Mum's enjoyment would be ruined because she'd be worrying, looking at the clock, waiting for me to return with the cake. It was funny I hadn't thought to tell Rachel that it was my birthday. I told her now as we wandered along.

'Why didn't you say?' she said, stopping in her tracks.

'I forgot.' It was true – being with Rachel had knocked it from my mind.

'We should celebrate.'

'How?'

She frowned, thinking about it, then she grabbed my arm and I laughed as she pulled me and we raced through the gloom, across the uneven ground, stumbling and holding on to each other, screaming and yelling at nothing.

We were creatures of the night, darting and weaving, brushing against bark, tearing through the brambles; and then we were spinning like overgrown children in dizzying circles, our arms wide and our faces turned up and we were falling, falling, down to the damp earth, where we lay waiting for the circles to stop.

'There's a cut on your knee,' I said. Blood oozed in warm droplets. 'Try this.' I pushed a leaf onto the wound.

She smiled and lay back, body abandoned, eyes closed, hair coiling across the earth.

Afterwards, we traipsed onwards through the murky light, past the old barn and I couldn't help noticing as we looked more closely that the owl had been attacked, its innards ripped and sprawling.

Now, when I recall that day I wonder, when we passed the barn, did we instinctively move a little closer to one another? Did we cast a look behind us and shiver? Did we have a sense of what lay only a few yards from our path?

If we did, I don't recall. I only know that the next day a body was found, hidden in a shallow grave, and after that the orchard was never the same. Neither was my relationship with Rachel.

17

1999

The shop assistant's lip curls as she packs the scarf and the flip-flops into a bag. I know exactly what she's thinking.

For a second I see myself through her eyes: thirty-five but looking older, all lumps and bumps and creases. I lift my chin and smile as if I'm completely normal, standing here. I'm an ordinary customer, making an ordinary purchase.

Outside, I take deep breaths.

The police officers have gone. I feel a foolish sense of relief. How stupid I am. They can't know anything. Not yet. I still have time to set the past straight; to consider how the next part of the story will play out. There are decisions that can be made.

I touch the grass-green scarf for courage and carry on along Cornmarket Street. Once, according to the stories, martyrs were imprisoned and then burned at the stake on these streets. They sacrificed their lives for their religion. I wonder where the burning happened. I think of the screams, the searing heat. How brutal life used to be. How brutal it still is. People having to make sacrifices for the injustice of the world. Would I have the courage to do the same?

I need a sugar rush. Turning into a side road, I find a

newsagent's. The bell jingles as I open the door. The shop is cramped and overstocked and I slope along the single aisle knocking into shelves.

Clumsy Elizabeth. Stupid Elizabeth.

Voices, like ghosts, flicker through my mind. I shake them away and focus on choosing a paper. Next, I select a glossy magazine and pick up a Twix. I am at the counter when I spot the rack of notebooks. I grab one of them and a pen. I should write down what's in my head, make sense, be prepared.

A group of teenagers tumble in as I'm waiting to be served. One of them knocks into me. She apologises and the rest laugh. They stare and nudge as I pay. It's probably my clothes, or it might be my size, or my thin hair, or it might be the glossy magazine. I can hear them thinking: *Why is a woman like her buying a magazine like that?*

Their voices babble inside my head and they remind me of the girls I knew at school. Different clothes, different hairstyles, same self-conscious desire to be part of a pack. It was only Rachel who let me in, eventually, and before her, Debra of course – the girl who had nothing, but thought she had everything. She was in a world of her own.

The shopkeeper is half asleep. He doesn't care what I buy. He doesn't care what I look like or how I feel as he packs my purchases into a red and white striped bag.

The girls are still giggling. I pretend I can't hear them as I leave.

Once outside, I head for the covered market where it's cooler and there's a pleasant, old-fashioned atmosphere amongst its maze of shops and stalls. I go to my favourite cafe – a narrow strip with a vinyl floor and Formica-topped tables and brown wallpaper in need of a good wash-down. The staff here change at a rapid rate and today I recognise no one. I ask for tea and an all-day English breakfast and then take my mug to a table.

Flipping through the newspaper, I read about the turn of the century, the year 2000, stories warning of bugs and computers, the value or not of the Millennium Dome.

How will I celebrate?

I probably won't, is the answer to that.

I find the article I want along with a photo of the orchard. My stomach flips as I examine the knotted trees and twisted branches. Squinting, I imagine one of those old demons hiding in a hollow.

Moving on, I read about the skeleton, unearthed by diggers exactly as Mrs Joseph had said. I read the article twice, three times, but there's no hint of identity, sex or age. There is only the mention of another body, an unsolved murder back in 1979. Could the crimes be connected, the journalist asks?

By the time the girl brings breakfast, my tea is cold.

I ask for another cup, stirring in two spoons of sugar which I don't normally have. Pale sausages, soft bacon and a pool of light-coloured beans. My appetite has gone, but still, I eat steadily, mopping up the beans with bread as thin as blotting paper.

Staring out the window, I spot the girls from the news-agent's hanging around, joined by a group of boys. I turn away before they catch my eye, eat the Twix and flick through the magazine, hardly taking in the stories, the fashion, the beauty, the sex. None of it connects to me.

Fifteen minutes later and the teenagers have gone.

I organise my belongings, noticing guiltily that I've stuffed my work overall inside my bag instead of hanging it on its peg. Pulling the overall out, I drop it on the seat.

'Hey,' says the girl at the counter when I'm on my way to the door. 'Is that yours?'

I shake my head. 'Not mine. It was there already.'

A theft and a lie. Not much, but even so.

I leave the cafe, thinking. It's been a few more hours since they found the skeleton. A few more opinions have been given. A few more brain cells have considered the who and the why and the when.

Are the police tracking me down, getting ready to pounce?

No. It's not possible. Still, suspicion chases me as I leave the market – so I walk a little faster and don't dare to turn around.

18

1979

It was all over the news.

A body in the orchard buried in a shallow grave behind the barn. A worker had unearthed it. Or rather, his dog had. Chasing a squirrel, it had come back with a human hand. At least, that was one rumour. There were others, too, and people speculating about cause of death: shot, stabbed, beaten. Organs cut out. Head missing. The stories grew more and more bizarre.

I watched the latest update on TV, appalled and fascinated. Three days before, I had passed this very spot with Rachel, ignorant that only a few yards away a woman had lain buried, and that same evening, when I had got home, Mum had wrapped me in her arms and told me how sorry she had been about the cake. She had made me one after all – pink and white, with a book made of icing resting in the centre. Bob had been and gone.

Now a photo of the victim flashed up on the screen. Twenty-eight years old, with long, dark hair and a thin face. Her name was Margaret Montague, a woman who had been reported missing nine months before. I shivered thinking about how long it would take a body to decompose, to become a skeleton. I leaned forward. The picture wasn't a good one. Still, there was something about the woman that seemed familiar.

The news moved on to the next item – talk about a nudist beach in Brighton outraging local residents, an ex-MP who'd faked his own death and been released from prison. There was a knock on the door and Mrs Joseph's voice floated through the house.

Poor woman . . . local, they say . . . a terrible business . . . Can you imagine . . . ?

The news turned into the weather. I pictured the victim again and because she had been found in the orchard, I placed her there in my imagination.

Out in the hall, Mrs Joseph's voice rose.

Missing . . . nine months . . . finally discovered . . . back of the barn . . .

The door slammed shut and Mum came into the room, straightening cushions, questioning what the world was coming to when people were murdered on their very own doorstep.

Nine months.

I counted backwards to November – last year when Dad had left. I didn't recall a story about a missing person, but then I'd been caught up in my own world. It had been freezing cold, I did remember that, because I'd been in the orchard on the very day he'd gone and I had seen that couple.

I closed my eyes, going over the scene: the voices and the slow rumble of laughter; the woman's winding hair; other footsteps and a tuneless whistling; the sense of someone else . . . watching.

A thought planted itself suddenly in my mind. I shook my head trying to dislodge it, but like a bad seed, it stayed.

I told Mum I was ill and went to bed for the rest of the afternoon. She brought me milk and toast on a tray to catch the crumbs and told me she was making a special meal, chicken wrapped in ham. It would make me feel better, she said. I had a sneaking suspicion it wasn't meant for me.

My suspicion was confirmed when I heard a knock at the door and a loud voice in the hall. Thirty minutes later Mum appeared with the news that Bob had come back for another visit and food was ready.

'I'm not hungry.'

'Of course you are,' she said. 'You need to keep up your strength. Besides, good manners cost nothing.'

I dragged myself out of bed and by the time I got downstairs, I could see that Bob had his feet well and truly under the table. Mum, flushed after a glass of wine, introduced us.

'This is Elizabeth,' she said.

'Hullo,' said Bob.

He was big, but not muscular like Dad. He had a flabby face and a belly that pushed against a badly ironed shirt which had a frayed collar and a button missing. He wore little round glasses, which he kept settling in place with one finger as if he was afraid someone would whip them away.

Mum was smiling again but her eyes were too bright

and she fiddled with the sleeve of her dress. 'Elizabeth's a bookworm,' she said.

'I know,' said Bob, dabbing at the corner of his mouth with a napkin.

It was one of the napkins, I noticed, with a golden crown embroidered in one corner – the napkins Mum reserved for special occasions.

'I've seen her. In the adult section.' He winked and I gave him a withering look. Naturally I was in the adult section. I was fifteen. What did he mean?

Mum seemed unsure too. Her smile slipped, but she quickly recovered, pouring wine for herself and Bob before suddenly remembering the food.

The chicken was dry and the ham was burned at the edges, but Bob proclaimed it delicious.

'A toast,' he said, raising his glass. 'To Phyllis and her new job.'

Mum lifted her glass too and I could see that Bob was thoroughly enjoying being in our house. At the end of the meal, he took his empty plate to the sink.

Later, when I was reading in bed, I could hear the two of them talking downstairs.

I switched off my lamp, but I couldn't switch off my thoughts – that bad seed had been watered by dark imaginings and now it had taken root.

Pulling the covers over my head, I distracted myself, thinking about Rachel. I went over our conversation. The way she had said *we* and how she hadn't wanted to be with anyone else and the fact that she had loved the den.

It had been so wonderful. Yet I couldn't dismiss my

earlier thoughts. The bad seed was growing, attaching itself to my mind, refusing to let go.

I got up and stole downstairs, letting myself into the garden. The sky was black stamped with stars.

At the back of the garden the wall shone pale in the moonlight. The trees in the field beyond waved their spindly branches, like a mass of winding hair.

Margaret. I knew who she was. At least, I had seen her before. I could deny it no longer. She was the woman in the orchard. The woman I'd seen on the same day Dad had left.

She had called out to me when I'd stumbled, but I hadn't turned around. I'd run from her and the man she was with and from the other person who had been watching me, watching them.

An owl hooted. Another answered. I looked at the sky. It was a perfect night for stargazing. I tried picking out constellations. The Plough, Ursa Minor, Cassiopeia. The words leapt about in my mind, but what did they mean? I'd forgotten what Dad had told me.

Laughter burst from the house, through the open door.

A hot tear slid down my face and slipped into the corner of my mouth. What I'd been afraid of most was happening. Dad had gone. Mrs Wright had stolen him, Mum had replaced him and I was losing my memories. They were disappearing like stars fading in the light.

There was only the face of the dead woman, and a knowledge I had no idea what to do with.

19

1979

The next morning, my sheets were soaked in sweat.

I had a temperature. Mum made a fuss, feeding me oranges, sponging my forehead, calling the doctor who pronounced mumps.

The last two weeks of my summer were spent in bed. A few days before I was due back at school, I recovered enough to get up. I went out on my bike wearing a bala-clava I'd found at the back of the shed and Dad's old donkey jacket.

The press had descended on the neighbourhood. Reporters were hanging about and talking to people, taking photos. A police car had parked at the entrance to the orchard and a few men with cameras had set up camp close by. I slowed as I passed the cafe. It was full of the usual builders and locals and some policemen.

Further along, outside the newsagent's, I stopped to read the headlines. They were all about the dead woman, speculating motive and method. I rode on, not daring to go into the orchard. Instead, I crossed the road and took a detour into the estate, heading for Rachel's house.

A cluster of reporters had spilled onto these streets too. One man with a camera had wandered into Rachel's road. Whilst I was watching, a car drew up. The woman with Farah Fawcett hair got out and leaned into the back seat to retrieve her son.

'Got a minute?' the man shouted.

'No,' she replied. 'And I told you that last time.'

'Did you see anything?' he persisted.

'What am I supposed to have seen? I said that last time too.'

'Anyone behaving suspiciously?'

She rolled her eyes and shook her head.

The door to Rachel's house opened and Mr Wright stepped out in his shirtsleeves. He surveyed the scene.

'Looks like the lady doesn't want to speak to you,' he said. 'So I suggest you move on.'

For such a big man he had a surprisingly melodic voice. His neighbour was gazing at him adoringly and my heart lifted. My dad might have done a bunk but Rachel's was right here, right now, a comic-book hero, an avenger, taking care of not only his daughter, but the people on the estate.

Another grateful smile and the woman took her son inside. Mr Wright on the other hand stayed put. Slowly and deliberately, he rolled up one sleeve of his checked shirt and then the other.

'All right, mate,' said the man. 'Calm down.'

Mr Wright blinked a few times, flexed his fingers and cracked them together.

Undeterred, the man levelled his camera. Mr Wright moved across, stuck out his hand and covered the lens.

'I don't think so,' he said. 'Do you?'

I held my breath, watching the scene play out.

'Take it easy.' The man edged away.

Mr Wright watched him go. I left quickly before he noticed me.

On the first day of term, even though two weeks had passed, the corridors buzzed with the news of the murder.

In assembly, a community officer called PC Newman came to talk to us. He stood on the stage with Mr Lee and spoke about how there was no need to panic, but we should avoid going around on our own, or hanging about late at night.

The atmosphere changed as people exchanged glances. Debra shifted, pushing her bony body close to mine. There was a stir of nervousness mixed with excitement. Already people were inventing new stories, moving on from the macabre description of the woman's death to speculation about what kind of person had done the deed. A psychopath, a serial killer, a man with a grudge, someone she had known.

When I thought of my own theories, my heart hammered. If I was right and the victim was the woman I'd come across that day, then I might have seen her murderer. Should I tell PC Newman, put up my hand right now and confess to being a witness?

But what was I a witness to? I hadn't actually seen anything untoward. I couldn't even be sure the two women were the same.

I slumped in my seat, my mind slack with indecision. Rachel sat a few rows ahead of me, next to Karl. I distracted myself: staring at the back of his neck; imagining firing poisonous darts into his flesh.

Mr Lee's booming voice made me jump. PC Newman had finished his speech, but Mr Lee was saying how he'd be available at the school all day in case anyone wanted to speak to him.

The rest of the morning passed slowly. We had double physics followed by the worst lesson of the week – swimming. Only the most confident of girls enjoyed those moments in the changing room. The rest of us, whether big like me or flat-chested like Debra, or painfully thin like some of the others, found it agony.

We were the last to get changed, Debra and me. Balancing on one leg, I thrust the other into my costume, while doing my best to cover myself with an inadequate pink towel. Debra didn't bother to hide and I could see quite clearly the bruises on the tops of her legs, and she was scratching, raking her arms with her fingernails.

Splashing through the foot bath onto the pool side, I asked her where the bruises had come from.

'Don't remember,' she said.

I didn't believe her. So many bruises, every day, it was obvious – Frank was knocking her about. Dad said that half the men in The Dog and Duck hit their wives and kids. I felt guilty because I'd been so absorbed with Dad leaving and trying to be friends with Rachel and worrying about a dead woman, I hadn't been looking out for my friend. I waited until she was in a race, losing catastrophically, and then I told the teacher.

By lunchtime, Debra had gone. John said he'd seen her crying outside the sick room. Had I been too hasty? No. I'd seen the bruises. I'd done the right thing.

*

On the way home, I stopped at the cafe.

It was practically empty, although dirty crockery littered the tables. A policeman with a thin moustache leaned at the counter chatting. When Maggie stopped to serve me, he moved across to sit with his mate at a table.

'Vultures,' said Maggie, handing me a Chelsea bun.

I glanced at the retreating policeman.

'Not him. New customers. A woman dies and they pick away at all the gory details.'

I offered to help clear away and she was grateful.

While we were busy, Mrs Joseph appeared in a swirl of multi-coloured scarves and shopping.

'Pilchards,' she said. The bag clattered with tins as she set it on the floor. 'Victor prefers salmon, but they're all out in Spar.'

'I've got some,' said Maggie. She turned to me. 'Would you mind, Elizabeth? Kitchen, middle cupboard.'

I put down my cloth.

The stairs to the flat led up from the messy storeroom out the back. The flat itself was warm and smelled of joss sticks and was full of interesting things: tapestries, candles, dream catchers. There were shelves of books too. When I was small, Maggie used to read to me. I recognised the myths and legends, the interpretations of portents and symbols. But there were other books about witchcraft and paganism and spirits. I shivered, running my finger across their spines.

I found the salmon and then mooched about, wasting more time.

The kitchen had painted orange cupboards and swirly green and yellow curtains. There was a pile of CND leaflets on the table, a framed poster of Che Guevara on the wall. Another leaflet for an anti-racist march in London.

I wandered to the window and then immediately stepped back. Rachel and Karl were in the street. Walking, not touching, but so close they might as well be. I practised spotting Karl's aura, narrowing my eyes and looking for signs of bad character, but nothing changed, whereas when I examined Rachel, her aura was shiny and sparkling. With a hint of something else. Some faded darkness. Or was it my imagination?

They crossed the road and stopped at the entrance to the estate. Karl was talking, leaning close to Rachel, who stood with her head bowed, listening. She lifted her head and my stomach flipped seeing the smile she gave him.

Stupid bitch.

I wouldn't forgive what he'd said even if Rachel did.

Across the street, Karl spoke again and she threw back her head and laughed.

My anger morphed into misery. She preferred Karl. The time we'd spent together in the orchard had made no difference. The two of us were as unalike as any two people could be. Her poise versus my clumsiness. Her beauty versus my ordinariness. Her *lovability* versus my *unlovability*. I was inventing words.

Karl pushed his hand through his new wavy hair and I had to admit I could see why Rachel liked him.

A moment more and they separated, Rachel heading to the estate and Karl going back the way they'd come. I watched him sauntering, hands in pockets.

A car passed. I visualised it veering onto the pavement and knocking Karl down. Blinking, I saved him, conjuring up a giant eagle that swooped and lifted him to safety. I congratulated myself on showing mercy. At the same time, I sent him a silent message that if he hurt Rachel, things would go differently.

When I got downstairs, Mrs Joseph had moved on to the subject of the murder. She was talking about the woman's husband. I went back to wiping tables.

'They lived by the river – well, he still does, I suppose, in one of those expensive houses with the lovely gardens that stretch down to the water. He reported her missing nine months ago – though some say theirs wasn't a happy marriage. Not at all.'

I carried a tray of crockery to the storeroom and missed Maggie's reply, but on my return, Mrs Joseph was talking about the husband's reputation. 'He's been in prison apparently, burglary with assault, and his wife was having an affair. A string of affairs by all accounts. According to the husband anyway. The police are asking for these men to come forward, to give an account of their whereabouts.'

'Gossip.' Maggie went to the till and opened the drawer, shaking her head as if she couldn't quite believe the amount of money there was inside. She handed me some coins. 'Wages,' she said. 'Come again.'

I thanked her and replied that I would.

She winked at me. 'And now maybe you could help Mrs Joseph home with her bags.'

*

On the way, Mrs Joseph complained about the building work. She talked about the action group she'd set up, Residents Against Estates, and asked if my mother would like to join. I doubted it, but I said I'd check anyway.

She invited me into her house, offered me a drink and deposited me in the front room.

Like every other time I had visited, I was struck first by the rancid smell and then by the sound of flapping and twittering. There were three bird cages set about the room. Seven canaries behind bars.

The room was lit by a standing lamp and the glow of the gas fire. The TV was on with no sound. Victor was watching from the same old chair in his usual burgundy cardigan and burgundy slippers.

I said hello and wandered across to the bookshelf: Hardy, Austen, Hugo, Poe. So many novels. Adult books, serious books that I was yet to discover.

I picked out *Tess of the d'Urbervilles*. Scanning the first pages, I stopped at the description of Tess. The style was dense, but I had already read *Jude the Obscure* and knew that I liked Hardy and I thought Tess was someone I wanted to know.

Mrs Joseph came in and set down the tray. 'Found the books then.'

'Are they yours?'

She shook her head. 'Victor's. You know, before.'

Poor Victor. I pictured him falling from that crane, arms spread like a bird. One moment and everything lost. Now Victor was shut away. Trapped like the canaries.

Mrs Joseph said that I was welcome to borrow the books any time.

'Really?' I could hardly believe my luck. So many other worlds to inhabit.

'And if you wanted to,' she added, 'you could read to Victor from time to time. It would be nice to hear a young voice in the house.'

She glanced at a photo of a boy in shorts. It was next to a picture of a quiet-looking man smoking a pipe. Her son and husband, I guessed.

The news came on. Mrs Joseph turned up the volume. More about the local murder. Margaret Montague had worked at a place called Trim – a hairdresser's in town. The reporter stood at the entrance to the orchard speaking into a microphone. From time to time the camera panned the watching crowd.

'Hey now. Would you believe it? Look who it is,' said Mrs Joseph.

I peered at the screen. 'Who?'

'Beatrice Collingdale,' she said, pointing. 'Works in Spar.'

The reporter was interviewing a middle-aged woman with a blue rinse. 'How do you feel about the murder?' he was asking.

'Shocked,' she replied. 'Everyone does. This is a quiet area. We're quiet people. Nothing ever happens here.'

The reporter nodded knowingly and again the camera panned the crowd. I leaned closer, recognising a teacher from school, and was that Mr Evans coming along with Nip? And there in the corner, almost out of shot, was Dave. A little apart, hands in his pockets.

The camera focused briefly and then zoomed across the orchard through the trees, crossing to the place

where I'd seen the couple and then beyond to the wasteland and back again to the barn.

Had it really been Margaret that day? What if the
man she had been with had killed her only hours, minutes, moments after I'd run away?

Or what if there *had* been someone else as I'd suspected, watching too? Maybe the watcher had waited
until she was alone and then killed her.

Maybe he had seen me and thought I had seen him
too.

What if, now, he was after me?

20

1979

There was a letter for me. I recognised Dad's writing –
his mix of small and capital letters.

Quickly, I tore it open.

Dear Lizzie. I expect Mum has told you by now.
I'm in Norfolk.

I stopped reading. From the kitchen came the sound
of laughter.

Bob was here. He had stayed the night. Mum had
warned me, sitting me down and explaining with pink
cheeks that he was coming for his tea and probably
wouldn't go home. I'd kept out of their way, going to
bed early and hiding beneath the blankets, reading with
a torch. In the morning, Bob had been at the kitchen
table, sloshing milk onto his cornflakes. Worse, he'd
taken my bowl.

Resentfully, I'd dragged out another from the cupboard and slumped into my seat. Mum had appeared
wearing a new dressing gown with rosebuds on the
collar. She'd smiled in a silly way and then moved about
the kitchen, touching Bob's arm, asking if he wanted tea
or coffee, perhaps some orange juice, a grapefruit.

I rushed back into the kitchen.

Mum was leaning over Bob's shoulder, arms hanging loosely around his neck.

She turned awkwardly as I thrust the letter under her nose.

'It's from Dad,' I said.

Her expression fell.

'Is he on holiday?' I demanded.

She didn't speak.

'Mum. What's happening? Tell me.'

Bob half rose as if to intervene and then, appearing to think better of it, sat down again slowly.

'It's complicated.'

'Mum,' I said, my voice rising. 'When's Dad back in London?'

'He's gone . . .'

There was something about her voice that made me panic. 'What?' I clutched her arm.

'He's gone there for a while.'

'To Norfolk?' I shouted. 'Why?'

'He's going to see if he can make a go of it.'

'Make a go of what?'

'His life.'

'He's got a life.'

'Yes, but he's going to try running his own pub. You know he's always wanted to do that.'

I stared at her. I didn't know that at all. Dad wanted to live in London or sail away to the middle of the ocean with me in the galley or go to California and work for Barry White. Those were his dreams. He'd never mentioned a pub.

Why didn't Mum care? Why wasn't she going crazy

at the thought of Dad and *that woman* making a proper life together?

Bob cleared his throat.

I gave him a bitter look. *He* was why. She was too interested in *him* to care about Dad – or me.

'When did he go?'

'A week or so ago.'

'I don't understand. Why didn't he come and see me?'

'He did.'

'When?'

'You weren't here.'

'Where was I?'

'It was Friday . . . after school . . . you were . . .'

In the cafe, probably, waiting for Rachel to notice me, wasting my time while Dad had been hammering on our door trying to see me.

'Why didn't he phone?'

'You know what he's like.'

He was a coward. That was all I could think. He had run away once without consulting me. Now he'd done it again.

'You should have told me.'

'I was going to, but I wanted to explain first, about him leaving and . . .' She stopped and now she flushed bright red. 'Listen, Elizabeth. It's not my fault. He was the one that left, who went off with that woman. I'm still here, aren't I?'

I knew that, but still.

'I know you've had a tough time. I've been talking to Doctor Clark—'

'What?'

'I said I've been talking to Doctor—'

'Yes, I heard you. What about?'

She glanced across at Bob, who'd fixed his gaze on the table. 'About you maybe going to see him.'

'Why?'

She blinked, pulled at the sleeves of her dressing gown. 'He thought you might want to talk about ... I mean, you've been having a lot of bad dreams lately.'

It was true. I woke most nights soaked in sweat. 'So?'

'Well ... I'm just wondering if this business in the orchard is ... disturbing you.'

Bob shifted in his seat. Why was she talking about this in front of him?

'I'm not going to talk to Doctor Clark. Tell me about Dad.'

There was silence. 'All right,' said Mum. 'We'll talk about it later.'

I glared at her. I knew I wasn't being fair. I knew that Dad had been the one that had left, but now he'd gone across the country, maybe for good, and Mum wanted to talk about it later? Why not now? If she could discuss my nightmares in front of Bob, surely she could talk to me about Dad? I willed her to change her mind, to get rid of Bob and speak to me properly, but she went across to the sink and Bob wasn't going anywhere. He looked at me sheepishly and smiled.

'What are you smiling at?' I shouted before I could stop myself.

'Don't be so rude,' said Mum, turning sharply.

'I'm not being rude. It's got nothing to do with him.'

'He hasn't spoken.'

'He doesn't need to.'

'It's all right,' said Bob.

He stood up slowly, holding out his palms as if appeasing a wild animal. I took a step towards him; he stumbled against his chair. Leaving one palm facing me, with the other hand he dragged at the napkin tucked into his shirt, putting it down as if it was a weapon. I wanted to laugh. Instead, all the upset that had been stirring inside me burst out. Grabbing the nearest thing, my mother's shoe lying in a pile by the door, I launched it at him, clipping the side of his head.

Nobody moved, not even Bob.

I turned and ran, out into the morning. Grabbing Dad's bike, I toiled along the street. With so many emotions storming through me, I didn't know or care which was the worst: anger, loss, guilt or revenge. I imagined them all swirling through my body, dark emotions thickening my blood.

Rachel answered the door, took one look at me and said, 'What's wrong?'

Tears started. I ran my fingers through my hair which was damp with sweat.

Mr Wright called from the kitchen. 'Who is it?'

Rachel pulled me into the hall and gestured for me to wait. She disappeared and I breathed deeply, absorbing the heat of the house, the quiet voices, the plush carpet beneath my feet.

A moment later and she was leading me into the front room.

With the curtains half closed, it was as dark and

warm as it had been before. Sinking into the settee, I relaxed, all my anger seeping into the springs. Rachel sat down opposite and I asked her straightaway if she knew about the move to Norfolk.

'Yes,' she said matter-of-factly.

'Don't you care?' I asked, leaning forward, my mouth parted with disbelief. Surely she must feel something.

'What's the point? Nothing's going to change.'

She fiddled with her cuff and I saw that the material was frayed at the edges. The dress was one of the long-sleeved shapeless creations she often wore. It was tie-dyed grey and white, giving the effect of a cloudy day. Even so, she still looked good. She was barefoot and I admired her toenails, which were painted the same lovely green I'd seen before.

Maybe she didn't care, but at least someone had had the grace to tell her the news. Mum had obviously known about it and kept quiet, while Dad was too cowardly to tell me any way other than by letter.

'But no one told me,' I said, my voice rising along with my indignation.

'What difference does it make?' she said abruptly. 'You have to face it, they've gone.'

I stared at her. Was this the same person who had run and laughed in the orchard, confided in me about the card, *entrusted* me with that card, even? What had happened? Why had she changed?

She plucked at the threads of her cuff. Her nails matched her toes, but the varnish was chipped and the nails bitten, the skin at the edges ragged.

I studied her face for a sign of what she was thinking.

Her eyes had taken on the grey colour of her dress and her skin was pale as stone. She made me think of those old women in the French Revolution calmly knitting beside the guillotine.

The kitchen door opened and, at the sound of it, Rachel got up and went into the hall. The warmth of the room pressed down on me. Sweat pooled beneath my arms. Maybe there was a heater I could switch off. My gaze fell on the photo, still turned around. Was it the disgraced Mrs Wright? I had a compulsion to know. A glance at the door. Now was my chance. In a couple of strides, I was at the mantelpiece.

It wasn't Mrs Wright. The woman looked like her, I had to admit. She had the same plump figure that stopped short of being fat, but she was fair-haired and didn't have the kiss curls. It was her sister maybe. There was a girl in the picture too, who was about four years old. The girl had red hair. Not Melissa; it must be Rachel.

The front door opened and closed. I put the photo back where I'd found it and ran to my seat.

Rachel returned with a can of Coke, crisps and custard creams. She was like an adult, the way she brought food and drink, the way she arranged the biscuits on a plate. The way we sat in the front room instead of in her bedroom.

As soon as I thought about her bedroom, I wanted to see it. I twiddled my thumbs, trying to distract myself.

'Has your dad gone out?' I asked.

She nodded. 'Newsagent's.'

'Does he mind me being here?'

'Don't think so.'

There was an edge to her voice. I glanced at her. She was protecting my feelings.

I blew my nose and asked if I could use the loo.

The suite was the same shade as ours. Aubergine. Rachel's underwear was strung out on the clothes horse next to her dad's baggy pants. I washed my hands and went out onto the landing. One of the three doors was open and I couldn't help peeking inside.

The room was a real mess. There were clothes left on the bed and stuff all over the floor. Rachel's magazines were on the bedside table and her school bag hung on the back of the chair. It must be her room, yet the clothes on the bed weren't her style. Tight dresses and skirts that were more likely to belong to Mrs Wright. Maybe Rachel couldn't bear to get rid of them. Maybe she held them at night like I sometimes did with the things I'd kept of Dad's.

Mr Wright was coming through the front door as I reached the bottom of the stairs. My heart was beating hard as if I'd done something wrong, which of course I had, snooping about their house.

At home, I was glad to see Bob had gone.

I thought Mum would punish me for what I'd done, but she contented herself with talking it over. She said Bob had understood my reaction but that she expected me to apologise. I promised I would and she turned her attention to Dad's letter.

'Speaking's hard,' she said. 'Writing's easy.'

Had she forgotten that she yelled at Dad whenever he telephoned and refused to have him in the house? I'd heard her tell him a hundred times that his writing was scruffy, that he couldn't spell, couldn't express himself.

I took the letter along with a local newspaper that Bob had left behind and went upstairs. Closing the curtains, I turned on the lamp and read the letter quickly, picking out all the bits of information, and then again more slowly, taking it in. I had to concentrate to work out all the words. Mum was right, Dad's handwriting was difficult to read. A lump formed inside my throat as I thought about him, scratching away with his pen, trying to keep his writing neat.

There was no mention of any pub. He wrote about a new job in a club. *People are just the same – same drunks, same thieves, same villains.* He didn't say whether he liked it any better or worse, or how he felt about not being in London. He did say he hoped I'd be able to come and see him soon, though.

I tucked the letter under my pillow and scanned the newspaper, looking for details of the murder.

The woman had been struck repeatedly with a heavy object. A hammer maybe. Brutal. A frenzied attack. Some of the facts I knew: she was a hairdresser, worked in a shop called Trim.

There was a picture of her and her husband on their wedding day. This photo was clearer than the one I'd seen on the news. I grabbed my magnifying glass, searching for clues. There was a niggle in my mind. I was becoming sure that this was the woman from the orchard, but something was bothering me. Had I seen her before that, somewhere else? Did I actually know her? I tried to focus, but the memory wouldn't come.

I concentrated on the husband instead, Lenny. He was short and slight with a quiff and definitely not the man who had been with her. Was he a villain like Mrs Joseph had suggested? Maybe Dad knew him. He knew all kinds of people around town.

Later, I went next door to read to Victor.

The birds were restless, twittering and brushing the bars with their wings. I began *Tess*. Victor's eyes were closed, so he might have been sleeping, or he might have been listening. From time to time I talked about the story. I babbled on even though Victor didn't reply. I started thinking about how much you can learn when you don't speak and let others fill in the gaps.

The news came on, and I took a break, tiptoeing across to the TV and turning up the volume.

There was more about Margaret Montague. The journalist was reporting from her house on the river. He described it as a dream house and interviewed a neighbour, a posh woman in a kaftan.

'How well did you know Margaret?' he asked.

'Peggy,' corrected the woman, rather primly. 'She preferred the diminutive. She didn't like Margaret at all.'

Tess fell from my hands and clattered onto the floor. Victor opened his eyes.

The woman was still talking, telling the reporter how she used to have her hair cut in Trim and that Peggy had been delightful, all her customers had loved her. She was friendly, interested. 'Didn't work there for the money, of course. Didn't need to. She liked people. It was the same when she worked in the hotel.'

'The Grand Hotel?' said the journalist.

'That's right. Not quite my style, but nice enough. Peggy wanted more, though, fancied herself in the beauty industry. Would have tried for her own salon one day, I'm sure.'

I sat down heavily, my mind whirring. Those dark eyes. That dark hair. She hadn't liked me – all that mess I'd made with the knickerbocker glory and the lie I'd told about needing to phone Mum. She'd liked Dad, though, been all over him. Touching his hand when she gave him the bill. Leaning close when she set down his food.

She'd worn her hair in a ponytail and been plumper, fuller in the face. She must have lost weight. In the photo on the telly, she was thin, her face gaunt. No wonder I hadn't recognised her at first. What would Dad say? Did he know?

I glanced at Victor, who was watching me now. Long legs stretched across the carpet. Lips pursed as if whistling along with the birds.

I should carry on reading, but I couldn't focus.

Things come back to haunt you, they say. How long would it be before the memory of Dad flirting with Peggy would stop haunting me?

21

1999

Memories curl around me like early morning mist. I haul myself back into the present and focus on the window display before me.

It's full of posters. Los Pueblos Blancos. The Hanging Gardens. The Blue Lagoon. The Taj Mahal. Glorious promises of exotic locations.

Inside, the shop is quiet with a lone travel agent and a man and woman choosing a cruise. They want to know every detail: every excursion available, every facility on board.

I browse the brochures.

More choices. The Caribbean. The Costa del Sol. Italy. Florida. Berlin. Sydney.

Dad has always said I should visit him. He's living his dream which I'm glad about, but I don't want to see it for myself.

I was nineteen, in that London bedsit, when he told me he was moving on from Norfolk. It wasn't a shock, since I'd always known he'd travel further. He'd found a dilapidated bar for sale on Bondi Beach. *Cheap as chips. Too good to miss.* He planned to do it up and give it a Seventies vibe: *disco nights and Barry White.*

I was glad that he was happy and, in a way, it made things easier. No more meeting and pretending life was normal. Charlotte sold the flat in Plaistow so they could afford it, which was a bit of a blow, but in the end, it was for the best.

'Come and see us,' he says each time we speak. 'You'll love it here.'

I never go. Never have. Not even when he bought a boat. Not even for his wedding. It would have been – would still be – too difficult. It's hard enough to hide secrets from acquaintances and neighbours, let alone from people you love.

He comes to England every so often. Charlotte and Melissa go to Norfolk to see the rest of their family and Dad spends time with me. He looks almost the same minus the platforms. Charlotte has grown as big as a barn and Melissa . . . well, she's the same as she ever was. Nothing like Rachel.

When I visit Mum, I relate it all, giving her the gossip, joining in with her tuts and grimaces. She forgives me then for the way she thinks I am: cautious, tight-lipped. Like I said, it's difficult to hide secrets and still be yourself.

I concentrate on the brochures.

Nice, with its dangerous, winding roads. Or Monaco, much safer with its perfect streets. How about a Greek island? The photos are appealing: haphazard villages built on slopes, yellow sunshine, a turquoise sea, the promise of music and dancing and tavernas stacked with dolmades and tzatziki and baklava.

Somewhere remote where you can be somebody else. Somewhere large enough to find work, yet small enough to feel safe.

The couple are choosing their cabin. The travel agent is stapling papers, sliding them into an envelope. Nearly done. Shaking hands.

I settle on Lipsi, a Greek island, simply because I'm charmed by the mythological connection. It's where Calypso imprisoned Odysseus when he was on his way back from Troy to Ithaca. A beautiful maiden detaining a man has the irony of reversal.

My phone rings.

I keep hold of the brochure and flip open my mobile.

'Elizabeth,' says Mrs Joseph. Her voice is high with excitement.

I switch the phone to my other ear. 'Hold on.' I nod at the disappointed travel agent, take a breath and walk to the door and out into the street. A moment more to collect myself. 'Yes?'

'They've found a knife.'

My stomach turns.

'Where?' As if I don't know.

'In the wasteland, close to the dip.'

'What kind of a knife?'

'The police haven't said.'

I wait a beat. 'Anything else?'

'Well . . .' She pauses dramatically.

'Do they know who the victim is?'

Stop. Calm down. I sound too eager.

Silence. I'm aware that Mrs Joseph wants to be able to say, *Yes, they do know*. She wants to be able to give me the gory details. But she can't because nothing has been released yet. Not even the sex, though of course the police will have identified male or female straightaway. What

else: height, build, ethnicity, maybe? I'm guessing, floundering, because I'm ignorant about this kind of thing. I
don't watch crime programmes anymore. I can't stand
the blood and the gore and the dreadful waste of life.

A young man cycles past. His pedalling is deliberate,
as if he's moving in slow motion, while all around the
world is speeding up, a blur of people walking past me,
disappearing, before I've focused on who they are.

Steadying myself, I lean against a wall.

'Elizabeth,' says Mrs Joseph. She sounds far away as if
she's stranded at the end of a tunnel. 'Can you hear me?'

'Sorry, yes. I'm outside.'

'I was thinking about Maggie. What would she say?
Another murder in the orchard, right on her old doorstep. Can you imagine?'

'Has she been in touch?'

'Not for years.'

'Is she still abroad?'

'New Zealand, I heard.'

Maggie sold the cafe and moved away not long before
I went to London. On her last night, I pushed an envelope through her letter box. It was only forty pounds,
but my guilt had never let it go. I wonder what she
thought when she found it, whether she had an inkling
of who it had come from or why.

For years, the new owners left the cafe empty, boarded
up, infiltrated by the local youth who spoiled it with graf-
fiti. I had a fantasy of going back, taking over. Living in
the flat upstairs. But of course, it never happened. Imagine
that view across the orchard; imagine those ghosts.

Mrs Joseph is still talking. 'Will you come home?'

'Why?'

'Well, it occurred to me that the police might want to talk to you.'

I blink hard, thinking. A student passes, her robe flapping behind her like wings. She moves on and disappears around a corner. A ghost. A memory of someone I might have been.

'Elizabeth. Are you there?'

'Yes, sorry. Still here. Why? Why would they want to talk to me?'

'I don't know.' She pauses and I'm pretty sure she's saying anything just to keep me on the line. 'I wonder if they're going to question people who used to live round here.'

'They can't speak to everyone. What would they ask?'

She's quiet and I imagine her gazing through her kitchen window at the small backyard, trying to think of a reply.

'Besides,' I say, 'they don't know how long the body has been there.'

'Skeleton,' she corrects. 'Not yet,' she adds.

'Are they checking missing persons?'

'I don't know, Elizabeth. I imagine they will. I can't think of anyone who's gone missing, though, not while I've been here. Apart from Peggy, of course. Do you remember?'

Yes, of course.

I wait a beat. 'You said they found a knife. Do they think it's . . . ?'

'The murder weapon?' Her voice rises. She's back on track. 'Well, they haven't said as much, but . . .'

'So, it could be any knife.'

'I suppose so.'

Am I showing too much interest? Does she sound suspicious, or am I just imagining things? My mind races through other questions. How long does blood stay on a surface? How can they know whose blood it is if they have no one to match it with?

There's another silence and then, 'Are you all right, Elizabeth? You seem . . . upset. Perhaps I shouldn't have told you—'

'Not at all,' I say brightly, interrupting. 'I'm fine. It's just odd . . . another death . . . you know.'

Satisfied, Mrs Joseph speculates on how easy or not it is to get clues from a skeleton. How much clothing might have been left behind. She stops once, to speak to Victor. Her voice is muffled, but I can hear the twittering. New canaries. They can't be the old ones. Not after all these years. It's a new generation of fragile bodies, trapped inside the cages, wings flapping uselessly against the bars.

Eventually, she tells me she'll ring again when she has more news. I thank her, trying not to sound too eager.

I think about going back inside the travel agent's but time is getting on. It's almost four o'clock and I need to get to the end of the story inside my head. I turn around and walk back the way I've come. Slowly, slowly, getting my memories straight.

22

1979

The dark-blue lantern hanging from the old building looked in need of a polish – the word *Police* more grey than white.

Should I go inside?

I'd woken thinking that I should. I had knowledge of the victim. It's possible I'd seen her days, hours, minutes before she'd been killed. Would I ever know? Could they ever pinpoint the exact day of her death?

A panda car drew up as I stood dithering and I moved swiftly away. That's when I saw him. Dave. Jogging down the street. Hands stuck in his pockets, eyes down, he didn't see me. Taking the steps two at a time, he disappeared inside.

I had no idea what he was doing there, but I didn't care. It was the excuse I needed to abandon my plan. I scurried away.

When I got home, Dad rang to say he was coming home for a day and a night and was planning to stay in lodgings.

Excited, I dismissed any remaining thoughts of talking to the police and made a list of exactly what I wanted to do: Dave's records. Lunch. A walk along the river (to remind Dad he wanted to sail around the world, not live in a pub in Norfolk). Shopping – Boots (to buy green nail varnish). The fair (because Mum and Bob had asked me and I didn't want to go with them).

In the kitchen, I was so absorbed in eating Frosties that I didn't notice Bob until he boomed, 'Good morning!' He was wearing a bathrobe. I turned away from his hairy legs and focused on my list. He went to the fridge as if he lived here, opened the door and peered inside.

'I thought I'd make scrambled eggs,' he said, 'for your mother. Would you like some?'

I shook my head.

He found a dish and cracked eggs. 'Looking forward to today?'

Obviously. What did he want me to say? I pushed back my chair.

'Are you then?' he persisted.

'Yes.'

'Great! What have you got planned?'

I mentioned lunch.

'What else?'

'The fair. Maybe.'

'Oh. I thought you didn't want to go.'

Shrugging, I stood up, just as Mum appeared in her silly rosebud dressing gown. Why couldn't she come down in her proper clothes like she used to?

'Do you hear that, Phyllis?' said Bob. 'Elizabeth's going to the fair. Without us.'

Mum gave me one of her hurt looks then bent to take plates from the cupboard. I moved to the door. Too late. She'd straightened before I could escape.

'I'm really not sure why you're seeing him and I'm really not sure why I'm letting you go.' She spoke in a rush as if she'd been storing the words.

I waited a beat before moving again. This was not going to end well unless I left now.

'Don't walk away.'

I clenched my fists and the list crumpled in my hands.

'What's on that paper?'

'Nothing.'

She held out her hand. 'Let me see.'

'Why?'

'Let me see.'

Reluctantly, I gave it to her. She frowned, reading, and I dug my nails painfully into my skin. Bob stopped beating eggs and scratched one bushy eyebrow. He looked from me to Mum to the shoes by the back door. I guessed he was worried I'd throw another missile. A bubble of laughter threatened to rise from somewhere deep inside of me.

'Don't smirk,' said Mum, noticing. 'It doesn't suit you.'

'I'm not smirking.' I scowled instead.

She wouldn't leave it alone. 'You do remember he left me for somebody else, don't you?' She stopped, but I knew what she was thinking. *And that means he left you too.*

I clamped my lips together, refusing to be drawn.

'I'm sorry, Elizabeth, but doesn't that mean anything to you?'

I glared at her. 'Please can I have my list?'

'Fine,' she said. 'I despair.'

'Don't be too hard on her,' I heard Bob say as I left the room. 'I know you're hurt, but it's not her fault.'

Dad was waiting outside Dave's in a pair of mirrored sunglasses.

I stared at my reflection and blinked.

'Hey,' he said, ruffling my hair, 'how are you?'

He gave me a hug and I mumbled, 'All right,' and followed him into the shop.

'I'm back,' said Dad, whipping off his sunglasses.

Dave came across.

'All right?' they said at the same time, slapping each other on the back and then returning to what they'd normally do: Dave with his headphones on, nodding in time to the music; Dad going straight to Barry White. I dawdled, picked out an album at random – Val Doonican: rocking chair, cardigan and pipe. Wasn't that how Dad was supposed to behave at forty-two, not like an aging pop star? I was sure his platforms were even higher than they had been before, and what about those sunglasses?

Still, I was just starting to relax, thinking all was right in the record world, when Dad shuffled across to Elvis Presley. Another alien move on his part. Especially when he pulled out *Blue Hawaii* and announced he was going to buy it. Well, if Dad was going to be different, I would be too. When Dad asked me what I wanted, I said Val Doonican.

'Are you serious?' he said.

I raised my eyebrows and looked knowingly at Elvis. *Are you?* We both knew it was a present for Charlotte.

Dave rang up the records on the till.

'How's business?' said Dad.

'So, so.'

'That's good.'

'Yeah. Not bad.'

'All right.'

'How's the security business?'

I lost interest and wandered across to the window. The hairdresser directly opposite was called Trim. I'd seen the shop, but not taken much notice of the name before. Mum cut my hair and had hers done in a posh boutique in town. Now I felt a jolt as I imagined Peggy being there. Trim was for *Ladies*, the sign said. Next door, there was a barber's.

While I was watching, a girl went inside followed by a middle-aged woman. It was busy. Maybe it had become more popular now Peggy had died. Vultures, Maggie would call them, sniffing about. Could vultures sniff? Did they have noses? Were beaks noses? I switched to thinking about Peggy. Who had taken her clients? I wondered if she'd had her own special place: seat, scissors, hair products, comb.

Dad and Dave were still talking. Dave was slipping the records into paper bags. Two bags for each one.

The door opened and my heart dropped as Mr Wright came in.

I looked across at Dad who was still busy at the counter. Had he heard the door open, sensed someone come in? He definitely hadn't registered who it was, although he must recognise him. How could he not?

Mr Wright was unmissable with his checked shirt and neat beard, not to mention his size.

If he went away now, Dad might not notice. I tried to communicate this using my best attempts at telepathy, but clearly it wasn't working; either that or Mr Wright didn't care because he went straight across to Country and Western.

'Stand By Your Man' popped into my head. Mrs Wright hadn't been very good at that.

Dad turned and his expression made so many rapid transformations it was like a dozen drawings of the same cartoon.

Even Dave's deadpan face showed a flicker of an emotion. What that was, I didn't know. You never could tell with Dave.

Slowly, Mr Wright picked up Tammy Wynette in one hand and Dolly Parton in the other.

'There you go,' said Dave, his voice louder than usual as he finished Dad's sale and handed him the records.

Mr Wright took one step forward and then another until he was right in Dad's face.

I held my breath.

He held up the records. 'Which one?'

Behind him, Dave cleared his throat. 'Tammy Wynette.'

'Agreed?' he said to Dad.

Dad nodded.

'How much?'

'Two pounds forty-nine,' said Dave.

Mr Wright got out his wallet. There was a long pause before he turned to Dad. 'How's my wife?'

After all the expressions he'd been through, Dad had

rejected the lot of them. Now he was a stone, rigid and pale, gripping the paper bags with solidified hands.

'She's fine,' he said in a strangled voice.

'And my daughter?'

'Fine too.'

'Good.' Mr Wright handed over a single pound note, holding on for a moment too long so that Dave had to pause, waiting for the moment of release.

Tension sizzled. The note crackled. Dave slipped it into the till.

Slowly, Mr Wright turned his back and left the shop.

There was a terrible silence, and then, 'You owe me.' Dave held out his hand. 'One pound forty-nine.'

Dad paid without a murmur.

From the window, I watched as Mr Wright crossed the road and turned in at the barber's.

Later we walked along the river and stopped on the bridge.

'He's not a victim,' said Dad, leaning his elbows on the balustrade. He was talking about Mr Wright.

'You see, Charlotte' – he paused to scratch his chin – 'she's more vulnerable than you think. She appears hard, but underneath she's mushy.'

I had no interest in what Mrs Wright was like *underneath*. Mushy or not.

'She's the victim,' he added.

'How?'

'It's hard to explain.'

I rolled my eyes. Things were always hard to explain when it came to Dad.

He tried again. 'There are men who treat women badly. Mr Wright is one of them.'

I kept silent. I liked Rachel's dad a lot more than I liked her mum, so I wasn't about to agree.

Dad pulled out a cigarette and took his time lighting it. I fixed my eyes on the moorhens darting at the edge of the water and hoped this wasn't going to turn into a chat about the birds and the bees. I had no interest in talking about sex with my father. Come to think of it, I had no interest in talking about sex with anyone. It was bad enough thinking about it: predicting when and where and with whom.

A boat came down the river, a middle-aged couple sipping wine at the prow. Dad's mouth curved into a smile. Did he still want to sail away? Would he take me with him? Or was it strictly Charlotte and Melissa: a two-berth cabin, no room for me?

'Men,' said Dad, as if the conversation hadn't paused, 'whose eyes wander.'

I stared at him. If anyone's eyes wandered, it was his. Maybe he twigged what I was thinking because he looked away sheepishly, mumbling, 'It's different.'

Was it?

'You don't understand.'

I sighed. It was a predictable response from Dad.

'Adult stuff,' he said, grimacing now. 'It's complicated – the reasons why a parent leaves.'

I frowned, working out what he was implying. Mr Wright had been unfaithful too. Was that it? He was certainly handsome, according to Mum, and women liked him. I'd seen how his neighbour had practically swooned when he'd confronted the reporter. Mrs Townsend too, when he'd rescued her at the school open day.

Dad was thoughtful, puffing away on his cigarette. He turned to me. 'Maybe I shouldn't say this.'

I waited, expecting more criticism of Mr Wright.

'Charlotte's not Rachel's mother.'

'Oh.' I blinked, processing this thought. 'Who is she then?'

'Her aunt.'

'Aunt?'

'Yep.'

The woman in the photo. She was Mrs Wright's sister, as I'd suspected, and now I knew she was Rachel's mum.

Dad was gazing at a rowing boat. *Pull*, said the cox through a megaphone. *Pull*.

I waited until the boat had gone and then asked why Rachel didn't live with her mum.

For a moment, he was distracted by a yacht. White and gleaming, *a beauty* he called this one. Then he told me that she'd abandoned Rachel when she was six years old.

'Disappeared. Went off the rails – apparently. Didn't tell anyone she was going. Not Charlotte, or Rachel for that matter. One day she was there. The next she walked out of the flat leaving Rachel on her own.'

'On her own? What happened?'

'Well, three days later, Charlotte called round. They'd argued not long before and I think she had it in her head they'd sort it out. No answer. Luckily she looked through the letter box and there was Rachel – sitting cross-legged in the hall.'

'What did Rachel say?'

'Not a lot. That she was waiting for her mum to come home.'

'What about her dad?'

He shrugged. 'Did a bunk when she was born. Her mum did the same thing then, apparently. Ran off, leaving Charlotte to take care of the baby, and then she turned up a few weeks later in the hospital. Tried to take an overdose.'

I frowned, thinking how terrible all that must be for Rachel. 'What was the argument with Charlotte about?'

He gave me a sidelong glance. 'Well. That brings me back to the subject of Mr Wright.'

'What do you mean?'

'Use your imagination, Lizzie.' He flicked his cigarette. 'Had an affair, didn't they? Him and Charlotte's sister. Why Charlotte forgave him then, I don't know. Hasn't now, though, has she?'

He changed the subject, pointing out another yacht on its way down the river. I was still thinking about Rachel being abandoned by her mother and Charlotte forgiving Mr Wright for his affair with her sister. I wondered if Mum would ever forgive Dad. I doubted it, not while she had Bob anyway.

We had lunch at The Grand Hotel.

It felt weird being there. I kept looking across at the entrance to the kitchen, expecting to see Peggy.

Halfway through my fish and chips I asked Dad if he remembered her.

He took a sip of his beer. 'Who?'

'Peggy. Long brown hair. She was here that day on my birthday.'

'Oh. Right. Yeah. Vaguely. Why?'

'Did you know she was murdered?'

He stared at me. 'What?'

'You know the body in the orchard?'

'Yes, we spoke about it.'

That was true. He'd warned me to stay away from the place, not long after the news had broken. At the time, I'd guessed Mum had put him up to it, insisting he acted like a parent, while thinking I might listen to him more than I did to her.

'But wasn't her name—'

'Margaret.'

'Yeah, so what about Peggy?'

'Same person.'

'Christ.' He stabbed a chip and examined it. 'I see. Peggy. Margaret. I didn't realise.' He frowned, chewing.

'Were you friends?'

'No,' he said quickly. 'What makes you say that?'

My stomach gave a little flip. He had the kind of expression he used to have when he came home late from The Dog and Duck and smelling of perfume.

I shrugged. 'I just remember you forgot your wallet and went back to speak to her and—'

He blinked. 'Did I?'

'Yes.' *Please tell the truth*, I said inside my head.

'Right.' He spoke slowly now. 'So, Peggy was the woman in the orchard?'

I nodded.

'Bloody hell.' He shook his head and sliced a piece of chicken.

Dad was in the loo when I spotted Debra outside.

She hadn't been back to school, but now she was walking with her mum and a sandy-haired man who I recognised from the open day. Frank. He was short, only a bit taller than Debra. Her mum was the tallest of the three and wore a dress that I guessed was the one Frank had bought. Only, it didn't fit the glorious description Debra had given. It was fancy, but even I could tell it was cheap – too many frills and the hem was coming down at the back.

What struck me was how happy the three of them were. Debra between them, chattering.

I bit my lip as something hard and sharp lodged inside my chest.

Envy.

There was no mistaking that.

23

1979

In daylight, the fairground lights shone sickly orange and yellow.

Crowds moved thickly across the field beyond the orchard, which had transformed into a whole new world with tents and painted caravans, stalls and roundabouts, dippers and wheels.

As we arrived, mucky children with candy-floss mouths held on to their parents' hands, and teenagers – most of them in packs – hung about on the dodgems and the big dipper. Couples travelled through the Tunnel of Love. Young men shot and threw and lassoed cheap toys. The air reeked with fried onions and burned toffee and echoed with screams from the top of the helter-skelter, the creak and swing of the Big Wheel, the organ music winding from the merry-go-round.

'Howzat,' said Dad as he knocked down a coconut. The stall holder handed it across and Dad threw it to me. I caught it, laughing.

We went on the ghost train. I screamed obediently when a piece of cloth dragged over my face, a skeleton dropped in front of me, a spotlighted figure leered from the darkness.

'All right, Lizzie?' said Dad in my ear as our carriage rocked through the tunnel.

I clutched his hand and pretended to be more afraid than I was. It felt good to have his attention.

The ride jolted to a stop and I insisted we went into the fortune teller's tent. A painted sign showed a picture of a wrinkled old woman with wispy grey hair and a crystal ball. The sign announced the fortune teller as Madame Beatrix.

When it was our turn, we pushed through the gauzy purple curtain. A woman in a long dress and shawl, hair hidden beneath a tasselled scarf, welcomed us.

Inside the tent, it was quiet, the shrieks and the beat of the music muffled by thick layers of tapestries, rugs and cushions. An attempt at the Middle East; it was cer-tainly hot enough – an exotic version of Rachel's house.

Madame Beatrix waited at a small, round table covered in a dark-orange cloth. On the table, there was a crystal ball and a pack of cards.

I sat on the seat opposite her. Dad stood behind me.

'Cross my palm with silver,' she said thickly.

Dad threw a few coins onto the table. I thought he should be more respectful and hoped it wouldn't count against me.

She was silent, looking at my palm.

I studied her face. She wasn't as old as I thought she should be. Not like the woman on the sign. She had blue eyes and strands of blonde hair escaping from her scarf. I focused on her aura. Nothing came.

Loudly she sighed and dropped my hand.

'That bad?' Dad joked behind me.

She drew her crystal ball close, moving her hands mysteriously across it, bending down, eyes searching.

'You will live a long time,' she said. 'And you will achieve your dream. Now your heart is full of loneliness. But that will pass.'

I held my breath.

'Yes . . . I see that dream very clearly.'

I wanted to ask what it would be.

'And pain and death.'

Not so good.

She looked up from the ball. 'But the pain will not necessarily be your own.'

I nodded, relieved at least about that.

Outside, Dad said, 'What a waste of time. Pain and death – applies to anyone.'

Still, when we got to the Big Wheel and I saw it towering and wobbling above me, I said I'd like to go to the hoopla instead.

Everyone was at the fair. I spotted people from school and then Debra with her mum and Frank, who'd been having a go at the hoopla. Miraculously, he'd won Basil Brush.

The woman on the stall was dark-haired and beautiful. I caught Dad staring at her. Frank was busy handing the stuffed toy to Debra. She looked at him adoringly as if he'd won the pools. I examined him, trying to get an idea of who he was. He was plain. Not handsome, not ugly, not large or small. He wore a diamond-pane jumper and jeans. Ordinary. Yet to Debra he was a god.

Dad was failing to win, but that was because he was trying to make the woman laugh. While he was busy, I looked around for Rachel. I hadn't seen her properly since we'd talked about Norfolk. Then I'd been mystified by her lack of response, yet now I knew about her mother, things made a bit more sense.

There was no sign of her. Karl was by the Hall of Mirrors with a couple of boys from school. It made me stupidly happy to think that he and Rachel hadn't come together. I was even more pleased when some girls arrived and they all started messing about, pushing each other and flirting.

I was still watching when a man bulldozed through the crowd. Short and lean with a quiff, he was in his shirtsleeves despite the cold, and walking with his arms out slightly to the side, fists clenched like a boxer.

For a moment, I thought he was coming for me. I ran through who it could be: teacher, neighbour, one of Dad's friends from work or from the record shop. Then it clicked. I'd seen him in the paper. Peggy's husband. What was his name? Lenny.

Dad showed no reaction – still chatting up the woman on the stand – until Lenny tapped him on the shoulder. He turned around and the colour drained from his face for the second time in a day.

Now I understood two things.

Dad had had an affair with Peggy, and he was terrified of her husband.

'You weren't the only one, mate,' snarled Lenny, 'but don't worry, I'm working my way through the lot of you. Think yourself lucky you pissed off out of this town. Otherwise you'd have got more of this.'

He rocked back and then forward and then back and then forward and then, with superb momentum, head-butted Dad.

Down he went, crashing into the stand, collapsing the table, scattering hoops and prizes.

Lenny stalked off.

Dad was left, sprawled on the ground, clutching his bloody nose. I couldn't help wondering if this was the pain and suffering Madame Beatrix had mentioned.

The day fizzled out like a faulty firework. We didn't talk about what had happened. There was no need.

Eventually Dad apologised in a nasal voice and we agreed to leave. He went off to his B & B and I went to see Maggie.

I'd started helping out regularly now. An hour after school a few times a week or else when Maggie was particularly busy. Today the cafe was empty apart from a small gathering of Residents Against Estates, but Maggie was behind with the cleaning up, so she asked me to lend a hand.

As I worked, I listened to the group talking. It turned out the wasteland the building contractor was after belonged to a rich old lady who'd emigrated to Australia. Her son by all accounts was trying to persuade her to sell.

Details shared. Notes written. The conversation turned to murder.

I half listened as I wiped down tables.

'I wouldn't be surprised if we had a serial killer in our midst,' said one man with a handlebar moustache. The rest of them adopted the theme, speculating about motive and evidence and police progress. Words slid across the room.

Beaten with a hammer ... buried in a shallow grave ... hardly covered in leaves and dirt ... a miracle it wasn't found before ...

I went to the counter with a pile of crockery.

'Gossips and scaremongers,' muttered Maggie. 'Hark at them dissecting every detail.'

She was right. Now they were talking about an item that had been found at the scene. The way they said *item*, I knew they meant condom.

Two policemen walked past the cafe and glanced in. Now was the time to tell them what I knew.

I didn't move and the policemen passed from sight.

I was an idiot and a coward.

What was stopping me?

I thought of the voices, the laugh, the whistling, the footsteps. The cold and the darkness. The woman's face. *Peggy's face.* I imagined her broken body. Her blood-stained clothes.

I thought of Dad. Blood dripping from his nose.

It was the result of having an affair with Lenny's wife.

Everyone at the fair who had witnessed it would think the same. What if one of them told the police? What if I then told them about Peggy in the orchard? Would they assume it was Dad? Would they think he had killed her?

They'd be wrong.

Dad wouldn't hurt a fly. Literally. I'd seen him shoo a bug through a window rather than kill it. (Mum on the other hand would swat it flat then wipe up its remains and disinfect everything it had touched.) I'd seen Dad shed tears at roadkill. (Mum tutted at the mess.)

Rachel and a group of girls passed the window. Some of them had stuffed toys. Rachel had a goldfish in a plastic bag. So she had been at the fair.

On impulse, I told Maggie I felt ill. I'd only been there for twenty minutes, but she didn't mind. I rushed out in time to catch Rachel as she was crossing the road.

'Hi,' I said, catching my breath.

'Hi,' she said back. 'You all right? I saw what happened.'

'Oh.' My face turned red. So had everyone else. I eyed the goldfish trapped in its bag and realised I had lost the coconut that Dad had won. I must have dropped it during the incident. The thought brought tears to my eyes.

Rachel noticed. 'Do you want to talk?'

I nodded miserably.

'Come on.' She beckoned me towards the orchard.

It was easy to get past the police, sneaking through a gap. Neither of us had mentioned the den, yet we headed there anyway. Crawling down through the bushes, we lay at the bottom of the dip. Dark and dense, the foliage muffled sound and wrapped us in a cocoon.

After a moment, I cleared away stones, found a branch, flattened the earth.

'Like a housewife,' said Rachel.

I turned to look at her. She lay there with her chin in her hands, the goldfish set on the ground. I wouldn't mind clearing up after Rachel. I'd cook and clean, do anything.

I expected her to mention the fair, but she seemed to have forgotten all about it and I was glad.

She pulled herself into a sitting position, scrabbled in her bag and produced a bottle. 'Gin,' she said, unscrewing the top and taking a swig. 'Are you shocked?'

'No,' I replied too quickly. 'I drink whisky.'

Immediately my cheeks burned. It sounded stupid. *I* sounded stupid, as if I was trying to impress her.

Still, she offered me the bottle and I took it. The liquid tasted as colourless as it looked. I made a face. Rachel was watching me, fiddling with her locket, a small smile on her face. Embarrassed, I sat down and handed it back. Rachel drank more. Soon her expression softened, her voice thickened. Smiling a little, she came across and laid her head in my lap.

My hand hovered, longing but not daring to stroke her hair. I listened to her chatter: the food she liked, the make-up she preferred, the records she bought – ordinary stuff. I wanted to ask her about her mother and how she felt about having been left all alone for three days, but the topic was too serious and I was afraid I'd break the spell.

From time to time she tapped my leg, saying, 'No one could find us here, could they? No one could take us away.'

I responded, 'Only if they had a pack of hounds, or an army of men and even then I'd fight them off.'

She laughed and called me *hysterical*. Then she dropped her voice. 'You'd do anything for me, wouldn't you?'

I stayed silent, my heart hammering, wondering if that was true.

After a bit, she changed the subject and talked about Karl. Now she spoke more personally, telling me how much he liked her and how she liked him. 'He wants to have sex.'

I flushed, not knowing how to respond. In the end I asked her if they were going out together.

She lifted her hand as if to shade her eyes from the light, though there was hardly any of it left now. 'I don't think I can,' she said.

'Why?'

She shook her head. 'I just don't think I can.'

Gently, I squeezed her hand. She looked at me, her eyes dark and green like the leaves.

'Thanks for being so nice to me.'

I promised I'd always be nice to her, although now my heart was beating so loudly and joyfully I thought she might not have heard.

24

1979

'I have an illness,' Debra announced proudly.

It was Monday. We were walking home from school. Debra was back and Rachel was absent.

The school felt empty without her.

'What's wrong with you?'

'It's called scurvy,' she said.

'Isn't that what pirates get, something to do with fresh water?'

'Sailors as well as pirates,' she corrected me, pleased that she knew more about a subject than I did. 'And it's to do with fruit. Vitamin C. I don't have any.'

'How do they know?'

She held out her thin arms. 'I bruise easily and I'm getting scaly.'

I looked at her dry skin.

'Frank says the reason we don't have fruit is because it's so expensive but he's going to get another job so that we can.'

We were passing Spar and I said I had to go inside. I bought a bag of oranges and gave them to Debra. She took them, eyes wide with disbelief, and carried them home like jewels.

*

I was due for a shift at the cafe. A couple of builders lounged at the tables and the moustachioed policeman was deep in conversation with Maggie.

'Turns out we were on the same demo back in seventy-four,' she told me brightly. 'Different sides, naturally.'

She laughed and I eyed him, wondering if he could tell I had information just by looking at me, but he was too busy slurping the tea Maggie had given him and sinking his teeth into a custard tart to spare me more than a glance.

There was nothing much to do, so Maggie suggested I tidy the flat. I started by washing up and then putting the cups on the hooks and the plates on the rack. I set about dusting the dream catchers, enjoying the sound of the wind chimes. Turning to the cluttered shelves, I found a wad of pound notes bound by an elastic band and weighed down by a crystal. It would buy Debra a lot of fruit, I thought, dusting all around.

Downstairs, Karl had arrived. He'd grown lanky, and his legs were too long to fit beneath the table so he'd stretched them along the aisle.

Grinning when he saw me, he gave an exaggerated thumbs up.

'Hey,' he said. 'Want a drink?'

'Drink?' I blinked back at him.

'Yeah,' he said. 'Why not?'

I watched him suspiciously. 'No thanks. Maggie needs me.' I gestured towards the counter.

'It's fine,' said Maggie, noticing. 'Take a break.'

Karl's grin widened. 'See. Have a seat.' He felt around for coins in his pockets. 'Coke?'

Reluctantly, I accepted and sat down. I wanted to get on with my jobs and wallow in my thoughts, sort out all the different bits of information I'd acquired lately about Dad and Rachel and even Debra. I still felt hot waves of guilt at thinking so badly of Frank.

Karl came back and sat in the same position, trapping me with his legs. I sipped from the can while he rummaged inside his bag, producing an exercise book and a pencil. I watched him through narrow eyes, waiting patiently for him to say what he wanted. Eventually, he cleared his throat and asked if I could deliver a note.

'Who to?'

'Rachel.'

I spluttered. 'Me?'

'Yeah.' He flashed me a persuasive grin.

'Why?'

'Well . . .' He stopped and fiddled with the pencil, sat back, raked his fingers through his hair. 'Her dad, you know.'

'What about him?'

'He might not be happy . . . you know . . . with me hanging about.' He grimaced.

I remembered the way Mr Wright had dealt with Karl's dad and the reporter and didn't contradict him.

'So,' said Karl, 'will you?'

I concentrated on my can. Why should I help the boy who'd insulted me? On the other hand, I felt a rush of pleasure because he thought I was so close to Rachel.

'I want to know she's all right,' he said.

I looked at him. His eyes flickered away. 'Why wouldn't she be?'

'I just want to know she's OK.'

He hadn't answered my question. I was quiet thinking about it. He looked at me properly again and I noticed his eyes were slightly different colours. One dark brown, the other more of a tawny shade. I warmed towards him seeing that imperfection. Maybe he wasn't so bad and maybe if I delivered this letter it would make up for the one that I hadn't. Rachel's card to Charlotte was still hiding inside my drawer.

'All right,' I said.

He grinned, wrote on the paper and folded it over. He held out his hand and then pulled back sharply. 'Wait. No envelope.'

'I won't read it,' I promised.

He hesitated, shrugged and then passed it across.

I pushed the note into my pocket, not caring what it said. I had another excuse to visit Rachel and that was good enough.

No one opened the door.

I kept on knocking and then calling through the letter box until eventually Rachel appeared wearing the same old-fashioned dressing gown.

'What's wrong?' I asked straightaway. Her face was red and blotchy, hair damp and plastered to her scalp. 'Were you in the bath? You look awful.'

'Thanks.' Automatically, she put her hand to her face and I saw that her fingertips were ragged where she'd bitten the edges; spots of blood had dried inside the tiny wounds. The sight made my stomach turn.

'You weren't at school.'

'I know.'

'I missed you.'

She smiled weakly and folded her arms, sagging in the doorway as she leaned against the frame.

'Have you got a temperature? Have you eaten?' I sounded like my mother.

'Probably and yes, I have. Sorry, Elizabeth, I can't do this now.'

Do what? I was only trying to help.

She went to close the door, but I wasn't giving up. 'Let me come in. I can keep you company.'

She sighed. 'I need to lie down.'

I softened my tone. 'I've got a note for you.'

Her curiosity was piqued. 'Who from?'

I paused. 'Karl.'

Her expression softened. She thought about it for a moment more and then let me come inside.

The front room was even hotter than usual and stuffy with the curtains closed. There were tissues dropped on the carpet. I picked them up automatically as if I was at home.

'Stop,' said Rachel, 'it doesn't matter.'

'But—'

'Leave them. Who cares?'

We sat down and I fished out the note and gave it to her. She read it and smiled a little, but then just as quickly the smile disappeared.

She drew a tissue from her pocket and blew her nose. Coughed. A glass of water stood on the table in front of her. I passed it across. She took the glass and as she drank, her sleeve slipped to her elbow.

My blood chilled. Cuts. On her forearm. Old cuts and new cuts, tiny slices across the skin. I stared, trying to work out what this was. Rachel saw me looking, and quickly dropped her arm. For a second she held my gaze as if daring me to speak, but I couldn't breathe. My throat felt swollen, my tongue glued to the roof of my mouth, and now it was too late anyway because the key turned in the door.

Quickly, she leaned forward and put the glass back on the table. I caught the smell of it. Not water. Gin.

She stood up and tightened the belt on her dressing gown. 'You'd better go,' she said.

I moved obediently, dazed by what I'd seen, out into the hall as Mr Wright disappeared through to the kitchen.

'Don't tell,' Rachel whispered on the doorstep.

I opened my mouth to protest.

'Don't,' she said.

'But you should . . .' *see a doctor*, I wanted to say, *tell Mr Wright . . . a teacher, anyone*, but none of the words would come.

'Promise me,' she said.

'OK.' But it wasn't OK. It was terrible. Those ugly marks on her beautiful skin.

She pushed me gently out of the door, closed it quietly without saying goodbye.

I stood outside the house thinking about what I'd seen. A couple of years ago a girl in the sixth form had tried to kill herself. She'd sliced her wrists and her mother had found her just in time. Why had she done it? I recalled the rumours about a boyfriend who'd left her for somebody else. None of us had known the absolute truth.

But Rachel's cuts were on her arms, not her wrists and anyway, they were a mix of faded scars and fresh wounds. Had she made the cuts herself? What had she used? A kitchen knife? A penknife? A razor blade?

How delicate her skin was, her wrists so tiny, her arms so slender. What was she thinking and how had I failed to notice?

25

1979

The next day, Rachel was away from school again.

Debra was cheerful, going on about how Frank had another new job, fetching and carrying at the market, getting cheap crates of fruit.

'I had a kiwi yesterday,' she said. 'I've never had a kiwi. Have you?'

I admitted that I hadn't.

'The doctor says I'm doing really well. Look!' She thrust her arm at me. The skin was flaky but better than it had been.

All through morning lessons, I could only think about Rachel, making tiny slices on her skin. Did Karl know? What if it wasn't Rachel doing it? What if it was somebody else? Was she a part of a cult? My imagination raged.

At afternoon registration, Mrs Townsend asked me to step into the stock cupboard. I followed her, expecting another lecture about Oxford and knuckling down, but instead she brought up the subject of Debra. She said that even though it was obvious I'd had the best intentions, I should think carefully before going around accusing people like that. I reddened. Obviously, all the teachers would know what I'd said about Debra.

'What you did could have had terrible consequences.

Sometimes it's good to take a step back and ask yourself, is this fact or is this fiction? Is it a serious issue or an exaggeration?'

The light was dim, and the cupboard smelled of new stationery. I could hear giggles coming from the classroom.

Mrs Townsend was still talking. 'Have you heard of *Billy Liar*?'

I nodded. 'Yes, miss. It's a film.'

'And a book,' she corrected.

'Yes, miss.'

'Well then . . . do you want to be like him, making everything up?'

I shook my head.

'Or do you want to take control, put the fibs away and knuckle down to work?'

I wanted to point out that I didn't lie, I only imagined things, but then the disembodied image of Rachel's scarred arm floated from a corner of the cupboard and hovered there, finger-pointing at Mrs Townsend. *Tell her.*

Why? She wouldn't believe me.

I shook my head to get rid of the image.

Mrs Townsend pounced. 'What do you mean, *no*?'

'No. I don't mean no. Yes. I mean, yes, of course.'

I apologised and told her I would most definitely work very hard at eradicating my imagination.

'Not completely, obviously, Elizabeth,' she said as we went back into the classroom amid whoops and cheers and wolf whistles.

*

Lessons crawled along. I zoned out for most of them. The only interesting moment was when Karl approached me in afternoon break to ask if I'd delivered the note.

It annoyed me how he did it. Waiting until the last minute after the bell had gone, making sure no one saw him as he came up behind me. He was embarrassed to be seen with me, I thought bitterly, but happy enough to use me as his messenger.

I told him stonily that I'd done what he'd asked.

I walked home from school feeling as if I had a cold weight in the centre of my body.

I tried to think of a rational reason for the marks on Rachel's skin. A disease maybe. Like Debra had. Nothing came to mind and then I thought: what if the situation got more serious? What if the cuts slipped down her arm to her wrist? I'd promised to keep Rachel's secret, but it was so dark and so terrible. What if she killed herself? It would be my fault.

I ran through the people I could tell. Not Mrs Townsend – she'd call me Billy Liar. Not Mum – she wouldn't want to be reminded of *that family*. Not Mr Wright – I wasn't brave enough to speak to him.

Dad, then. Maybe he would tell Charlotte and they'd both come rushing back from Norfolk.

The thought made the world seem a little less grim. Dad would know what to do.

I stopped at the phone box.

'Hi,' I said, when Dad picked up.

There was a pause. 'Elizabeth. What is it?'

My heart dropped. He sounded impatient. 'Nothing.'

'Nothing?'

'I just wanted to talk.'

I heard the sigh, imagined him sitting down, brushing his hand through his hair as he resigned himself to speaking.

'I miss you,' I said after a bit.

The telephone box smelled of piss and stale tobacco. Cards with semi-clad women offering massage services had been stuck to the glass.

'Yeah, I know, Lizzie. I miss you too.'

'When are you coming home?'

Another silence. I focused on a crack running the length of one pane.

'I don't know. I've got to work and . . .'

He stopped.

I waited.

'And I . . . we might be going away for a bit.'

'Away?'

'Only for a holiday. Nowhere grand.'

The pips went. I shoved in another coin.

'Where?'

'What?'

'Where are you going?'

'Great Yarmouth.'

'But it's still school . . . Doesn't Melissa—'

'Yeah, no, we're going a bit early and then staying . . . for Christmas. Charlotte's got some relatives . . .' His words tailed away.

I swallowed hard and passed the receiver to my other hand. I wouldn't see Dad this Christmas either.

'Can I come?' I asked in a small voice, knowing the answer.

'I don't think it's possible. I mean, it's sorted now and . . .' He paused. 'They've . . . the relatives, you know, they've only got a small cottage. A couple of rooms.'

'What about Rachel?'

'What about her?'

'Will she be going with you?'

'No, I don't think so. I mean, no, she won't be coming.'

Now was my chance to tell him. I took a breath. In the background, I heard a door bang and then a voice. A question: *Who is it?* Dad must have mouthed my name because next there was the sound of walking and then another door closing.

I traced the crack on the glass with my finger. Would Rachel forgive me if I gave away her secret?

'I saw her the other day,' I said tentatively.

'Who?'

'Rachel.'

'Oh.' He spoke again more quietly to somebody else: 'OK. I'll be there in a minute.'

I pushed the tip of my finger harder against the crack. Blood bubbled to the surface of my skin.

Outside, a gang of boys was clowning around with Karl at the centre. He caught my eye. One of his friends squashed his face against the glass leering in at me. I moved instinctively, pressing my back against the oppos-ite side of the box, tears rising.

Mr Evans appeared. He paused as if waiting to use the telephone and the boys moved on.

'Dad,' I said, more urgently now. 'Can I come and see you before you leave?'

'I don't . . .' He broke off. I heard more words in the background. Someone said, *We've got to go.*

My cheeks burned with embarrassment. Nobody wanted me. Nobody. 'Dad?'

'I'm sorry, Elizabeth, now's not a good time.'

The pips went. I had no more change.

'When we get back, I'll call you, OK?'

'But what about Christmas?'

The line went dead.

I ran back to Rachel's house thinking that I would ask her to explain what was going on and that I would tell her I didn't think I could keep her secret unless I knew more.

I arrived hot and flustered and stood for a moment, recovering my breath. The house appeared empty and unwelcoming, walls silent and cold, curtains tight. How different it was inside. The sofa that sucked you in; the heaters turned up high.

I knocked. No answer. I looked up. Was that the twitch of a curtain in the upstairs room? I waited longer and sure enough, the door opened.

Mr Wright was in his work clothes: mud-splattered jeans and an old shirt. His hands were grimy, nails caked with dirt. Even so, his hair was neat, his beard trimmed. A thought flashed through my mind: he and Mum would make a handsome couple. He was far more attractive than Bob, more interesting too, always helping people out. I had a sudden flash of living with Rachel in the same house. How good would that be?

He spoke first. 'Rachel's not well.'

I slowed down my thoughts. 'Can I see her?'

His eyes slid across my face and over my shoulder. 'Sorry, but I don't think so.' He made to close the door.

My stomach dropped as I guessed what was happening. After seeing me in the record shop with Dad, it had reminded him of what my family had done. Now he wanted to eradicate the memory, starting with banning me.

'Please.' I spoke loudly, hoping for another miracle.

The telephone rang. He half turned, but didn't move to answer it. I could see the coat stand – Rachel's coat, his builder's jacket, shoes on the floor. The door to the kitchen was shut fast. What if it was Rachel who didn't want me in the house, not her dad? She might have told him to keep me out. I'd seen the cuts and she was ashamed. The thought made me desperate to speak to her. I needed to tell her that I would help in any way that I could.

My miracle happened. PC Newman was passing the house, wheeling his bike. 'Either of you got a puncture kit?' he called out cheerily.

I seized the Paracord from my pocket and dangled it before him. 'Yes!'

He raised his eyebrows. 'How does it work?'

I explained and Mr Wright had no choice but to help, and then to let me into the house to use the toilet when I asked.

The door to the front room was ajar. No Rachel. In

full view of the men outside, I didn't dare go in the kitchen. Instead, I coughed loudly and ran up the stairs, hoping that she'd hear me.

The bathroom smelled of bleach. Mr Wright's razor was abandoned on the sink, bits of hair and foam caught on the blade.

At least Bob was tidy. The other day he'd been vacuuming the stairs, whistling tunelessly. Dad had never done jobs in the house. Even when Mum had been rushing around all day after the charges, Dad had sat with his feet up, reading the newspaper or watching the telly. He'd never made the tea or done the shopping. Bob had even brought his toolkit and fixed some shelves. I'd heard him hammering early one morning.

On impulse, I opened the door of the cabinet above the sink. There was a packet of unopened Dr White's, a can of shaving foam, a bottle of TCP. A box of the same sleeping pills Mum used. Blades for a razor. A bottle of Brut nestled beside a bottle of Tramp. *That doesn't surprise me*, I could hear Mum saying. Tramp was cheap. It suited Mrs Wright down to the ground. Bob had bought Mum a bottle of L'Air du Temps, for no other reason than that he had felt like it. He had bought me a chain too, with the name Elizabeth hanging from it.

I flushed the toilet, turned on the tap and opened the bathroom door. Had they finished mending the puncture? I looked down the stairs – no sign – but I could hear the drift of their voices.

Tiptoeing along the corridor, I knocked gently on Rachel's door. Maybe she was asleep.

The bed and the floor were still strewn with Mrs Wright's clothes. No Rachel. I went in. One of Rachel's dresses hung on the wardrobe door. I couldn't resist taking it down and holding it against me. Grass-green. My heart constricted as I touched the material, catching the scent of apples.

Putting the dress back, my gaze fell on the bedside table. The white wood was stuck all over with shiny pink and purple stickers. A book of fairy tales lay on the top. It was battered and worn with its cover hanging off. Opening it, I found an inscription. *To Rachel, Love Mum.* Inside the back cover was Karl's note.

If it had been folded up, I told myself, I wouldn't have read it. As it was, the words were in plain sight.

There's no hurry. I can wait.
I ❤ you
Karl xxx

Wait for what? It was obvious what he meant.

The drawer of the bedside table was partly open.

If it had been closed, I told myself, I wouldn't have opened it.

Inside, there was a glossy magazine, some pens and badges. An envelope.

At first, I thought it was full of sweets, but then I realised they were pills of all different shapes and sizes.

An alarm was sounding inside my head.

Barely breathing, I put the envelope back and closed the drawer.

Behind me, somebody coughed.

Swiftly, I turned. Mr Wright was there, watching me from the doorway. 'I was looking for Rachel,' I said quickly. 'I thought she'd like some company.'

He was silent.

I babbled some more, filling the gap. 'I wanted to tell her ... I mean, to ask her if she needed anything, like, you know, a magazine, fruit, books ...' My voice trailed away. 'Sorry,' I added.

I went towards him, trying to act as if nothing was wrong. He didn't move, only carried on looking at me. 'I told you she wasn't well,' he said.

'Yes.' My heart thumped. He turned sideways as if he was a door opening, letting me through. Considering his size, he moved lightly, stepping back as if it were a dance. It was another part of him I couldn't help admiring. He had a kind of grace.

In the hall, I was dying to go into the kitchen to see if she was there. I nearly asked for a glass of water, but in the end, I didn't dare. If Rachel didn't want to see me and her dad had had enough of me, what could I do?

'Will she be at school tomorrow?' I said.

There was a beat as his gaze slid away from me, to the coat stand, to the carpet, to the kitchen door. 'I don't think so.'

'What exactly is wrong with her?'

'Sick. Stomach bug. Up all night – slept all morning.'

I bit my lip. 'Would it be all right if I popped in then ... tomorrow I mean ... after school?'

'No,' he said. 'I don't think it would be.' He gazed sadly down at his hands. 'I don't think it would be a good idea ...'

I went hot, knowing what he was going to say.

'. . . to come back for a while.' He gave a sigh.

'Why?' I asked. My voice sounded pathetic. 'Is it because of . . .' I hesitated.

'Yes.' He closed the door quietly behind me.

I was banished. The daughter of the enemy. I clenched my fists, hurt spiralling into anger. It was Dad's fault running off with that stupid woman. Now I'd never know the warmth and comfort of the house again.

If I couldn't visit Rachel, how would I be able to help her?

26

1999

I walk fast, out of the past and into my future, through the sticky streets towards the High Street.

A homeless woman huddles in a doorway. She's vulnerable, like Rachel was.

I think how badly I blamed myself for not seeing those cuts on her arm, for not guessing what was wrong. There were so many signals, then.

Now I'm more forgiving of my child self. Fifteen. I *was* only a child and I was young for my age. Naive. Trying hard to fit in with all those magazines I read and beauty treatments I used to do. It was like kicking off from a crumbling bank and trying to swim upstream.

Vulnerable people . . . they hide things well. Those dresses she used to wear. Those long sleeves.

I give money to the homeless woman. She nods, but doesn't smile. Why should she? I lay my gabardine beside her. It's a sacrifice that suits me. Is there any other kind?

At the stop, a woman in a wide-brimmed hat and sunglasses is reading a paperback. A couple are talking earnestly. Students huddle in groups. I try not to resent how normal they are, going about their usual business. I try not to be bitter. I made my choice, my bed, whatever you want to call it, a very long time ago.

For a second I visualise another me, leaving here, going back towards the station. I see myself waiting for my usual bus and then lumbering on; the heat lessening as we pull away, onto the familiar, straight road; and then the breeze from the fields, slipping through the open window, stirring my hair as we pick up pace.

I imagine getting off at the village, carrying on as normal: choosing food from the Co-op, maybe a bottle of wine, and then taking my shopping home, feeding Jude, enjoying the comfort of her body winding round my legs; and there I am – throwing the brochure into the dustbin, trusting in luck and destiny, the quality of mercy and all that.

I shake my head. I know it's a fantasy. Society isn't so forgiving that you can slide in and out of its doors as easily as that.

The bus comes and I get on.

It's a twenty-minute ride along the Cowley Road through slow-moving traffic.

No seats, I stand with my back against the window, skin sticky with sweat, bags shored up around my feet.

The floor is littered with bus tickets and sweet wrappers and bits of gum. I turn my mind to Lipsi and paint a picture – a child's picture of a sky that's a brilliant blue, and a sea that's a transparent turquoise, and a huge sun and a bright, white moon.

Two girls in school uniform sit at the back of the bus. They talk behind their hands, burst into laughter at the slightest thing, trying to prove they're happy; they don't need anyone else.

I think about what they are like. One of them confident, dominant even. The other a scramble of insecurity – so painful. As soon as they separate, she will walk home, going over their conversation, hoping she hasn't been stupid.

They catch me looking and stare back – unsmiling, challenging my right to exist. I'm dated and dreary. Quickly I turn away, but I can hear them sniggering at their next joke. On me, probably.

I'm glad to get off the bus, even though the air is dense, the sky leaden.

In the supermarket, I buy a last supper. I choose steak and baby potatoes, salad and fruit. Apples. I wonder briefly what apples are like in Lipsi. They will have apples, won't they? I know they'll have melons and peaches and plums. But apples? I take a couple more just in case.

There's a park between the supermarket and the flats. Not a park, exactly, more a playground within a square of green.

Finding a bench, I settle, placing my bags beside me.

Despite the sticky heat and the low-slung clouds, the playground is full. Mothers standing around in clumps, in dresses and flip-flops, chatting to their friends and sometimes to their children in quiet, heat-strained voices.

Ordinary people living their lives.

The sky shifts from plum to almost black.

Some of the mums look at their watches, call out, *Five more minutes*, while their children jostle and cry.

I know I should move on, decide what will happen

next. But it's so hard and it won't do any harm to wait a little longer. I pull out the notebook, my fingers trembling as I take the pen. Not that I've written anything. It's still inside my head.

Nearly there. At the end of the story.

Just a little more time while my mind slips to the end.

27

1979

At home, Mum had left a message to say she was working late.

I kicked about the empty house. In the kitchen, I peered into the fridge. Mum was preparing meals again, but it wasn't the food that Dad had liked – no shepherd's pie and steak and kidney pudding. Instead, Mum made pâté and stroganoff and chicken chasseur. She was trying to impress Bob.

I rang Dad. No answer. Why would there be? He'd gone away. Still, I dialled again, letting the phone ring for ages, imagining the sound winding through the empty house in Norfolk.

In the end, I decided to see Dave. Maybe the sight of him would fill this aching gap.

He was behind the counter wearing his headphones. I smiled at him, then shuffled across to Barry White, picked up an album and gazed into his warm and lovely face.

'Dad has betrayed us both,' I whispered. 'You and me, Barry, we've been abandoned.'

A fat tear splashed onto the record sleeve, drenching Barry's ear. I wished Dad would come back so that things could be like they used to be. I wished he was here now, tapping his feet in time to the music. I wished he hadn't chosen Norfolk and Mrs Wright over this town and me.

Another tear splattered onto Barry's nose. Dave came across and took the album gently, patted my arm before going across to the turntable and putting the record on. I watched him, sending it spinning, moving the stylus with a practised hand. His hands, I thought, were kind. Long, slim fingers, smooth palms. When the record had finished, Dave slipped it into two bags, stroked it lovingly and held it out to me.

I mumbled about not having any money.

'S'all right,' he said, touching my shoulder. 'Have it.'

It was the most he'd ever spoken to me. I smiled weakly and he asked about Dad.

'He's gone away,' I said. And the thought of that brought a fresh new pool of tears. 'Great Yarmouth.'

He nodded sagely as if Great Yarmouth was the most remarkable of places to visit.

It all came out. I told him how Dad had taken Melissa, but not me, that I'd been left here with Mum and Bob and it wasn't fair. I told him how I wanted to be friends with Rachel but she was too ill to come out of the house and that I'd upset my good friend John because I hadn't wanted to go to the Little Chef. I said that Debra didn't appear to be holding things against me, but she probably was, which meant I had no one. No one.

Soon I was blubbering and dashing the tears from my eyes and opening and closing my hands dramatically as if I wanted to release my feelings, but couldn't quite let them go. I knew I was crying not only about Dad, but about Rachel because I'd thought somehow that knowing her would make up for Dad being gone, but in the end she didn't want me. She wanted Karl. She had terrible scars all over her arms and I had no idea why.

I didn't tell Dave that last part. I concentrated on Dad, and as Dave listened, he raised his eyebrows, higher and higher until they almost disappeared. He'd had another haircut, I noticed. With shorter hair, he seemed younger. In fact, now I came to think about it, he was quite good-looking. It was amazing to me how different he seemed: I'd always thought he was Dad's age, but now I realised Dad was older.

I finished talking and his eyebrows came back down. He nodded thoughtfully and went behind the counter. A thick black jacket hung over a chair. Reaching into the pocket, he pulled out a handkerchief.

'It's clean,' he said.

I took it gratefully and then started crying all over again, thinking how once I'd given Rachel my handkerchief and she'd given me a tissue.

'Sorry,' I mumbled, blowing my nose.

I followed his gaze, out through the window at the street. He looked unhappy suddenly and that was my second revelation: not only was Dave a good-looking man, he also had feelings. It was weird to think about him being an actual person. Dave was just Dave. I practised spotting his aura. It was all fuzzy and warm. Sad. Confused. Or maybe that was just me. Now I felt a great surge of love. My Dad's friend. *My* friend. *He* hadn't abandoned me, gone away to start a new life. Dave was Dave and he was here. I had to stop myself from throwing my arms around him.

'Who's this girl you're talking about?' he said after a while.

'Rachel.'

'The Wright girl? The red-haired girl?'

I nodded.

'I saw her. This morning.'

'Where?'

He nodded across at the barber's next to Trim. 'I was having my hair cut. She walked past the window with her dad.'

'Are you sure?'

'Sure.'

I thought about this, going back over what Mr Wright had said. Hadn't he told me she'd been sleeping all morning?

I blinked. Two more revelations. Dave cared about his appearance and Mr Wright had lied.

I left the shop. A man with a handlebar moustache was coming out of the barber's. I recognised him from Residents Against Estates. He'd gone on about there being a serial killer in our midst. Maybe he was one of the ghouls Maggie despised, visiting places where victims had frequented.

Catching sight of my reflection in the window, it came to me how all my intentions to improve my appearance had resulted in nothing. My hair was too long, almost at my shoulders. Flat. Lifeless. It had no bounce. Layers, that's what I needed. A bit of fluffing up and then I'd be walking down the street in slow motion like an is-she-isn't-she Harmony Hairspray girl.

Dismissing the suspicion that I might be one of the ghouls too, I went into Trim.

A young woman with sparkly purple eye shadow and spiky eyelashes like insects stood at the desk.

'Yes?' she said.

'Can I make an appointment?'

She scanned the book. 'Who with?'

'Um . . . Last time I had Margaret.'

Why did I say that?

The woman's plucked eyebrows shot up. 'Peggy, you mean?'

'Yes.'

'When? You do realise . . .'

'Um, it was ages ago. Two years.'

'Oh.' She was recovering now. Coughing, she said, 'We have a replacement.' She nodded across at a woman with a bleached perm. 'Claire. She do?'

'Fine.'

'Now? She's free.'

I felt in my pocket. 'How much?'

I sat in the chair waiting for Claire with shampoo in my ear and water down my neck. How odd to think this could be Peggy's vacated place. There was a set of brushes and combs laid out before me. Were her fingerprints on the handles? What about the mirror? Was her reflection imprisoned inside?

My gaze fell on a key left on the table. It was attached to a ring replete with a charm – a silver skeleton with rubies for eyes. It was Peggy's, I guessed, remembering her skull jewellery.

On the radio, they were playing 'Bohemian Rhapsody'. Freddie Mercury singing about his mama, a fantasy and killing a man. I listened, biting my lip and wondering what it must be like, to murder someone, to smash their head in with a hammer like Peggy's killer had done. What emotions had been running through their mind? I thought about Peggy. How had she felt? I remembered that day – how gloomy the orchard had been, full of shapes and shadows. Imagine being alone there; imagine sensing someone hiding amongst the trees, and then the sudden movement, the swing of the hammer, the pain and the blood seeping into the ground.

'What are we doing today?'

I jumped. Claire was standing behind me. My thoughts quietened.

'How much off?'

'An inch?' I replied, guessing.

She frowned, thinking hard. 'Do you know what? I reckon a Purdy cut would suit you.'

I looked at her blankly.

'You know, Joanna Lumley, the *New Avengers*?'

I knew what a Purdy cut was, but would it suit me? 'Are you sure?'

'Yep. Let's go for it.'

I agreed, reluctantly, and watched her pick up a lock of my hair and snip it in half. She talked a lot, telling me she'd only been at the salon for a few months. I listened, but didn't ask her any questions. I was practising my new art of being silent, letting other people fill in the gaps, and soon enough, she started talking about Peggy, lowering her voice. Claire wasn't that old, late teens. The rest of the women were older. Maybe she didn't get to gossip that often and was making the most of it now.

'You know what,' she said, stopping and catching my eye in the mirror, 'it's a bit weird being here. I mean, here. Exactly.' She pointed at the floor.

'How?'

She made a face. 'It's like she's watching me. You know what I mean?'

I nodded. I knew exactly what she meant.

She continued. 'Her husband came in – Lenny. The boss called him thinking he'd want to collect her things. Sat right here.' She gestured to my chair this time. 'Don't you think that's a bit creepy?'

I nodded again. It was definitely creepy.

'But he didn't take any of it away. None of her brushes and stuff. She had a few keepsakes too, lucky mascots, photos, that keyring.' Claire pointed at the skeleton. 'Why wouldn't he take them? I mean, the key's just a shop key – opens the storage room – but the keyring. That's personal.'

I shrugged. Keeping quiet was paying off.

'Well ...' Claire opened and shut the scissors a few times. 'It turns out she was having an affair. At least, everyone here says so. And the police came, asking us questions.' She glanced at a door which I guessed connected Trim with the barber's. 'Apparently, the police wanted to see a list of their customers. I reckon they must have thought she was having an affair with one of them – or maybe more. Though I don't know why she did that because Lenny's loaded. *Loaded.*' She paused dramatically, did some scissoring again. 'Dodgy money. Apparently. But still . . . and . . . do you know what?'

I shook my head.

'It was rumoured . . .' She hushed her voice. 'They said Lenny knew all about the lovers and he did things to them – for revenge. Makes you wonder why anyone would take the risk.'

I thought of Lenny headbutting Dad.

'Trophy wife, I reckon,' said Claire. 'Picked her for her looks, didn't expect her to turn out like she did.'

'Did he wonder where she'd gone?' I said quietly, risking a question, hoping it wouldn't put her off. 'You know . . . when she disappeared in the first place?'

'Well yeah, everyone wondered, but they just thought she'd gone off with one of her blokes – run off without telling Lenny. She probably knew what he'd do.'

'Do you think he cared about her being dead?'

Claire shrugged. 'Doesn't seem like it, does it? Maybe it was just pride. He didn't want her but no one else could have her either. Some blokes are like that.'

'You mean . . .' Our eyes met in the mirror.

She shrugged and looked away. 'I'm just saying that she'd done the dirty on him and he didn't care whether she was dead or alive.'

I waited a few moments while she snipped a lock of my hair. Then I asked her if she'd ever actually met Peggy.

She shook her head. 'Nah, but she wasn't popular here. Took the piss a bit too much, I heard, if you get what I'm saying. People don't like to be laughed at, do they? 'Specially men. Think how Lenny must have felt. Her taking the piss like that?'

I nodded wisely.

Dad. The man in the orchard. Who else had she had an affair with?

I asked Claire, trying to keep my question vague. Did she have a theory?

Maybe she suddenly realised how young I was, maybe she thought she'd said too much. Maybe it was because the connecting door opened and one of the barbers, a pimply boy with a Mohican, came in and tipped a wink at her. Or maybe she just didn't know. Whatever the case, her expression changed. No more chat, she carried on sculpting my hair.

28

1979

I went down the side of the house. There'd been no answer when I'd knocked and this time I wasn't giving up. I was determined to speak to Rachel.

The garden was the same size as all the others on the estate, but while the rest were neat and trim, this one was abandoned and ugly. Overgrown grass, brown patches dead from the sun, a pile of rubbish left in the corner. An empty washing line stretched from fence to fence, slicing the space in half. A decomposing mouse splayed on the path. It was so different from the comfortable clutter of the house.

Next door I could hear a woman humming. A child calling. The sound of a washing machine. Voices on a radio. The ordinary sounds of the estate.

The back door was closed. I pressed my face to the frosted pane and rapped on the glass. No answer, and yet I couldn't help thinking Rachel was inside. That old sixth sense I'd been cultivating, making the hairs on my arms rise.

I went around to the front again and called through the letter box. In frustration, I pulled out a scrap of paper and wrote a note. I asked Rachel to meet me in the den. Tomorrow after school at four o'clock. I said she needed to talk to me and that I wasn't sure I could keep her secret.

I pushed the note through before I could change my mind and then stood there regretting it, worrying that Mr Wright would find it before Rachel.

I banged on the door, calling through this time, telling her what I'd done.

At home, Mum had a headache and after a long look at my new hair, she went to lie down. Bob was making tea, wearing Mum's apron, following a recipe from the Cordon Bleu.

'Beef bourguignon,' he announced, peering at me over the top of his reading glasses.

'Never had it.' I sidled to the door.

'Can you pass the mushrooms?'

Reluctantly, I grabbed them from the fridge.

'How about giving them a wash?'

I made a face, but did it anyway, standing at the sink, scrubbing at each one.

He was chopping meat, thumping away with a cleaver, slicing easily through the dark red beef. I tried not to look at the stained board, his mucky fingers, nails grimed with blood. I had visions of Sweeney Todd.

Finishing, he wiped his hands carefully on a cloth, poured oil into a pan and while it heated, peeled an onion.

'How's school?' he asked as he worked.

'Fine,' I replied.

'What's your favourite subject?'

I sighed. I didn't want to have this kind of conversation with Bob.

'I bet you're good at English,' he said.

I shrugged, waiting for him to tell me what a waste of time it was.

'Best subject,' he said. 'Books. Stick with it. I can tell you've got a talent. There's no other kids in the library choosing from the adult section.'

Was he laughing at me? I checked, but he was busy concentrating on chopping the onion, wiping his eyes when they stung.

'Thanks,' I said, oddly pleased.

'Your mother knows,' he added. 'How much you like it. Very proud she is. Very proud.'

The onions must have been affecting me too, stinging my eyes. I leaned forward, focused harder on the mushrooms.

I sensed him behind me and then his hand was resting on my shoulder, heavy and warm. I bit my lip to stop myself from sobbing. Already, the tears were dripping into the sink.

'It's not easy, Elizabeth, all of this. But you'll get there, don't you worry, and your mum ... well, she's been badly hurt, but she'll get there too.'

I nodded and finished washing the mushrooms.

Bob took Mum's food to her on a tray and the two of us sat quietly in the kitchen eating ours.

'I hear you had a puncture,' he said.

How did he know that? The bike was back in its

hiding place behind the shed, still with its makeshift repair.

'Mr Evans mentioned it,' he explained.

'Oh.' Did Mum know too? I thought not, since she would have gone mad if she'd twigged I was riding Dad's bike.

'Don't worry,' said Bob, reading my mind. 'I didn't tell your mum.'

'Thanks.' I focused on my food. It was surprisingly good, the sauce tasty, the meat soft.

'I can help if you like. I was a dab hand at mending punctures – when I was a boy.'

I sniffed and looked at him. Why was he being so kind? Was it a trap? But he was watching me seriously, no hint of humour. I focused on chewing the beef.

Afterwards, Bob did the dishes and I dried them. He asked me if I had any dirty washing. Embarrassed, I fetched a few T-shirts and a pair of jeans and, as an afterthought, Dave's handkerchief. He'd been so nice to me, I'd take it back tomorrow. Now I helped Bob work out where to put the Daz and how to switch on the machine.

'By the way,' he said as I was leaving, 'that haircut suits you.'

I blushed, feeling surprisingly pleased with his approval.

Later, after deciding Dad's bike needed attention, I wheeled out my old one and headed for the river: riding fast, pedalling furiously, bumping over potholes and stones, trying to untangle my thoughts.

At the river, I stood on the path catching my breath. It was odd to think how nothing had changed since I'd been here with Dad that day when Peggy had been alive. The same scenes: ducks and swans scrabbling for bits of bread, groups of people I vaguely knew.

The houses on the bank opposite were of varying shapes and sizes, expensive, with gardens that stretched down to the water where boats were moored.

I walked along thinking about which one Peggy had lived in and after a few minutes, I spotted a blue house with a terrace running around it, glass doors and a yacht moored at the end of the garden.

Strange to imagine how she had gone about her life on that last day, walking through the house in her dressing gown, brushing her hair, eating toast, making plans, not knowing she wouldn't be coming back.

A man came out the door and walked across the terrace. Pausing, he shaded his eyes. With his slight frame and quiff, I recognised Lenny. He looked about him slowly, deliberately. Then he headed further down the garden towards an unlit bonfire. It was a pile of clothes. Some bits of furniture. I watched as Lenny shook a can over the pile and held my breath as he lit a match and threw it down. The clothes and the wood went up in flames while Lenny stood there watching, warming his hands in the bonfire breeze.

The temperature dropped and I shivered. Mum may not have destroyed Dad's possessions but she'd put them in boxes and given them away. How easy it was to annihilate a life. I wondered why Lenny had chosen this moment to do so. Was he burning evidence? No, that couldn't be true. The police must have gone through Peggy's stuff already. How far had their investigation got? According to the papers and Mrs Joseph, the answer was *not very far*. They'd interviewed *people of interest* but no one had been arrested. Lenny must have an alibi.

I looked at him, standing with his arms folded, staring grimly at the fire. Death. The ultimate end. The final act. From the opposite side of the bank, I watched the memories of Peggy's life burn and, in my own kind of way, I mourned her.

29

1979

The next day, I tried not to think about whether Rachel would come or not.

Time trudged along. I kept looking at my watch and the teachers kept saying, *Are we keeping you, Elizabeth Valentine?*

Around the school, I saw Karl with his friends. I avoided him, stuck with Debra, listened to her going on about Frank and yet another new job. A couple of the men on the building site had left without notice. Frank had jumped at the chance. It was so much easier for him to walk across the orchard to get there, instead of catching the bus like he had done for the chicken factory.

Last lesson of the week was RS. Keeping my head down, I cruised through to the bell, thinking only about meeting Rachel.

By the time I'd fitted all my books into my bag and Mr Hinton had told me that I might not have a home to go to, but that he did, I was the last to leave. Debra had gone early for a doctor's appointment. Still feeling awkward after the Little Chef incident, John had left too.

Karl leaned against the wall in the corridor.

It was typical. He wanted to talk to me, but as usual

he was doing it when no one else was around. It was embarrassing to be associated with Elizabeth Valentine.

He asked if I'd seen Rachel and I told him sharply that I hadn't.

'I keep phoning,' he said, 'but no one answers.'

'She's sick.'

'What's wrong with her?'

I shrugged.

He scratched his head. 'Look,' he said, in a conciliatory voice. 'We want the same thing, don't we?'

Did we?

'I'm sorry for what happened in the past. But that was ages ago. We both want to help Rachel. Why can't we do that together?'

'What do you mean, help?'

He frowned. 'I can't work her out.'

I rolled my eyes. Was this about his stupid note? I started walking down the corridor. He followed, still talking.

'I don't know where I stand. She's moody. Changes her mind about stuff.'

I snapped. 'What stuff? Sex?'

He stared at me. 'What are you talking about?'

I shook my head and carried on walking. My face was burning. I had made a mistake by saying that. He would guess I had read his note. Now we were out of the building and heading for the gates. I walked faster to get ahead of him but as we approached, he grabbed my arm.

'What's wrong with you?'

'Nothing.'

'Are you jealous? Is that it?' He gave a nasty smile.

'No.' I shook him off. I thought he had changed but he hadn't. He was no better than he had been when he'd called me a bitch. How could I have admired his eyes? They had the same mean look in them as before.

'You're a liar,' he said.

'I'm not.'

'Everyone knows that you are. Tell me . . . why do you tell so many lies?'

My cheeks flamed harder. 'I don't,' I snapped back.

'Is it because you're obsessed with her?'

'What?'

He gave a laugh. 'You're obsessed with Rachel. Always following her about. Watching her. I've seen you at school. Everybody has.'

Tears stung my eyes. Karl knew nothing about the bond I had with Rachel, or the scars on her arms. That was our secret. Rachel had entrusted me. Not him.

A car passed, going slowly. My old, dark thoughts were rising. How easy it would be to reach out and push his chest hard until he fell back into the road. I clamped my arms to my side, clenched my fists to stop myself from moving.

'Do you know what I should do?' he said.

I swallowed hard. 'What?'

He shook his head. 'Forget it. Why would I bother?'

I thought he'd leave then, but he stayed there, hands jammed in his pockets.

'Listen,' he said. 'I don't know why you thought . . .' He hesitated. 'I'm not going to tell you . . .'

He was struggling, forcing himself to speak.

I kept silent, letting him fill in the gaps.

He blurted it out. 'I think there's someone else.'

I frowned. I hadn't expected him to say that. 'Who?'

He shrugged. 'I don't know. It's just a feeling.'

Mr Hinton came out the gates and gave us one of his sarcastic smirks. 'What are you two doing? Is there something I should know?'

Karl gave me a look as though it was my fault. My anger rose knowing that for him, even a joke about being connected with Elizabeth Valentine was disgusting.

Mr Hinton left and we stood there in silence.

'Just tell me if you hear from her,' he muttered as he walked away.

I went straight to the record shop.

Dave was busy, talking to a man in a tasselled leather jacket.

As I waited for him, I stood at the window. The receptionist came out of Trim and tottered across the road. Spotting me through the glass, she frowned as if trying to remember who I was. I pretended not to notice. Dave was still talking, but he gave me a wave and I held up the handkerchief which I'd ironed carefully. Dave smiled and gestured at his coat behind the counter.

Edging round, I surveyed the shop. Maybe this was my future – an entrepreneur, a music magnate, a record producer. I would make loads of money and entice Dad home: appoint him as manager of my empire. Across the shop, Dave laughed. A deep jet of sound. The bubble burst. It was a pipe dream. An empty fantasy like all my dreams. Whatever happened, Dad would never return.

Sighing, I bent down, tried to tuck the handkerchief

into Dave's coat pocket. My hand grasped something woollen. A black hat. I stuffed it back in and put the handkerchief in the other pocket. Straightening, I noticed a bunch of keys. I blinked. The keyring was exactly the type of thing that Dave would have – a skeleton embedded with ruby eyes. Yet ... hadn't I seen this skeleton before? Wasn't it the same as the one in Trim, attached to Peggy's key?

Dave and his customer were talking about the merits of Iron Maiden versus Motörhead. It wasn't often I observed Dave happy, but now he was laughing again. It was a low, rumbling sound, growing louder as if the volume was being slowly increased.

He looked across to see what I was doing and our eyes met. A tall man in a black jacket with his hat pulled down, covering his hair. Of course. No wonder I'd thought the man in the orchard with Peggy was familiar. It was Dave.

30

1979

The trees were bare. Fruit picked and leaves fallen.

I walked aimlessly, killing time, passing the barn where Peggy had been found. The police were long gone. A scrap of blue tape fluttered from a branch like a flag marking the place. Cheap flowers wrapped in cellophane leaned against the side of the building. They were all rotten save for one fresh bunch of roses.

I read the messages.

A good friend.

A wonderful neighbour.

A much-missed colleague.

There was nothing about being a loving wife.

I wondered if the roses were from Dave. I supposed that now he had nothing to hide. Lenny must know about him in the same way he'd known about Dad. I couldn't think of a time when I'd seen Dave with any bruises or broken bones, but I remembered what had happened to the shop. Had Lenny got his revenge by breaking the window and wrecking the display?

Dave had been at the orchard when they had found the body. I thought of seeing him on TV, standing at the edges of the crowd. Had he been afraid that it was her? Had he been heartbroken? You never could tell with Dave.

A crow took off from the top of the barn, flapping noisily. It was after four. The light was fading.

I quickened my pace. It was creepy in the orchard with the trees creaking and the wind stirring their branches. Making my way to the wasteland, running across the open ground and then crawling into the den, I felt safe. Cool and calm.

Voices and sounds carried from the building site. The thrum of machinery. The clash of steel. Soon, they'd be packing up for the day. Men marching across the field, heavy boots tramping the ground. Taking the shortcut through the orchard to home.

The estate was getting closer, encroaching on my space, and it occurred to me that if it continued, if the contractors ever got their way and bought this piece of land, my den would be flattened. I imagined a house built smack bang on top of where I was sitting now.

Time passed. It was gone four. Would Rachel come? She had only been to the den twice. What if she couldn't remember where it was?

I scrambled up the side and crawled through the bushes. Dark clouds scudded across a slate-coloured sky. Rain was coming. The wind grew stronger. It rattled the trees and crows flew out as if shaken from their perches.

The sounds of machinery, and men working, had stopped, but around me I could hear the skitter and scramble of creatures burrowing in the bushes.

Should I go home?

If only she'd come.

The air changed. There was movement and male voices. The builders were coming across the fields, their shadowy shapes sharpening as they came closer. I spotted sandy-haired Frank, surrounded by men all taller and wider than he was. They were laughing and joking. I saw Frank offer a sandwich, take a cigarette. A hand slapped him on the back. 'Hey, Frankie.' There was something about him. Ordinary and mesmerising. They loved him just like Debra did.

I stepped out of sight and the group moved on, their laughs and shouts lingering. I blew on my fingers to keep back the cold.

Where was Rachel?

Suddenly, she appeared at the edge of the orchard, dress catching on the brambles, face pale in the gloom. She stood a while, looking around like a hesitant deer.

I stepped forward. Raised my arm. *Hey, Rachel*, poised on my lips.

There was a sound. A low, tuneless whistle drifting from the fields.

A late builder on his way home – or doubling back.

A man. A low whistle.

A low whistle.

Stop. Rewind.

The wind picked up, chilling my bones.

The light slipped further into darkness.

That day. Peggy's last day. It had been the same. The same slanting light, the same cold wind, the same birds imprisoned and struggling in the branches.

The same low whistle.

The watcher.

It was him. I was sure. And he was heading for Rachel. I held my breath.

A figure loomed, large and solid, coming from the building site, crossing the wasteland like a fairy-tale giant. Hefty steps that shook the ground. I relaxed. I was wrong – he was a saviour, not a threat.

Rachel was motionless. Her jacket, the colour of earth, her dress like green leaves, her hair a burnished vine. Rooted. Arms crossed against her chest. I thought of the slashes on her skin. Imagined the blood like resin oozing from the wounds. The damage she'd done. Why?

I held my breath.

Unsure.

Mr Wright stopped whistling.

He strode onwards, reached Rachel. Neither of them noticed me standing in the shadows, surrounded by the long grass. Spying again. Should I step forward, make my presence known?

He slid one hand around her arm.

A small movement.

It might have been a gesture of affection.

Only.

Rachel flinched.

Dread skidded all the way down my spine.

She stepped backwards, but he didn't let her go.

I wanted to move, but my feet were anchored to the ground. I tried to call out, but my throat was dry and my tongue felt swollen.

He spoke so quietly, I barely heard him. I strained to make out what he said but the blood was rushing too loudly inside my head.

I quietened and the words came slithering on the breeze.

'What are you doing here?'

Silence.

Clutching harder, he pulled Rachel towards him.

'Did I give you permission to leave the house?'

'No.' A single word, full of fear.

'So why are you here then?'

'I came to find you.'

No. That wasn't true. She'd come to find me. This was my fault. I needed to tell him that so she wouldn't get the blame, but still I couldn't move; it was as if one of my old woodland devils held me in its grip, just as Mr Wright held Rachel in his.

Releasing her arm, he turned as if to walk away, only he didn't go; instead, he just stood there, looking at his hands.

Suddenly, he spun around. 'I don't believe you,' he hissed. 'You've never come to meet me before.'

'But it's true,' said Rachel. 'I wanted to see you.'

Sweat prickled beneath my arms. I could feel Rachel's fear. It was living and breathing. As real as the empty trees and the dark sky and the cold wind. I didn't know why I'd never seen it before.

Quick as a whip, he lifted his hand and slapped her face. I sucked in my breath. She staggered with the force of it while, with his other hand, he steadied her, like a father protecting his child.

He was talking again, fragments of his sentences shearing away like bits of bone; hard, sharp-edged words: *punish, bad girl, just like your mother.*

Your mother.

Not Charlotte. *Your mother.*

Rachel spoke, her words soft and frayed: 'I don't want to, please, not now, I don't want to.' She was crying, sobbing, pleading. He took her arm once again and she struggled to break free, but he wouldn't let her go.

I had to do something. I had to help.

At last, I shook away my paralysis and broke the Devil's spell.

Throwing myself from my hiding place, I raced headlong, across the space between us, straight into his hard, broad back. A battering ram. Enough to make him stagger. Surprised, he let her go and swung around to face me.

'Run,' I yelled to Rachel as he grabbed my wrist. 'Run.'

A moment's indecision and then she did. Hitching up her dress, turning and sprinting across the wasteland.

I was alone. With him. Pain stabbed through me as he tightened his grip.

'You little bitch,' he said. 'I told you not to interfere.'

He was the Devil and he'd found me at last. But still, I sank my teeth into his hand. Yelping, he stepped backwards and I broke free, and set off running too, into the orchard, leading him away from Rachel.

On I went, through the lines of trees, stumbling across the stones and the roots. Behind me I could hear the heavy thud of his footsteps.

I tried to order my thoughts. I had to lead him away, find a telephone box. Call the police. Mum. Bob. Get to the cafe and tell Maggie.

But there were no telephone boxes here. No police either. There was only the orchard and the wasteland and the half-built estate. I was going in circles. I knew this place but panic had set in and I was lost.

I stopped, leaned against a tree, breathing hard, wiping the sweat that trickled from my brow. Where was he? I walked on slowly, getting my bearings. Now and then I imagined a footfall. I shivered and turned but there was no one there. I carried on, forcing myself to think.

The orchard became familiar. A tree with dead rot. A hollow. A crevice. I quickened my pace. The wasteland was closer than the exit.

Where was Rachel? Maybe she'd gone to the den, too shocked to go further.

Maybe she was hiding, waiting for me, knowing I'd come.

I slowed, catching my breath. A few more steps and I was out from the trees, crossing the wasteland, hoping I was right.

A hand grabbed my arm, yanking me back.

'Got you,' he wheezed in my ear.

I screamed.

Another hand went straight over my mouth, and then he was dragging me.

I tried to shake my head but I couldn't move.

I tried clamping my teeth onto his hand, but my mouth wouldn't open.

I tried anchoring myself with my feet, but he was too strong.

In the distance, I could see the uneven outline of the housing estate getting further away as he dragged me.

We stopped. He lay me down on the ground. His face was calm now. His lips moved. I couldn't make out what he said, but he sounded just like he always had done. His words melodic, soft and soothing. Those dark eyes that Mum had so admired staring into mine. Only his expression was empty. His breath on my face, sweet and rotten, as his hands crept around my throat.

Time slowed. Images came and went. A bed covered in Mrs Wright's clothes. No room to sleep. Rachel's sadness. Her faraway looks. The scars on her arms. Her quiet, her ease – which turned out to be dread. Her fingers, skittering. Fiddling with her locket. Playing with her hair. Movements that betrayed her calm.

Hands about my throat. Thumbs digging in.

I was slipping. Falling. Fading.

A movement close by. Wood snapping. A badger or a fox.

A rushing of blood in my ears. His breath.

I concentrated on his bloated face so close to mine as he leaned over me. The look that slid from place to place now fixed firmly on me with one intention.

Uselessly, I summoned the last of my energy and pushed against his chest. But he was so huge. So huge. And as wide as he was tall.

My eyes were closing. My mind was shutting down. My body failing. I could only smell the sweat on his skin, only hear his breath rasping as he focused on his task.

And then something else.

A low growling. A creature in the shadow. It was a fiend. The Devil's accomplice coming to finish me off.

Fingers loosening as the snarling grew fiercer. There was a curse, a yelp of pain. He jumped up and let me go. I gasped for breath, forced myself to sit upright as my vision cleared, and I saw that he was kicking out, not at a fiend, but at a dog. Nip – teeth fastened around his leg.

Somebody shouted my name and there, ahead of me, was Rachel, emerging from the bushes surrounding the den. I tried to yell at her, but my bruised voice failed. I tried to stand, but my strength had gone.

She stopped and she waited. Anger sparking, he headed straight for her, Nip yapping at his feet.

He didn't see the penknife in her outstretched hand.

He didn't see her aura, fierce and defiant.

He ran straight into the blade. Stopping, grabbing his belly with surprise, he stumbled, staggering forward a few feet more. One more step and then he collapsed, falling, crashing into the den.

31

1979

How long did we stand there?

It seemed like hours. The birds – nesting now; the trees sighing; the shabby wasteland; the rise of the half-finished houses in the distance.

The orchard had settled, gone quiet.

Even Nip had raced off on another quest.

It was as if nothing had happened.

Yet it had. I felt it in my body. In my burning throat, in the tender skin where his fingers had been. In my scratched hands and bruised arms. This was no fantasy. It was real. Rachel held the knife. It was smeared with blood. Was he dead or badly injured?

What had Rachel done?

I wanted to run, to find an adult to make all of this go away. I wanted my mother, just as I had done years before. I wanted her arms around me and to know that everything would be all right. But Mum wasn't here, and something terrible had happened and the instinct that had made me run to her then now made me stay.

But we couldn't do this on our own.

'We need help.' My voice was raw.

Rachel, stupefied, snot and tears and dirt on her face, was silent. Her eyes gazed blankly at the space at the top of the den where Mr Wright had been. I imagined him sprawled in the dip, the blood pulsing out of him.

'Rachel,' I said, as loudly as my broken voice would allow. 'We need help. We need to get help for . . . him.'

She turned to me and blinked, amazement etched onto her face. 'What?'

'We need help.' I clutched at her arm. 'We can't do this on our own. Please.'

'I had to stop him,' she said, still not registering.

'I know. But we need help. *He* needs help. You've done . . . we've done something . . . only I don't know how bad it is.'

She frowned and looked at the knife in her hand as if she couldn't understand how it had got there.

'Rachel, please, listen to me.'

Nip had been here which meant Mr Evans must be somewhere close too. He could help us. Where was he? Maybe it was too late and he was already on the opposite side of the orchard, calling for Nip, hooking him back onto his lead, taking him home. I spun around, listening and hoping. But there was no sign. No sound. Nothing but this deadly quiet. Even the birds and the animals had shrunk away, I thought, hiding from the horror of what they'd seen.

'It'll be all right,' I said again, my voice shaking, 'but we need to get help.' I shook her arm. 'We need to tell someone.'

'No,' she said suddenly. 'We can't do that. We can't *tell* anyone.'

'But we can't just leave him, he might . . .' I stopped,

took a breath, started again. 'We don't know if he's alive or . . .'

She stared at me, her eyes wild. 'Or what?'

I lowered my voice. 'Dead.' I looked nervously at the den again. If he wasn't dead or badly injured, he could appear at any moment and come after us. Whatever was happening, we needed to act now.

Rachel was shaking her head. 'He isn't dead. He can't be dead.'

'You stabbed him, don't you see?'

'Yes, but I wanted to stop him. That's all. He isn't dead. He can't be dead.'

'Then what do you mean that we can't tell anyone?'

She hung her head, dropping her arms. 'What he did.' Her voice was barely more than a whisper now. 'What he did to me. We can't tell anyone *that*. He won't like it. He said I should never tell. Never. If I did, he'd punish me.'

My breath came in shallow gasps. There was blood on her hand and smeared on the front of her dress.

'He'll come back,' she said. 'He'll come home and then – if I don't tell, he'll forgive me and we can go back to how it was.'

'Forgive you? No. You've done nothing wrong.'

She looked down at the knife again. 'I had to stop him,' she repeated, 'from hurting you.'

'I know. And we'll tell . . . my mum, the police, and they'll believe us and everything will be all right.'

'No,' she said, taking a step away from me. 'It won't be all right. It can never be all right. Please, Elizabeth. Promise me.'

'But—'

'Please.' She dropped her voice. 'He killed before. He would have killed you too.'

A chill swept through me. 'Who did he kill?'

She lowered her voice. 'The woman in the orchard.'

I knew. I knew. The low whistle, the heavy tread. The watcher. I knew the moment I saw him walk across the wasteland. Yet still, I was shocked, hearing it from Rachel.

'How long have you known?' I asked, shivering.

'Not long,' she whispered. 'I wanted to leave him, to go to Charlotte, but he wouldn't let me. He told me what would happen if I did. He told me how he'd killed Peggy and would do the same to me. He said he'd kill Charlotte if I breathed a word. And Melissa. I had to protect them.'

'Why?' I said. 'Why did he kill Peggy?'

She leaned towards me. 'They were having an affair.'

The slashed tyres. The burnt-out van. Lenny must have known about him, too.

'But Peggy got rid of him and found someone else.'

Dave.

'He was jealous,' she said.

'Jealous enough to kill?'

'I don't know.' She covered her eyes. 'I don't know why he did it.'

Darkness blurred the edges of the trees. A few late birds sang evensong. A fox appeared, stepping daintily out from the orchard. It stood, staring across at the two of us, before moving slowly, arrogantly, away.

Nothing here had changed.

You'd think it would have done. After what had happened.

I focused back on Mr Wright. I wanted to agree with Rachel, that he wasn't dead. He had a flesh wound. It was only a penknife. A small blade. Still, he'd need a doctor, perhaps the hospital. Whatever Rachel said, we had to call for an ambulance or the police. We had to sort him out and then I'd take Rachel home with me.

I'd tell Mum.

Dad would come.

Everything would be all right.

He was alive. I was sure he must be. Shocked, maybe, bleeding. Hurt enough to stop him from lumbering out from the den.

I needed to check.

'Rachel,' I said, my mind still churning.

She stood there, arms hanging down at her sides. Gently, I took the knife from her clasp and dropped it on the ground and we leaned together.

'I have to go down there,' I whispered finally.

She nodded because she knew there was no choice.

In my mind the wasteland still rang with angry words, the earth still shuddered beneath heavy footsteps. I felt the grip of his hand on my arm, smelled the sourness of his breath, saw the purpose in his eyes.

Yet now he lay on his front, sprawled out as if he was sleeping. Head twisted and pillowed on the rocks.

I wanted to be sick, but forced it down. I didn't know what to do. I blinked, getting used to the gloom; stood for a moment, hands clasping and unclasping. My instincts told me to run, away from here, away from the cold and the devils and the orchard, back to Mum and safety. Yet I couldn't leave Rachel. It wasn't an option. I pictured her above me, afraid and trembling, willing me to return.

Deep breaths. I would pretend he was sleeping. I must be quiet, not to wake him. Inside the plastic bag was my torch. I grabbed it and flicked on the beam. He didn't move. He must be dead. Still, I knelt beside him, shining the light. Leaning down, I peered at his face. No breath. No flicker in his staring eyes. I put out my hand. His skin was still warm. I shone the light more carefully. The rocks and stones were covered in blood that was dripping from his head. Once again, the sickness rose and this time I gave in to it, retching on the ground.

'Elizabeth.' My name whispered in the dark. Rachel calling for me.

I pressed the back of my hand to my mouth. 'It's all right,' I croaked.

Slowly, I stood up and edged away. He looked so peaceful lying there. I felt sorry. I wanted to kneel back down and ask for forgiveness for my part in what had happened, but then I remembered. What he had done to Rachel. What he had done to Peggy. What he had tried to do to me.

I climbed back, breathless. At the top of the dip, rain splashed on my skin. Rachel stood where I'd left her. Rigid, peering through the gloom.

She could tell from my face he was dead.

'But he can't be,' she whispered. 'What will . . . what will . . . happen?'

'I don't know.' I was shaking, trying to blank out the image of his body.

She looked at me with wild eyes, her disbelief transforming into fear. I tried to stay calm, but what we had done was stark and dark and horrifying.

'We have to do something,' I said, as if it was a new thought. 'We can't just leave him. My mum will know what to do.'

'No, Elizabeth. Please.' She was begging me, clutching my arm, her fingers squeezing the same place as his had done.

I closed my eyes, steadied myself. 'The longer we leave it . . . the worse it will be. If we go home now, if my mum calls the police now, then maybe—'

Rachel grew still. 'You won't tell them I stabbed him?'

I swallowed. 'I'll tell them it was self-defence. I have bruises on my throat and on my arm. And . . . I don't think it was the knife that killed him. He hit his head. They'll believe us.'

'They won't, Elizabeth. Please. They'll take me away, put me in borstal.'

Would they do that? Lock her away with murderers and thieves? How would she cope? I thought of the scars on her arms. She'd die. She'd kill herself.

Her eyes fastened onto mine, willing me to promise.

'But Rachel,' I said, 'we can't deal with this. We're just . . .' I wanted to say children. But looking at her now, she didn't seem like a child. I had thought it before, those times in her house, the way she'd been, so poised and secretive. In the end, I had put it down to what had happened with her mother. Now I understood there was more.

'I don't know what to do,' I said. There was a crack in my voice. I was failing, faltering.

She jumped on my indecision. 'Please don't tell. Please. I don't want people to know. I'm ashamed, Elizabeth. People will blame me.'

'They won't,' I said, forcing myself to think clearly. 'They'll say he deserved it.'

'They will,' she insisted. 'I'm sixteen. I *chose* to stay with him.'

I waited, letting the truth of her words sink in.

People *would* blame her. The gossips and the vultures. Wasn't that what Maggie said? They always blamed the victim. Even when they'd found Peggy, beaten to death, people had focused on her affairs, asked why she was in the orchard. As if she deserved to be hit on the head with a hammer.

Rachel *had* chosen to stay behind after her aunt had left. She *was* sixteen. She and Mr Wright weren't blood-related. How would she prove what he'd done?

I wanted to convince myself and Rachel that it wouldn't happen like that, but how did I know for sure?

The body was hidden. Down in the dip. No one needed to know. Not now, at least. Later. Maybe. Once we had worked things out. It was Rachel that mattered. She had stabbed him to save me. Not herself. And she hadn't meant to kill him. She'd simply protected me and now it was my turn to protect her.

We clung to each other, half running, half stumbling over the ridges and the furrows, through the orchard, as the rain fell about us. It was as if the trees were guiding us, pointing their skeletal branches, nudging us onwards with their blunt boughs. An owl called. We followed the sound. A fox barked close and then further away. Leading us. Bats zigzagged the path ahead. For once the demons were gone.

Lights were on in Maggie's flat. The curtains were open.

I wavered.

Maggie was different. She believed in women's rights and freedom and would never blame Rachel.

A figure appeared at the window – a man. Spreading out his arms, he closed the curtains. In that second, I recognised his face. The thin moustache, the lean look of the policeman.

Quickly, I pulled Rachel across the road and we headed for her house. The rain was coming down in sheets and by the time we got there, we were drenched.

Inside, mind numb, I led her up the stairs and into the bathroom, ran a bath and helped her slip off her clothes, all the while soothing her with whispered words. *It wasn't your fault. I'll look after you . . . you know I will.* I soaped her soft skin and the dark cuts, watching the dirt and the blood from her hands mixing with the water, and then pulled the plug, seeing how the rivulets swirled and disappeared.

But the blood didn't stop, slipping down her legs as she climbed from the bath. When she started to sob, I wrapped her in a towel. I found a nightgown, but she stood so straight and stiff, I had to lift each of her arms to put it on and then, clearing away the clothes and shoes and bags from her bed, I helped her ease beneath the covers. But still the blood came. Faster, stronger. I fetched a sanitary towel, but it was soon soaked, so I took a towel from the airing cupboard and put it between her legs to take the flow. 'What's happening to me?' she whispered.

I didn't know – I could only imagine. I was a child watching a child losing a child. It was only later that I understood.

'My stomach hurts,' she said.

I found aspirin, stroked her arm, and then, when she was calm, I asked her what had happened.

'You won't tell.'

Did I have a choice? I shook my head and urged her again.

At first, she wouldn't say; she only cried, silently into her pillow, but little by little, I coaxed the story out. Charlotte had warned Rachel she was leaving, said she was taking Melissa and that she should come too. Rachel had been angry, disbelieving that she wanted her, accusing Charlotte of abandoning her, like she'd been abandoned by her birth mother. She'd said at least Mr Wright had never threatened to leave. He was solid, dependable, always there. The father she'd always craved.

'We had a row about it,' Rachel said, her words threaded through with grief, 'and then she told me that I was wrong about him, that he was a liar and a cheat. He'd had affairs, including one with my mum, her own sister.'

My eyes filled with tears, knowing it was true. 'Do you think that's why your mother left?'

Rachel sighed. 'I think so now.'

'But she never even got in touch.'

'Charlotte thought she'd had a breakdown, that she'd thrown herself off a bridge or taken an overdose. She said she'd tried it before. When I was a baby.'

Dad had told me that too. The overdose, the turning up in the hospital.

'In the end, Charlotte admitted defeat. She said it was more important to take care of me and as I was her niece, I suppose the social workers let her.'

'And Charlotte forgave ... *him*.' I couldn't bring myself to say his name. I didn't know what to call him anymore.

'He said he was sorry. Charlotte told me how charming he was, and that I was stupid and that I couldn't see what was going on in plain sight. He wasn't what he seemed.'

She was crying again, huge tears spilling down her cheeks. I took her hand and tried to comfort her. I thought of the card, still in my drawer, and Rachel saying she'd changed her mind, wanted to live with Charlotte after all. If only I'd given it to her. She might have rescued Rachel in time.

I lay beside her on the pink bedspread, staring at the ceiling, following the pattern, the icing-sugar swirls. I took in the whole room, the purple hearts, the stickers on the bedside table, the candy-floss walls, the lava lamp that made orange patterns on the wall and the white teddy bear with the words written across its chest. *I* ❤ *you*. A present from Karl. Probably.

Now I understood why Rachel had kept him away.

I asked her when the abuse had begun.

She turned off the lamp and whispered in the darkness.

'He told me I was lovely. He said I was lovelier than Charlotte. My eyes were more beautiful, my skin softer. He said he was glad she'd gone because now he could concentrate on me. He bought me clothes that Charlotte would have liked. And make-up. Jewellery, magazines. He didn't *do* anything. He was nice. That was all I wanted. I didn't realise . . .' She let out a sob.

I thought of Bob, gentle and kind, and my own eyes filled with tears again. I'd got him so badly wrong. Now it was too late. Everything was too late.

'What happened after that?' I whispered.

'It was Christmas. He told me he was lonely. He cried. I stroked his arm. To make him feel better. I didn't realise that was a signal. I didn't, Elizabeth. I didn't know until afterwards when he said it was my fault, that I'd led him on, that I was no better than my mother or any of the others.'

I clenched my teeth, listening to this. I grabbed her hand and insisted she was innocent. It was his fault. Not hers. She cried again and then, through her tears, she told me all the ragged details of what he had done and how she had felt when her period hadn't come. She cried and she cried, and I cried too. She made me promise not to tell. He was dead and it was our secret. If the police believed Rachel, what more could they do to him? But if they didn't believe her, there was so much to lose.

Inside, though, I raged and I hated myself for not having helped her before. For not having sent that card when she had asked me to. Her cry for help. Right at the beginning. Maybe I could have prevented it all.

'What will I tell people?' she said at the end of it. 'Where will I say he's gone?'

'I don't know,' I admitted, 'but I'll think of something.'

Then because she was weeping again and wouldn't sleep, I fetched the sleeping pills from the bathroom cabinet and went downstairs to warm some milk. It was odd doing a normal chore in Rachel's kitchen. I ground a couple of the pills into the milk.

I stayed with her until she fell asleep.

Later, I tiptoed out of the room, went downstairs and telephoned home. Bob answered. I took a breath to steady my voice. 'I'm at Debra's,' I said. 'Her mum said I could stay the night.'

'Are you all right?'

I stopped for a second. *No. I'm not all right. Come and fetch me. Help me. Please.*

'Elizabeth? Your voice sounds strange.'

'I'm fine.'

I told him that the line was fizzing and I couldn't hear. I told him that Debra's mum had made cocoa and that I had to go.

I went back to Rachel, took off my clothes and pulled on one of her huge nightgowns. Lying beside her, I stared at the icing-sugar ceiling, listened to the drumming of the rain, imagined it soaking Mr Wright in his watery grave. I hoped that hell existed. I hoped that he was there right now, burning in the fires. I hoped I wouldn't go to hell because of the part I'd played.

I was trembling so hard, my teeth were chattering.

I edged closer to Rachel's warmth. Beside me she stirred. I put out my hand and laid it gently on her side.

How would we cope? I had no idea. My thoughts wouldn't stretch that far. I could only think about what was happening now. What it felt like to be lying beside Rachel, feeling her warmth, trying to comfort her. I'd have to come up with a proper plan. People would ask questions. Mum and Bob, Dad and Charlotte. Karl. I had to think of something.

I *would* think of something.

Tomorrow.

Tomorrow. Everything would be fine.

32

1979–1999

I take a breath and I'm back in the present.

Around me, the lines of the slide and the swings are blurring. It's early, but still the sky is black and the light has almost gone. The mums, the children, have left now. There's only me. Alone and thinking. Faint images coming back.

That night, when I lay with Rachel in her bed.
The storm raged and the rain fell heavily all night long. For a while, I listened to her breathing. Then I eased myself away and tiptoed to the window. My body ached: arm sore where he'd grabbed me; throat painful where he'd laced his fingers; hands badly cut and bruised from the brambles tearing me when I'd fled.

I breathe again, as the wind picks up, stirring the bushes, plucking at my hair, urging me to move on from the bench.

But I can't. The images are growing stronger. They're taking shape, forcing me to remember.

That night, when I lay with Rachel in her bed.
When the storm raged about the house, grabbing at the windows and the doors, gradually calming and

282

blowing itself out. When the dark room grew lighter with the windswept blush of dawn. I thought, what if I'd been wrong and Mr Wright hadn't been dead? Maybe he was hammering on Maggie's door right now and she, horrified, was letting him in and the policeman was running down the stairs, tucking in his shirt, taking control.

It couldn't be true. He had been so still. There had been so much blood.

Yet the thought wouldn't leave me. It burrowed inside my brain. I was exhausted but, as soon as I fell asleep, I jolted awake. Time and again.

In the end, I got out of bed and walked around, and while I was walking, I pretended that I lived here and I imagined I was an adult going about the house, washing and cleaning. Taking care of Rachel.

So, I began to do exactly that, brushing crumbs off the kitchen table, rinsing a coffee cup left on the side. Strange to touch the cup, to think about Mr Wright's lips on the rim, his fingers grasping the handle. I plunged it into hot soapy water and imagined the traces of his body disappearing – his saliva, his prints – and I thought again how easy it was, to erase someone. Like Mum had with Dad. Like Lenny had with Peggy.

Afterwards, I collected items Mr Wright had left lying around – gloves, a newspaper, a lighter – and I put them in a plastic bag. Quietly, I opened the front door. It was dawn, and the birds – grateful after the rain – were singing. Next door I could hear the child crying. The woman appeared, Farah Fawcett hair deflated, early morning cigarette in hand.

'Oh,' she said.

'Hi,' I said, trying to make out it was the most normal thing in the world to be staying in Rachel's house, to be wearing one of her nightdresses.

Dropping the plastic bag into the dustbin, I told her that Mr Wright had gone to Norfolk. I was keeping Rachel company. I said he'd gone to work there for a while.

She believed me. She had no reason not to and, I suppose, she wasn't that interested. That's when it came to me that Rachel could just carry on living in the house until the rent ran out; that so long as we could convince people that Mr Wright had definitely gone away, no one would ask questions. People – parents – abandoned their children all the time and Mr Wright wasn't even Rachel's father. Plus, Rachel was sixteen. Later she could go somewhere else, though I wasn't sure where that place would be.

One step at a time.

Get rid of his personal possessions: in one big sweep like Mum had done with Dad, or gradually?

The house was heavy around me, walls pressing in. The clutter, the heat making me sluggish.

Slowly, I went upstairs to his bedroom.

Opening the wardrobe, I examined his clothes.

Forcing myself, I dragged a bag from the top and filled it with shirts, toiletries, pyjamas. Not too much. I'd do things gradually.

What next?

Rooting through a drawer, I found a box of papers: rent and bills. I pulled the whole drawer out and set it on the floor. Kneeling beside it, I searched through. But it was too daunting. How could I ever work this out? I'd never been sent a bill, let alone paid one, and what did you do about rent?

I sat back, mind spinning. What had made me think that I could do this? It was impossible. I wasn't equipped. I was as useless as all the teachers had told me I was.

I pressed my palms into my eyes. My head felt tight. My throat sore from that man's hands. I ran down to the kitchen, found the aspirin, shook out two and tossed them down with a glass of water. Slow and steady. I leaned against the sink. My gaze fell on a knife, discarded on the side, and the image of Rachel came back, with the penknife covered in blood. I set the glass back down. *Concentrate*, I told myself. Rachel needed me. She had no one else. I went slowly back upstairs.

In the box, there were letters. Some from Mrs Wright – sent from London, or Norfolk, talking about practical things. Asking for money for Melissa, mainly, which it didn't look like he was paying. Good. It meant she wouldn't miss the money now he was gone.

The last letter was dated November '79. It was Charlotte's leaving note. She wrote:

I forgave you for your affair with my sister. Worse, I blamed her. Now I don't know where she is, so I can't even say I'm sorry. Rachel wants to stay with you. Fine. There's not much I can do about that. I've told her she can have the flat in Plaistow when I move on. I'll send the key.

I read and reread, my eyes focusing on the phrase *when I move on*. The meaning was clear. Charlotte had always known she'd take my dad to Norfolk. I blinked hard. It didn't matter. Nothing about them mattered anymore. It was only Rachel. Only this. Besides, I knew now that we needed Charlotte. There was only so much we could deal with on our own.

I found another box, this time full of receipts. A glass bottle filled with pennies. Money. We needed money. As much as we could find.

I pulled out jackets and coats and trousers, searched the pockets. No wallet. Of course not. He'd have that with him. I cursed myself for not taking it last night. In an ordinary jacket, a plain, dark brown jacket, I found a jewellery box. Curious, I pulled it out and opened the lid.

Inside, there were two chains. The first was silver. I picked it up and let it swing. It was a pendant: a bull's skull. It didn't take much to search inside my memory to remember where I'd seen it, hanging from Peggy's neck as she leaned across the table, serving food. I dropped the chain, tried to think clearly, but my mind was running backwards and my imagination was churning, filling in the details.

The past dissolves.

A moment of quiet.

The park is full of changing light, shadows creeping all around me.

A van parks beyond the gates and a man in a dark green uniform gets out. Young, in his twenties, maybe, with hair cut close to his head. He stands on the pavement, on the other side of the railings, checking a clipboard, scratching his chin. He looks about him and sees me.

The park is deserted.

I am alone, but not nervous.

Not like Peggy must have been. That day.

That day when I saw the couple. Peggy and Dave.

The footsteps. The sound of voices. The low rumbling laughter and then someone else. Whistling tunelessly. Mr Wright. Coming home from work, stumbling across his lover with somebody else. Hiding. Watching. Seeing me there too. Perhaps.

I watched them. Peggy and Dave. They heard me as I stumbled. *Who's there?*

I ran, leaving them alone, except they weren't alone, were they?

What happened next?

The picture grows inside my head.

Dave left first to avoid suspicion. Peggy's husband was a villain after all. He was dangerous. He'd already vandalised the record shop. Slashed Mr Wright's tyres. Burned out his van. Soon he'd find out about my dad and attack him too.

So Dave left first.

What was Peggy thinking as she waited amongst the bare trees for the coast to clear? Was she considering how her life was so empty that she had to fill it with men? Or was she happy because she'd found someone she really wanted at last, and was planning to leave Lenny for good? Perhaps she was smiling to herself as she waited, dreamy-eyed, thinking back to those moments with Dave.

Perhaps.

But then.

Something changed. Something shifted.

Did she notice how eerie the silence had become, how the light had darkened? Did she hear the rustle in the undergrowth, the crack of branches underfoot and wonder what that was? Did she believe, like I used to, in devils and demons hiding amongst the trees?

Perhaps, heart beating hard, she searched for a cigarette to give herself courage and while she was rummaging in her bag, he struck. So quickly, she didn't know what had happened. Or was it an argument that went badly wrong? He loomed out of the shadows and confronted her, grabbed her arm. Maybe she pushed him off, or maybe she laughed at him in that way she did. He couldn't stand that. He never could stand that. So he pulled out a hammer from his builder's bag and he struck her. Just like that, and she fell. He struck her again. And again. Grunting, sweating, he dragged her to the barn and he hid her, covering her body hastily with branches and leaves, and then . . .

He leaned down and ripped the chain from her throat.

His trophy.

Perhaps.

At least, that's what I've pictured over the years. That's what's crept into my dreams. That's what I imagine now.

And the second chain in the jewellery box?

My memory stutters when I think about that, because it was familiar too. A locket. The same as the one that

Rachel wore. With a photo of Rachel in one side and a photo of her mother in the other.

I don't know the truth of the story, of course, and I don't know for sure that he killed her. I only know it took months before I found the courage to show Rachel. That when I did she broke down and I held her up as best as I could. I was mindful of the cuts she'd made on her skin. Of the envelope of pills I'd found in her room. Of her mother's history. Neither of us knew what to do. We'd gone so far down our road we didn't know how to get back. The mind has a way of blocking thoughts to cope with a knowledge that you daren't confront. Because if you do, the horror will be too much to bear.

At least that's how it was for me.

Breathe, I tell myself, as my thoughts skitter across time and space and my heart pounds. It's because I'm so close to the end.

Inside my bag, the brochure rests. Inside my head, my confession burns.

Which way should I go?

The van door slams.

The park keeper walks through the gate, litter picker in his hand. He eyes me carefully, sitting there on the bench. Too smartly dressed to be homeless. Too lonely to have a child somewhere playing. Too unappealing to be waiting for a lover.

He watches me, but he doesn't approach to ask if I'm all right. Perhaps he thinks I'm not worth the trouble. Perhaps he wants to finish his work and go home.

Slip, slip, slip to the end.

33

1979–1999

That night, when I lay with Rachel in her bed.

It came to me.

I should have taken his wallet and all the things that I'd left in the den. I should have picked up the knife, too.

I had to go back.

I pulled on my clothes, found a scarf to hide the bruising, checked that Rachel was still sleeping and let myself out the door.

Early morning. The estate was deserted. I walked quickly through the streets. On the main road, I paused.

Which way?

I could turn right. Go home to Mum and Bob. Mum, who would give me one look and know there was something wrong. She would take me in her arms and tuck me into bed and listen to my story. She would tell me none of it was my fault and then she would call Dad and he would come rushing back to me. Maybe he would stay.

I thought of the heat of Mum's arms, the new kindness I had found in Bob. The safety.

Then I thought of Rachel, waking. The first few moments of peace before the memory of the orchard filtered into her consciousness. She would wonder where I was. Maybe she'd call out and then go downstairs looking for me. But the house would be empty and slowly she would realise that I had abandoned her, just as everyone else had done. She would sit cross-legged in the hall just as she had that time before until the police came knocking.

It wasn't going to happen.

Rachel was a part of my story now and I was a part of hers. We were in this together. The crazy girls.

It was cold beneath the trees, with the mist rising about me like ghosts. I ran, stumbling over roots, and still I kept thinking what if I'd been wrong and he wasn't dead?

The birds cried out as I approached the den. I had no time to stop and listen, or to change my mind. I dropped to my knees and eased through the bushes, down to the dip.

He lay there still. Blood dried and crusting. Carefully, I crouched over his body. Holding my breath, I touched his skin. So cold. Like marble. I recoiled. The trick was not to think. Moving my gaze from his face, I quickly searched his pockets and found his wallet. I took his keys too. It was instinct moving me forwards. I thought of his work bag. Where was that? Would people miss him at the building site? No. Men left all the time. They came and they went. No one would care.

I went to the place where I kept my provisions and took them too, then, I grabbed leaves and branches, stones and clumps of grass and lay them across his body. It was the best I could do. Scrambling up the side of the dip, I scanned the wasteland. I found the work bag at the edge of the orchard. I searched and searched for the knife, tried to identify the exact place where I'd stood with Rachel, but my mind was blank. The wasteland was different in the early morning light. In the end, I gave up.

The cafe was open by the time I left the wasteland. I went in as the policeman came out. 'You're early,' said Maggie, giving me a smile.

I told her Mum had a headache and that I'd come out to give her some peace and did she want any help?

She looked at me. 'Your voice sounds scratchy.'

'Sore throat,' I replied, touching the scarf.

As soon as a delivery man came with a tray of cakes, I took my chance, mumbling about fetching clean cloths and then racing up to the flat.

I took forty pounds from the bundle on the shelf. I hoped Maggie would be confused and not notice, or that she'd understand and forgive me if she did. I vowed to pay it back as soon as I could.

By the time I got downstairs, the delivery man had gone and Mrs Joseph had come in, on her way to Spar. I fiddled about, wiping down the counter, listening, trying not to think about what I'd done.

They were talking about the housing estate. Mrs Joseph said she didn't want to be triumphant yet, but the old lady in Australia wasn't budging. The building company would be lucky if they got their hands on any land while she was still alive.

Afterwards, I went home. Mum was still in bed. Bob had gone to work. I raced to the bathroom and washed, changed into fresh jeans and a high-necked jumper. I gathered school clothes, toiletries.

I asked Mum if I could stay with Debra for a few more days. Debra hadn't been well recently and she could do with a friend.

Mum was mildly surprised, but she didn't mind. She thought it was nice of me to help out Debra. I guessed she was glad that I had a distraction and she had time with Bob.

I went to Spar and bought bread and cheese and apples and took them back to Rachel.

When she woke, first she smiled and then she cried. 'I thought it was a dream,' she whispered, 'but then I remembered.'

She pushed back her cover. Blood was leaking through the towel and onto the sheets. I soothed her, rubbing her back until she was calm, then I took away the towel and replaced it with another because she was still bleeding, although now I thought the blood had slowed.

'Will everything be all right?' Rachel whispered.

'Yes,' I whispered back. 'I'll protect you. You know I will.'

'What will you do?' she asked.

'Anything,' I replied, but she was asleep already.

The next morning, I took the bag I'd filled with Mr Wright's clothes, his wallet and his keys and I caught the first bus to the river. No one saw me or, if they did, I was sure they wouldn't care. I was Elizabeth Valentine, the girl of no consequence. I was invisible. I always had been.

At the river, I walked far enough to be out of sight of

any houses. There I opened the bag and filled it with stones. A few swans drifted in the shade by the bank, weed streaming around them like tangled hair. I took the bag, looked about me, made sure I was alone, and then, leaning forward, I dropped it into the water. Shivering, I heard the splash, watched the ripple.

It was only the beginning. Gradually I'd take the rest of his things, his clothes, his tools, little by little, dumping them in public bins, rivers and canals, annihilating his existence.

Rachel stayed in bed. She slept and the bleeding slowed and I fed her and soothed her as if I was an adult and she was my child.

I tried to make plans, but my mind was numb. At night, my dreams were filled with visions of a cold, hard body rising from the dip, wrenching away the branches, shaking the leaves from its hair. In the daytime, everywhere I looked, Peggy's face was there, her eyes reproaching me for not telling what I knew.

Gradually and together, Rachel and I went through the box of papers, trying to understand. The rent had been paid until the end of the month. That meant we had time to work out what was next, to contact Charlotte with a story.

I reread her note and thought about the flat in Plaistow.

Rachel summoned the strength to phone Charlotte, telling her that Mr Wright had gone away and hadn't told her where.

'Good riddance to bad rubbish,' Charlotte said. She

asked Rachel to come to Norfolk, but Rachel said she wanted to leave school, take the flat in Plaistow, make a go of it there. She practically read out the script I wrote for her, and held my hand as she made the call.

'You're sixteen,' Charlotte said. 'You can do whatever you want.'

I think she was glad to help her niece, but relieved too that she no longer had to take responsibility for her. She contacted the school, made the necessary arrangements for her to move into the flat. When the time came, she swept down from Norfolk and sorted out the furniture in the house.

By then I had got rid of most of Mr Wright's clothes and toiletries and Charlotte was convinced he had gone elsewhere. She didn't want any of what was left, she said, even though most of it was hers. Mr Wright had contributed nothing, hadn't even paid any rent. Typical. He was a leech. No doubt he had moved on to the next woman he could live off. She was only sorry she had stayed with him for so long.

That first day when Rachel moved to London, I went with her, helped her settle in. We sat in the dingy living room hardly registering each other, feeling the memory of Mr Wright slithering between us, along with our guilt. Still. We'd made it this far and we had to keep on going.

She got a job. A shop girl in Fenwick's, selling make-up. She had the perfect face.

In the park, a breeze quickens, shadows move.

There's a rustle in the bushes behind me and when I

turn, I see the dim outline of a figure. It's a young man, with eyes of slightly different colours. There's another figure behind him, roll-neck jumper, platform shoes, tapping his foot to the rhythm of Barry White. Then comes a procession of ghosts, released at last from the prison of my mind – there's Mum and Bob; John and Debra and her mother and Frank; and Charlotte and Melissa and Dave, headphones on, nodding to the beat. Peggy, bits of grass and earth and broken twigs sticking to her hair. Mr Wright. As he was. Large and real, with hands held out to grab me. He dissolves, flesh dropping from his body until only his bones remain, and then another figure appears. Rachel's mother – distant, face blurred, holding out her hands for help.

'You all right?' says a voice.

It's the park keeper, standing in front of me, the litter picker still in his hand. I smile at him gratefully as the tears fall.

He shifts, scratches his chin. Confused. How could he know that his words have catapulted me right back to the beginning?

'It's clean,' he says, holding out a handkerchief.

I laugh, taking it. 'Thank you.'

He nods. 'Are you coming?'

'Yes,' I say, getting up.

I relax as I walk with him back across the grass and through the gates.

'Do you have far to go?'

I smile at him sadly. 'That depends.'

I don't tell him what it depends on and he doesn't ask. He drives away in his van, giving me a wave from his window before settling back into his own life. One more connection severed.

Afterwards, I walk slowly down the street with the dark sky pressing down and the hot, sticky air holding me tight, still uncertain of what will happen next.

34

1999

The flat isn't far from the park.

At the entrance, I wait. Soon a woman in a pink tracksuit comes out, and holds the door open.

She smiles as I step inside. No questions asked. I keep that smile along with the kindness of the park keeper.

The block of flats was built in the 1960s and is nothing like that old house in Plaistow. It's more like the places I rented in London.

I was stronger then. We both were. Not like in those awful early days, when every footstep, every letter through the door, every look or gesture made us think we'd been discovered. It hardly seemed possible that the world could keep on going, its cogs and wheels grinding and groaning, while at the bottom of a murky hollow, Mr Wright's body lay.

The days turned into weeks. We became a little less jittery. Rachel recovered from her miscarriage. She was lucky. The pregnancy had been in its early days. It was only a question of time before the last of the blood seeped away.

Of course, I had to go home. I had to go back to school too, on the Monday, three days after he'd died. I tried my best, I really did, acting away like the best of them. John saw through me – at least he thought he did.

He knew I was pretending, but he couldn't work out what it was I was trying to hide, and he never quite forgave me for that. Debra on the other hand didn't notice, wrapped up as she was in her perfect world. Then Frank got a better job in a better place and whisked her and her mother away. Happy ever after. I was glad that at least one fairy tale had come true.

Home was harder than school. Those first weeks, coming in as if nothing had happened, sleeping, knowing Rachel was alone in her house, going to see her whenever I could. Keeping Karl away.

I sometimes wonder how I fooled Mum. Maybe it was because she and Bob were so in love. I enjoyed Bob's company too. His quiet companionship and our long talks about books. Maybe it was because I'd stopped worrying so much about Dad. It wasn't that I rejected him, exactly, but if I thought about him, then I'd think about Charlotte, and that led to thinking about Mr Wright – so it was easier not to consider any of them at all.

The weeks turned into months. Rachel had gone to London. Still the knock on the door didn't come. No police officers appeared demanding what I knew about the body in the orchard. No one questioned what had happened to Mr Wright. They all accepted the story that he'd left Chelmsford, gone away to find another job. The men on the building site came and went. It was that kind of work. He was grief-stricken, probably. Embarrassed, even. That's what people said. Who wouldn't be when their wife had humiliated you like that, gone off with another man?

I thought, how could something so momentous remain undiscovered?

But remain undiscovered it did.

O levels. A levels. I got average marks. Even though my dream of Oxford hadn't gone, the sense that I deserved to be there had disappeared. I didn't try. Mrs Townsend despaired of me and then gave up on me.

Since university didn't work out, it was obvious that I should move to London and be closer to Rachel, in case she needed me. She'd done the unthinkable, protecting my life. I would do anything for her in return, if it was necessary. We were finally connected, just as I'd always dreamed. The crazy girls. It was just that no one apart from us knew how crazy we were.

I announced my intention to Mum: I wanted to be independent. I got a job in a bookshop tucked away in East London – Newham. Mum gave me her blessing. She had decided herself to try something new. She was going to teach English, replacing her charges with older kids. All those evening classes had expanded her knowledge. It was time to take that forwards. Bob gave me cash to start me off and I was grateful because in the end I had realised he was a good man. One of the best. Like Frank.

I lived in the bedsit in Canning Town. Far enough away from Plaistow to give Rachel space, close enough to be there if she needed me. At first, she wanted to see me. We sat quietly together in the flat, eating and watching TV. It was a relief for both of us not having to pretend. But as time went on, we both knew it was better not to think about the past. We both knew, too, that we had a terrible knowledge that would bind us forever and for that reason we had to stay close.

So that's what I did, dropping by from time to time, offering my friendship and support and she, depending on the way her life was going, couldn't help leaning on me. Funnily enough, it was Rachel who first came to Oxford: when Charlotte sold the flat, she decided she wanted to get out of London, so she stuck a pin in a map and ended up in Oxford. I followed, of course. My city of dreams.

In the block, someone is playing the piano. The music is sad and beautiful, like water rippling. I stand for a moment as my eyes fill with tears.

A few minutes pass and then I take the stairs.

First floor. Deep breaths, I knock.

The door opens and Rachel stands there. It's been two years. Her hair is shorter than it used to be. She is thinner, too, and there are soft lines showing on her face, but she looks well. Barefoot, she wears a dress – loose. Pale green. Nails painted to match. Still bitten.

'Elizabeth,' she says, her expression changing from surprise to pleasure. We both ignore the hint of darkness we always feel at the sight of the other.

She invites me inside, and I step into her flat, so cool and airy after the heat outside. It's decorated with light-coloured furniture, wooden floors, glass and chrome, the minimum of fuss. The opposite of the house she shared with *him*.

'You should have told me you were coming,' she says, leading me to the kitchen to offer me a drink.

I show her my bag of shopping. 'Hungry?'

She laughs, shrugging. 'Why not?' She pours wine while I start work on the meal.

Because it's the last supper, I want to make sure that I get it right: the steak how she likes it, the salad dressed, the potatoes crisp.

While we talk, she chats about her life. Her latest boyfriend has gone the way they all do – fizzling out after a couple of months.

'But I've got a new job,' she says, 'managing a boutique. It's very exclusive and of course I get a discount on clothes and accessories.'

She swishes the skirt of her dress, shows me the silver bangles on her bony wrists. I admire them and say how much they suit her.

She doesn't ask me why I've appeared so suddenly. I don't mention how much weight she's lost.

When the food is ready, we sit down and because she asks me about work, I tell her I've left my job.

'It was going nowhere.'

'The museum?'

'No, I left that a while ago. I was working in a cafe.'

'A cafe?' Her eyes widen. 'Why? You're wasted on a job like that.'

I shrug. 'It was a stopgap. Money. You know. Needs must.'

'You should go back into education,' she says.

I sip my wine. 'Maybe.'

Outside, the air is changing; a wind is stirring the trees, lifting the leaves, swirling bits of rubbish into tiny tornadoes in the street. There's going to be a storm; this heat will break at long last.

Rachel drinks wine, but hardly touches her food. She talks about her latest psychologist.

'I didn't know you'd switched,' I say. 'What was wrong with the other one?'

She wrinkles her nose. 'She asked too many questions.'

'Aren't they supposed to?'

'No. They're supposed to listen.' Eyes serious, Rachel fixes me with her gaze. 'This guy . . . he tells me to shake off my past and look to the future.'

I nod and drink and wish it was as easy as that.

The wind blasts the window open, making us jump. Rachel hurries to close it and we clear away and, as we do, I imagine the two of us living together in a stone cottage with a view of the sea. The dream takes root and for a moment flourishes before it withers and dies.

To distract myself, I produce the presents I've bought for her: the grass-green scarf, the flip-flops, the magazine.

'It's not my birthday for another month,' she says but I can tell she's delighted, the way she holds the scarf to her face and admires the flip-flops and flicks through the magazine.

Her face brightens as she remembers something. She rushes out the room, coming back with a parcel.

'I've had it for ages,' she says, 'just in case you popped by. Bought it for your last birthday, actually.'

'I didn't know you knew when it was.'

'For goodness' sake, Elizabeth, of course I do. Why do you put yourself down?'

I flush, knowing she's right, knowing that it irritates her when I do.

'Besides, we met around the time of your birthday. August. Don't you remember? You fell off your bike.'

Of course I remember. I never dreamed that she would too.

'Open it then,' she urges now.

I pull the ribbon and carefully peel off the paper, grinning like a child. I gasp when I see what's inside. It's a first edition copy of *Jude the Obscure*. I can't stop the tears brimming in my eyes, silently rolling down my cheeks.

Rachel is beaming. 'You did say you might go back into education.'

I laugh. 'I didn't say that!'

'You said *maybe*. I've always thought you should and, if you ask me, it's not before time.'

I shake my head in disbelief. 'Oh, Rachel,' I say, holding the book to my chest. 'This is the most wonderful gift I've ever had.'

Outside, the weather gives way to rain.

Falling softly on the windowpane.

Increasing its momentum.

And since I can't put it off any longer.

I tell her.

It's a shock getting bad news, even when you're expecting it, even after twenty years.

When Rachel gets hers at the end of a hot August day,

with the rain drumming on the leaves outside the window, and the scent of summer perfume fading away, she takes both my hands in hers.

Despite everything, I feel lost as I stare into her dark green eyes, as I think about how much I've loved her and for how long. As I think how nothing – no one – has ever compared to Rachel. I don't know if that's because she makes me feel needed or if it's because of what she did for me or if it's because she looks at me and sees who I really am.

I think about how difficult it's been to stay away from her and how each time I come back it's as if we've been apart for no more than a day. I think how terrible it is that such darkness should be the reason for the thread that has connected us and will connect us forever.

'What shall we do?' she says, her eyes glistening, her fingers moving to the locket round her neck.

I swallow hard, trying to keep my emotions in check. The rain falls harder. There's a flash of lightning. Thunder rolls. I paint her a picture – the one I'll hold in my mind when she's gone. A young woman beneath a dazzling sun, beside a turquoise sea. The fluttering of a grass-green scarf. She's smiling and she's free.

'You must find someone,' I tell her, 'someone special who will take care of you.'

'What do you mean?'

I take out the brochure and put it in front of her. I tell her that I have money, I can buy her a ticket. To Lipsi, or somewhere else if she prefers. She can work there, get a job in a shop or open a boutique of her own, maybe, one day.

Still she frowns, trying to understand.

'Why?'

'Because they'll look for you when they find . . .' My voice catches. 'When they find out who it is.'

She is quiet. 'Do you think that they will – find out?'

'I don't know. Perhaps.' I think of the knife. Will that really be proof? A few scraps of cloth, whatever is left of his clothing, twenty years on. Surely it will have rotted by now, been devoured by animals. Like his flesh, I think, shivering.

'Oh.' She twists her hands in her lap. 'Do you think they'll try to find me?'

'If they find out who he is, yes – you, Charlotte, Melissa. My dad.'

'And if I tell them what he did?'

A scatter-gun of rain hits the glass. 'You can't prove it,' I say quietly.

'But I was pregnant.'

'You didn't tell anyone apart from me. You didn't tell anyone about the abuse. How can you prove it?'

I don't tell her what else I'm thinking: that if she's questioned, she'll crumple. The police won't be like her psychologists, skirting around the subject. They'll be clinical, brutal, uncaring. They'll delve and discover that she lived in the house alone. She never reported him missing. Even if they believe her story – accept manslaughter – she won't get through the process. She's too fragile.

'Have you lost weight?' I ask suddenly.

She shrugs. 'Maybe.'

I'm silent and then I push the brochure towards her. 'You must go.'

She blinks back her tears. Opening the brochure, she leafs through, smiles a little and I think she's going to agree, but then she shakes her head. 'If they decide to look for me, they'll find me, eventually, wherever I am. What's the point of leaving?'

'They won't look for you if they don't need to.'

'What do you mean?'

I moisten my lips. 'I'll be here. I'll tell them.'

'Tell them what?'

I'll tell them it was me.

She shakes her head, understanding.

'No, Elizabeth,' she says quietly. 'And anyway, they won't believe you. Why would they? What would your reason have been?'

'I'll say it was an accident. I'll say he was abusing *me*. I'll tell them about Peggy. I've got the chain. They'll know it was him.' Even as I say it, I know it's not true. The chain is no proof at all. Any more than the locket is proof that Rachel's mother is dead.

Unconsciously, Rachel's fingers go back to the chain around her neck. 'No. Your life is not worth less than mine. Why should you sacrifice your freedom for me?'

I want to tell her that I owe her. That I don't deserve her friendship. I never have.

'Elizabeth?' she prompts me gently.

'Because . . .' I stop. 'I'm stronger.'

'No.'

'And because . . . I'll do anything for you.'

'You don't need to.'

I open my mouth and she puts her finger to my lips. 'He was my abuser,' she says. 'I stopped him then and

I'll stop this now. Besides, they may never identify him and then there's no reason for them to come to me. No one reported him missing. No one cared enough.'

They're the same thoughts that I have had, but I don't want to risk it. I tell her this. I insist she must leave, that I will deal with it all.

Tears pool in my eyes again and she smiles gently.

'You, dear Elizabeth, have helped me for so long, but this is *my* battle and *you* are going to carry on with the education you should never have stopped.'

She pushes *Jude the Obscure* towards me and I rest my hand lightly on its cover.

'You can use your money for that. Forget all about this – and me. It was never your fault. You're a bloody marvel, Elizabeth Constance Valentine. And don't you forget it.'

Maybe she's right. Maybe there is a chance that I could achieve the dream I once had.

Or maybe my dream has changed.

The night moves onwards as we sit together. The thunder clears, the rain lessens, gentle now against the windowpane. The storm has gone, but the thoughts remain raging inside my head. I think about how no one can harm Rachel. Not the scientists who may one day identify the skeleton of a man who no one cares about. Not the police who may one day hunt Rachel down and question what she knows.

Because if that happens, I will rise up.

I will tell them that he left. I will tell them that I saw him pack his bags. He was a good man. A kind man. A gentle man. There were plenty of people who thought that. Plenty of people who witnessed his chivalry. His charm. Why would Rachel want to hurt him? *How* could she hurt him? A young, frail girl.

Whatever Rachel says, I won't leave her. If she steps forward, I will step ahead.

Because we're connected. It's our dark secret.

Nothing and no one can change that.

Acknowledgements

Thank you to my wonderful agent, Sophie Lambert, for her wisdom and creative flair, and to the brilliant team at C&W.

To my editor, Sam Humphreys, whose creativity and tactful approach have made this novel stronger. As always, it has been a delight and a privilege to work alongside her. Thanks to the amazing team at Mantle and Pan Macmillan, especially to Samantha Fletcher and Philippa McEwan and to Katie Tooke for the stunning cover.

To early readers Alex Birtles, Jan Dacre, Helen Hathaway and Stephen Walcott for their honest and insightful response. Thank you, Alex, for being a constant champion and friend.

Thank you to the writing community, to readers, authors and friends. To Anna Davies at Curtis Brown Creative and to bloggers, booksellers, reviewers and librarians who do such an excellent job. Special thanks to Bill Buckley and Audrey French at Radio Berkshire. Taking part in the book club has been a joy. Thanks also to Rachel Edwards for her friendship, long lunches and shared radio shows.

Thanks to my oldest friends, Gary Leary, Jules Pipe, Alison Shepherd and Alisoni Wagner, for keeping me grounded with their realism and wit.

To my brothers, Peter, David, Christopher and

Acknowledgements

Michael, who have given me so much encouragement and good humour along the way. To my cousin, Hilary Hawkes, for lunches and bookish chats.

Gratitude and love to my parents, Joyce and Jack Quintana. Your memory is captured within the pages of each book I write.

To my beautiful, clever and funny children, Stephen, Amelia and Olivia, whose light shines on me every day and makes my life worthwhile. And to my warm-hearted stepson, Dominic, the finest of young men.

Finally, to my husband, Derick, whose love and patience, kindness and unfailing support have helped me to arrive at the place where I always wanted to be. Love, always.